# HOLIDAY HEARTS VOLUME 3

## SWEET HOLIDAY ROMANCES

## JOSIE RIVIERA

# HOLIDAY HEARTS VOLUME 3

## SWEET HOLIDAY ROMANCES

JOSIE RIVIERA

# JOSIE'S NEWSLETTER

To keep up on newly released ebooks, paperbacks, Large Print Paperbacks, audiobooks, as well as exclusive sales, sign up for Josie's Newsletter today.

As a thank you, I'll send you a Free PDF ... The Beauty Of ...

Josie's Newsletter

*Did you know that according to a Yale University study, people who read books live longer?*

# INTRODUCTION

Dear Friends,

A heartwarming story is the hallmark of a romantic holiday. Savor the magic in *Holiday Hearts Volume 3* with three sweet holiday contemporary romances in 1 boxed set.

*Holiday Hearts Volume 3* is available in ebook, Paperback, Hardcover, and Large Print Paperback.

Individual books and audiobooks sold separately.

This collection includes the following books:

### *Sweet Peppermint Kisses*

There's no place like home. Until the heart gallops off in an unexpected direction…

After Chiara passes her RN license exam, she plans to leave Virginia and return to her beloved Kansas hometown for good. Except her home health client's handsome brother makes her consider changing her plans.

Between his job, his sister's injury, and his horse ranch, Vance has no time for Christmas. But Chiara's delight in the season makes him willing to do anything to keep the enchanting smile on her face.

When it comes down to asking her to stay, can he let go of his painful past, throw his heart over the fence, and follow it toward a future together?

Sometimes the best gifts are hiding right under your heart.

### *A Chocolate-Box Christmas*

Love is sweeter with a touch of mischief.

A short book for a quick and sweet holiday read.

Judging a chocolate-making competition for the women's shelter's annual fundraiser should be an easy, even pleasurable, assignment for Maise, new food critic for the *Bloomingfield Daily Dispatch.* Too bad just the smell of chocolate makes her stomach roil.

By the time she reaches the last table, she hopes her face isn't as green as her holiday sweater. But the tall, square-jawed man behind piles of fudge makes her want to linger, even savor the moment along with his chocolate-coffee-flavored confection.

Except there's something Ben Elliot is hiding behind his piercing blue eyes and lazy grin, and her reporter's nose senses a story worth exploring. She finds herself longing to discover the secret ingredient sweetening their mutual attraction.

### *Holly's Gift*

Miracles don't always come easy. Sometimes it takes a secret wish to light an angel's way.

When Holly steps into a homeless shelter looking for an MIA piano student, she notices a distinct lack of Christmas cheer—because a handsome building inspector is forcing the shelter to temporarily close down.

Holly knows bad guys—she was married to one. Yet when the man asks her out, she finds *absolutely not* warring with *absolutely yes.*

Tim Stewart doesn't hold his breath waiting for God to answer prayers. He went from homeless desperation to television stardom to relative obscurity while God stayed silent. But when Holly barrels into his life, her steady faith sparks hope for a dream of his own. Even if it means praying for a Christmas miracle—one last time.

Cozy up, enjoy, and lose yourself in the wonderful season of love.

# PRAISE AND AWARDS

**USA TODAY bestselling author**

**#20 Amazon Bestseller Romance Anthologies (Books)**

**#34 Amazon Bestseller Romance Collections and Anthologies**

**#24 Amazon Bestseller Romance Anthologies (Kindle Store)**

# 5 STAR READER REVIEWS
## HOLIDAY HEARTS

**Amazon Review by Barbara W.:**

5.0 out of 5 stars

"I have read each of these stories and reviewed them separately. These three stories are full of things that happen to everyone. They bring us to hard truths, to fun times, to grief of friends gone too soon, of overcoming tragedy of the past, and learning to love again. I enjoyed each of these and hope you will, too!"

**Amazon Review by Bernadette C.:**

5.0 out of 5 stars

"Three great Christmas stories in one volume. If you like clean Christmas stories, these are for you. "

**Amazon Review by wn CB:**

5.0 out of 5 stars

"Needed stories that not only had happy endings but also reaffirmed God's love for us all. Thank you very much."

*This book is dedicated to all my wonderful readers who have supported me every inch of the way.*
*THANK YOU!*

# JOSIE RIVIERA

## Sweet
## PEPPERMINT
## Kisses

# 5 STAR READER REVIEWS

**Amazon Reviewer**

5.0 out of 5 stars

"Come meet Peppermint the horse who loves....peppermint candies plus spend Christmas at the ranch.

A wonderful, well written story mixing disappointment, loss, fear to love again with faith, determination, friendship and love plus the magic of Christmas making an enjoyable read."

**Amazon Review by Deb O.**

5.0 out of 5 stars

"This was my first Josie Riviera. This is such an awesome book Christmas book to get you ready for the season. It's a fast easy read with a great plot twists and turns, intriguing characters. I loved the romance between Vance and Chiara. Chiara is a nurse who is hired by Vance to help care for his sister. Vance is a computer app developer. Vance and his sister have not been celebrating Christmas, he lets Chiara bring the Christmas spirit and cheer in the house. Vance and Chiara's romance starts to blossom but has some bumpy roads, but in the end love finds away. I loved all the Christmas descriptions of the town, the house and all the horses, I especially loved Peppermint the horse, they made the story come alive! I highly recommend this book you will enjoy it like Idid and you need to grab a copy to see how they get their HEA!!! I will definitely be reading more of this author!!!"

Amazon Review by Stacy K.

5.0 out of 5 stars

"Chiara moved to Virginia three years ago for a guy and then she broke up with him and since she was already in school so she waited and this Christmas is the last time she is away from her family on Christmas. Vance is divorced and determined not to marry again and then he meets his sister's new nurse try as he might he can't get his mind off of her and now he and Gertrude are celebrating Christmas because of Chiara. Pregnant horses, two people who are scarred by love don't believe they can find it again is like watching a Hallmark movie but in actuality reading a Josie Riviera book. Awesome, well written and the characters are amazing."

# CHAPTER 1

*C*hiara Johnson sat on a chair near the chrome table in her kitchen, inhaling the enticing scents of vanilla and almond wafting from the oven as her cookies baked. Sighing, she peered around her modest apartment. Although she categorized the first day of December as the beginning of the holiday season, it didn't feel much like Christmas.

"Sugar cookies," her mother had always said, "were the answer to all life's problems."

Well, maybe they were.

Nostalgic images of baking with her mother and sister brought misty tears. These pangs of nostalgia erupted at the oddest moments, although in December, homesickness was justifiable.

Of course, she would volunteer at the women's center. Chiara believed in giving back, especially to an organization that had indirectly affected her. Adeline, one of her co-workers, had been homeless for a while until she secured a job. The shelter had enabled her to get back on her feet.

Besides, Chiara thought, volunteering gave her a sense of purpose.

It was just ... well ... she hadn't imagined herself still living in Turning Point, Virginia after three years.

Sure, she'd made friends. Adeline had even launched a book club that met in town every Friday evening, and the women were a delight to be around. However, with Chiara's work schedule, she had attended only a couple times.

She turned the volume louder on her cell phone as "I'll Be Home For Christmas," the 1943 version sung by Bing Crosby, came on. One of her favorite holiday tunes, she sang along to the last few bars: "If only in my dreams."

Dabbing the tears from her eyes, she stood to check on the sugar cookies.

Her cellphone rang and she answered, recognizing the incoming caller's ID.

"Hi, Emma," she said as she settled back in her chair.

"Are you sure you can't move home by Christmas?" her younger sister asked.

"You read my email? Yes, I'm positive." Chiara cradled the phone to her ear. "I accepted a full-time job for December to help pay off my last tuition bill."

"Couldn't someone else in your nursing agency work instead of you?"

Emma was a typical nine-year-old girl. She had a lot to say about every subject, couldn't see any side of the story except hers, and regarded Chiara as the world's best sister.

Chiara smiled. It was wonderful to feel adored.

"Everyone else in the agency either has a significant other or children or both," she replied. "And they all had holiday plans. I didn't, and I was available. Plus, the agency was scrambling to fill the position on such short notice."

"Mom and Dad said you're an awesome nurse. They say you genuinely care about people."

"Thank goodness parents put us on a pedestal, right?" Chiara laughed. "Between classes and other expenses, I've worked hard to make ends meet. Right now this job is necessary."

Wasn't *that* the understatement of the year?

Obviously, she couldn't ask her parents for money. Due to the recent economic downturn, they struggled financially. The Midwest had been hit particularly hard.

However, Chiara was determined to succeed. She'd studied nonstop to earn her RN degree at a high-quality Virginia university and planned on securing a stable, well-paying position.

"So, you start your new job right away?" Emma asked. She was chewing on something, presumably a fruit snack. The little girl ate fruit snacks endlessly.

"Monday is my first day, and it's a live-in position, so I'll be saving rent money," Chiara said. "My client is a woman recuperating from a fall and a concussion."

"Did she trip or something?"

Chiara went to the sink to run water into the mixing bowls. "She was riding a horse. The woman lives on a horse ranch."

"Horses? Lucky you! I want a brown and black pony for Christmas."

"Umm, horses are way too big for my liking and can be extremely dangerous. Also, it's not my ranch, and I won't be riding any horses."

"Maybe Santa will bring me a horse from the ranch. Tell him."

"I'll be staying in a guest apartment over the garage, and I probably won't run into Santa."

Chiara wondered if the over-the-garage apartment would be an improvement over her current home. The bland beige walls in the galley kitchen screamed for a colorful face-lift, and the vinyl flooring was outdated. A dose of Christmas decorations should have been on her to-do list. Unfortunately, between her classes and home-nursing appointments, she was beyond exhausted.

"Doesn't Santa come to Virginia?" Emma asked.

"I'm sure he does, although I've never seen Santa ride a horse."

Emma paused. "Do you think you'll see one of his elves?"

"You never know."

"Well, one of his elves riding a horse is almost as good as the real Santa."

"I agree."

"Just in case, I'll tell Santa I want a pony when I see him at the mall."

Chiara chuckled. "You do that." Homesickness welled again. She blew out a breath and kept her voice light. "I'll Skype all of you on Christmas Day, okay?"

She envisioned her parents and Emma attending the festival of lights exhibition in Kansas City. Oh, how her family delighted in the festivities, marking off the four Sundays before Christmas on the Advent calendar, skating every weekend on the city's outdoor rink. Emma would be the first one on the ice, gliding fearlessly, not afraid to fall.

Her chest squeezed. Family togetherness was the most significant part of the holidays, and she'd once again miss those days with the people she treasured most.

As she listened to Emma's excitement about the cool Harry Potter book she was reading, Chiara opened the oven to an eruption of heat. According to the recipe, the cookies were done. According to her eyes, they weren't. However, the last time she baked cookies, she had burned them until they were unrecognizable.

To be prudent, she removed the raw-looking cookies

from the oven and set the trays on the stove. Hopefully, they didn't taste the way they looked.

"Are you still there? Did you hear what I said?" Emma asked.

"Yes. I'm overjoyed you're liking the Harry Potter books." Chiara nodded into the phone. "I'm baking sugar cookies for my agency's holiday party and had to take them out of the oven."

"Remember how we test different recipes for our ginger-bread houses?" Emma giggled. "And how they always collapse?"

"We'll experiment with another recipe this year, an easier one." Chiara bit into a cookie before realizing it was burning her tongue. Gingerly, she chewed, swallowed, then groped for a glass of water. "Royal icing will stick the pieces together like cement."

"When? If you're not here, we won't be able to build a gingerbread house."

"I'll be home by New Year's Eve. This nursing gig is only for December."

*If* she lasted that long. The last wealthy family she'd worked for had treated her poorly. She remembered them well—five people residing in the same home, each settled into their separate spaces and hardly conversing with one another, disregarding her as nothing better than invisible hired help. Defensive, she'd managed her job professionally and kept to herself.

What gave some people the right to be so dismissive to others just because they had money?

She pushed away the memory and finished the cookie. It had hardened already and tasted delicious even without icing and sprinkles.

"Promise?" Emma was asking.

"Absolutely."

"And if you see Santa at the horse ranch—"

"I'll mention your pony request." Chiara glanced at the clock. "I should get ready for the Christmas party, so we'll talk soon. I love you."

"I love you too and I'm giving you a cyber cuddle."

This was Christmas, Chiara wanted to say. She needed more than a cuddle. She needed to be with people she cherished.

"Be good and tell Mom and Dad I send my love." She returned Emma's blown kisses and then ended the call.

That squeeze in her chest again, an ache of loneliness. Lips pressed tight, she moved to the counter where her laptop sat and switched her computer on. Quickly, she scrolled through the job listings on the nursing agency's website.

There it was. Her one-month gig.

*Home Nurse. Temporary live-in position assisting a woman with self-care, companionship and everyday tasks. Immediate opening.*

The agency's report stated the patient was recovering from a concussion and broken ankle after missing a vault in a high-stakes horse competition.

Just like Kevin.

Despite her efforts to never think about him, her mind brought up an image of her ex-boyfriend. Of course, his concussion and broken wrist hadn't been the result of a horse show. It had been the result of a bar fight.

Why, why, why were his violent tendencies so clear in hindsight? Fortunately, he'd never hit her. But if only she'd had that knowledge beforehand, had understood that a man's online dating profile didn't necessarily reveal who the man really was. Despite her parents' reservations, she had left home and relocated to Virginia to be near him. A few months after their relationship began, she realized he wasn't the guy for her and broke it off.

Although she longed for all things Kansas, by that point she'd enrolled in a nursing degree program and secured a full-time job.

So here she was, three years later. Overdrawn on her bank account, in a town she didn't consider home, not so much as a hint of a boyfriend, and celebrating Christmas by herself.

Focus on the future, not the past, her favorite pastor had once preached, and bring your views on life into context. A home was more than a building, more than a place. A home was where she was a participant, not a consumer who followed from the sidelines.

As she contemplated this, a message from V. Thatcher popped into her inbox:

"Miss Johnson, a change in plans. My sister has a late morning doctor's appointment. Please report for your position on Monday afternoon after lunch."

"Is four o'clock okay?" she quickly typed. "It would be better for me and give me more time to pack my things."

She pressed send, then felt her body freeze in place.

*Since when did a person who'd just gotten a job tell her employer what hour was best to meet?*

An immediate reply appeared.

"Make it five. The front gate will open when you drive up. Thanks. Vance Thatcher."

ON MONDAY AFTERNOON, Chiara heaved her suitcases into the living room. She tugged on red patent leather boots and buttoned her new cream-colored jacket, which had been an early Christmas gift to herself for completing her degree.

Peering into her bathroom mirror, she styled her blonde curls into a side bun and applied natural lip gloss. She wore no other make-up, so there was nothing she could do about the vivid spots of pink on both cheeks. She was eager, she told herself, anticipating her newest job. Or, she realized with a wry grin, she was punch-drunk from exhaustion.

As a result of late-afternoon traffic and bad weather, her trip took longer than expected. She drove her ancient Ford Escort slowly along the rain-slicked roads.

Strings of garland adorned the businesses on Post Avenue, the main street in town. Streetlights added a mellow glow to the silver puddles, and a sign advertised horse-drawn carriage rides.

All this fanfare because the town of only 20,000 inhabitants had been voted one of the most festive in America.

She couldn't contain her smile. The description was so fitting, notably at Christmas.

Sometimes, she marveled at how the townspeople did it. A week earlier, harvest flags and gourds had been everywhere. Now there wasn't a pumpkin in sight.

So why had she never seemed to belong, forever pining for Kansas's flat grasslands, the fields of wheat, the meat-falling-off-the-bone barbecues? The likelihood of a white Christmas in Kansas City was generally assured. In Virginia, December was commonly a rainy month. Turning Point averaged seven inches per year, so snow at Christmas was hit or miss.

If she were honest, she didn't even like snow, except between Christmas Eve and New Year's. Nevertheless, she loved four distinctive seasons, and Virginia had that commonality with Kansas.

Minutes later, her cellphone's map brought her to a street address at the north point of town. Her agency had detailed the property as an equestrian estate and, as she drove past, limitless tracts of farmland looked untouched. As she neared the final turn, she slowed and then stopped at a red light.

Further down, she sighted a gated driveway leading to a luxury log cabin mansion, sitting on acres of land and resembling a wooden lodge. The ranch even had a name—Wellington Acres. And according to the agency's information, the home bordered a pond.

So large. So beautiful. Despite the fluttering in her gut, Chiara dismissed her intimidation. She could do this.

Several horses grazed in pastures, and one tossed its head toward her. Behind the fencing, a white horse with big brown eyes seized a mouthful of grass, then greeted her with a whinny.

Emma would love it here—outside in nature, with all this open pasture to run wild and play. Age-old pine trees lined muddy trails. Whatever else happened, Chiara thought, Wellingon Acres was an extraordinary place to spend the holidays.

Perhaps she'd purchase a miniature evergreen tree for her garage apartment and spruce it up with bright gold tinsel. For Christmas, Emma wanted Judy Blume books, a portable piano keyboard, and a hair straightener for her unruly blonde curls. With part of her salary, Chiara could give Emma a special Christmas, and the items would easily fit into her luggage.

Except for the pony. Chiara grinned. Well, her sister would need to wait, unless ponies learned how to fly.

She fiddled with the radio while she waited for the light to change. On the other side of the highway, a bright-red Corvette sped toward the light, apparently intending to run the yellow. Despite the rain and swiftly falling darkness, the car had no headlights and was cruising well over the twenty-five mile per hour speed limit. The teenage boy behind the wheel glanced down, undoubtedly studying his cellphone. Then he gestured to another teen boy in the passenger seat.

A drumming sound grabbed Chiara's attention. A large black horse had galloped onto the road. Wildly, she looked around. Where had the horse come from?

The Corvette sped closer. The horse's eyes were wide with fright as it whinnied in terror.

The driver of the Corvette looked up in time and slammed on the brakes. The car fishtailed on the wet road, coming perilously close to the horse. The driver overcompensated, and the car swerved off the road, hurtling through a pasture fence. The horse spun in a circle and loped away.

Noise exploded all around Chiara—horses in the pasture neighing, the boys screaming.

She jerked her car over to the curb, shut off the ignition, and dashed across the road. The sharp cold air seemed to slice through her as she raced to reach the boys.

Clearly shaken, they emerged from the Corvette. One was crying as he wiped at his bleeding forehead. The other was shaking and whimpering. As she pulled her cell phone from her purse, he pleaded for her not to call his parents.

She didn't know his parents' phone number, she thought to reply. Instead, she stayed quiet, and, with disciplined focus, she examined them both for injuries and spoke quietly to calm them. Then, supporting the wounded boy's head in her lap, she punched in 911.

# CHAPTER 2

$\mathcal{V}$ ance Thatcher sat in his favorite wingback chair across from his younger sister, Gertrude, in the living room of their childhood home at Wellington Acres. Between them, the fire crackled and burned cheerfully in the stone fireplace, bringing warmth to a massive room that boasted a twenty-seven-foot-high vaulted ceiling.

"How's the beta phase going for your new computer app?" Gertrude asked.

He could go on and on about how he thought his dating app would revolutionize matchmaking since he was using broader parameters than other dating sites, such as similar tastes in movies, books, and foods, as well as mutual friends.

He didn't say a word, though. Legs outstretched, he settled back in his chair and surveyed the pine-paneled study across the hallway. His thoughts ran together, reflecting on all the responsibilities he had left to accomplish before the day was over.

"If you have to make any business calls …" Gertrude was indulging in her nightly glass of red wine, set on a table beside her wheelchair.

"My phone calls can wait a while longer." He pushed to his feet and glanced at his watch. "Chiara Johnson should have been here at five o'clock."

"It's only a couple hours past."

"She obviously doesn't need a job if she keeps prospective employers waiting this long. Her credentials are outstanding, her references were verified, and the nursing agency highly recommended her. Apparently, everyone was wrong." He had little patience for people who weren't dependable. If she decided to show up, he was going to tell her all that and more.

Gertrude brushed a strand of hair from her face. She had pulled her long hair into a ponytail, highlighting the startling contrast between her black hair and pallid complexion. Her freckles nearly jumped off her skin.

He studied her, searching for the same bright eyes and flash of adventure in the sister who seemed to have disappeared. Her cheeks were ashen, her eyes dull.

*Ever since the accident.*

His heart thudded a solemn beat.

A daredevil, Gertrude surely longed to be outside doing what she loved best … skiing in Colorado, gliding through a canopy of trees on a zip line, riding fearlessly on her favorite horse across the open pastures. All while his warnings stuck in his throat and he ordered his lips to stay sealed. Otherwise, she'd accuse him of over-reacting.

Instead, she was confined to a wheelchair, a result of a broken ankle and a cumbersome cast, and further incapacitated by a concussion.

"Vance, you should get back to your office in town," she said.

He'd thought the same thing about a million times. "I can work from home. I've been able to accomplish just about everything from here."

"'Just about' isn't enough, at least not for you. And then you played hooky from work today to drive me to a doctor's appointment." She went for her wine, sipped, swallowed. Typical Gertrude, his dramatic-pause sister. "I could've rung a taxi."

"Absolutely not. Cognitive testing was scheduled during your neurology examination."

"And it wasn't necessary. My memory and concentration are outstanding. Your start-up business app isn't going to start up by itself."

She was right, but he didn't want to leave her. He couldn't help himself. It was necessary to ensure she was able to rest, both physically and mentally. In the first couple of days after the accident, she'd been so badly confused, she could barely function.

And that had scared him.

He strode to the large picture window, leaned his shoulder on the frame and gazed outside. Nighttime had gathered, casting the pastures in a dark charcoal hue. Their five-bedroom home afforded panoramic views of the fields, horse barn and bordering pond. He and Gertrude had inherited Wellington Acres from their parents. Along with the property, though, had come unexpected debt.

He studied his parent's wedding portrait over the fireplace mantel, an overly large black-and-white photo. They held themselves straight, staring into the camera, not even holding hands. Had they ever been in love, especially after the debts started rolling in?

Next month would have been their fortieth wedding anniversary.

"Perhaps Mom and Dad didn't know how to handle money," Gertrude said, reading his thoughts. She too gazed at the portrait.

"Perhaps?" He turned to her. "More likely, they

19

completely disregarded a mortgage and property taxes since they were too busy jet-setting."

In his mind, Vance ticked off the chores he intended to discuss with the ranch manager, Joe Brown, before he left for another late night working alongside his computer programmers.

A fence was down in an outlying pasture, a result of all the rain. The horses, he thought ruefully, were the easy part of running a ranch.

His cell phone pinged. Vance glanced at the text from one of his investors. The investor was reminding Vance about their meeting in Turning Point the next morning at ten o'clock. He acknowledged the message with a quick response, then shoved the phone into his pocket. He'd much rather be writing code than talking to businessmen, trying to drum up financial support.

"Vance." Gertrude's delicate chin lifted. "I can certainly handle this interview by myself."

"I won't leave you alone until I know there's a nurse in place."

"Amanda's here."

"She's not a nurse, she's a housekeeper, as she has reminded us very politely one hundred times. Besides, at sixty years old, Amanda has enough to do. Suppose you require—"

"Since I got home from the hospital, you've never been more than two steps away from me." Gertrude's lips trembled as she held back a laugh. "All this hovering is getting on my nerves."

For a moment, he stared at her, too startled to speak. *He was hovering?*

"I can stay, really," he replied.

"No, you can't. Besides, you've accomplished more than enough already when you should've been involved in your app's beta testing phase. Instead, you're in your study paying bills, or making phone calls, or ensuring I'm comfortable—"

"You're making me sound like a helicopter brother."

"That's a term used for parents who are excessively protective of their children, although the description aptly suits you." She grinned, then sobered. "Our ranch is finally productive. I never thanked you, and I should."

"You're welcome." He nodded. "By the way, I fixed the pregnant mare's paddock fencing."

"And how was Peppermint this morning?"

"You know her, the official greeter of the horse world in all her snowy white splendor. Even being six months pregnant, she's as social as ever. She's no bother, and neither are you."

In truth, he wanted to do more for Gertrude. Ten years his junior, she looked so young and frail, so different from the wild, anything-for-a-dare sibling he'd grown up with. If their parents were alive, she undoubtedly would have added to their gray hairs.

Or not. They'd been so busy on their travel adventures, they probably wouldn't have noticed the scrapes their daughter got into. In fact, he couldn't recall when their parents were around for more than a few months at a time.

"Vance, really. Go."

He wavered, peered at the clock, and then went to get his parka hung on a brass rack in the foyer. The December 31 deadline for the official presentation of the app to his investor group was coming fast.

"Amanda can help me get into bed," Gertrude assured him when he returned. "And tomorrow we'll place another Internet ad."

"Miss Johnson should have called, or texted, or—"

"It's the Christmas season." Gertrude checked him in mid-sentence. "People are busy. Just because we don't observe the holidays doesn't mean other families don't."

They'd rarely celebrated Christmas. As a boy, he'd heard vivid descriptions of Santa and his flying reindeer from his classmates, but Santa never rode his sleigh to the Thatcher house. The Thatchers never put up a tree or exchanged presents. If they had, his parents probably would have hired a personal shopper to buy their gifts.

Briefly, Vance closed his eyes and sighed. He'd always liked Christmas—the snippets of traditions he gleaned from his classmates and friends, the endearing movies on television, the beloved music. And church. He remembered attending services with his family when he was young, hearing about Bethlehem and the wise men and the birth of baby Jesus.

But they stopped attending church regularly, then not at all.

When he'd asked his parents why, he never received a clear answer. He'd only been a kid then, and after a few years, it didn't matter. It was just the way things were done in their house.

"When Miss Johnson replied to your email," Gertrude said, "she requested her interview time be changed. Maybe she had family commitments."

From what he'd gathered from her agency's report, she wasn't married, nor had children.

He paused, shuffled his feet, eyed the majestic grandfather clock in the corner.

"My accident wasn't your fault," Gertrude said softly. "Don't keep blaming yourself."

"I should have been there for you."

"Like you could've stopped my horse from throwing me." She waved her hand. "Don't be ridiculous, Vance. You can't solve all the world's problems."

"Only half." Grinning, he strode to her and grazed a kiss on her shiny hair. "If Chiara Johnson happens to show, text me. In the meantime, I'll grab a flashlight and take a walk to the stable."

As he was about to leave, Amanda rushed into the room.

"Mr. Thatcher? Miss Johnson has arrived. And she brought someone with her."

Gertrude looked up, her gaze puzzled. "Who?"

Amanda hesitated, catching her breath, tucking strands of silver hair into her bun. "A police officer who wishes to speak with Mr. Thatcher."

"Police? Why?" With a slight shake of his head, Vance wondered again about the audacity of a woman who not only ran two hours late for a new job, but decided to arrive with a police escort.

Gertrude launched her wheelchair forward. "Is the woman hurt?"

"Wait here." Vance placed a hand on her arm to stop her, then draped his parka over the wingback chair. "I'll go see."

"No one's hurt, Miss Thatcher." Amanda clasped her hands together. "Although Licorice broke through the pasture fence and caused a car accident down the road."

# CHAPTER 3

"**M**r. Thatcher?"

"Call me Vance."

"Vance. I … I assume we should cancel our meeting." Chiara stared at the dark-haired, slightly bearded man wearing jeans and a heather-gray T-shirt. He and Officer Bennington, the policeman who had accompanied her to the residence after the accident, had spoken privately while she had ducked into the marbled powder room off the foyer to wash her hands and face. Now she faced the man who was supposed to be her employer.

"Why cancel now?" Vance extended his hand. "I presume you're Miss Johnson."

"Please call me Chiara. And yes, of course, you're right. Why cancel now?"

Oh, my. He was so good-looking. She didn't mean to gawk, but he radiated the casual refinement she recognized in the well-to-do. Just the type she dreaded—supremely confident, prosperous and privileged.

This close, she caught the scent of him—open air and cedar and fine leather.

Feeling totally out of her element, she glanced around. The home reminded her more of a getaway retreat for the Vanderbilts than a real house.

He assessed her in turn, and she imagined what he saw. Wrinkled black slacks, muddy boots, her cream-colored jacket stained with blood.

Entirely self-conscious, she accepted his outstretched hand. His fingers were callused and firm, not the fingers she imagined for a moneyed man who ran an equestrian estate this size. She assumed he sat parked behind a desk all day and issued orders to his employees.

But no, evidently not.

"I apologize for my lateness. There was an accident."

Ridiculous. Of course, he was aware of that. Why couldn't she think straight around self-assured men? She avoided dating guys like Vance because they made her feel like a minion.

"Please. No apologies." His eyes, the color of deep mahogany, held her gaze. "Officer Bennington briefed me, and my manager called to say he's safely secured our runaway horse. Licorice is my sister's horse, actually, and very tame." He glanced at the policeman, then returned his attention to her. "I'm sorry I wasn't notified sooner. I could have helped." His gaze flicked to their hands, still joined.

"Miss Johnson was certainly an asset." Officer Bennington offered her a brief salute. "She knew precisely what to do. Fortunately, the teenage boys weren't hurt—only some surface wounds and scratches. They've been transported to the hospital in town, their car towed, and their parents notified. You're well-trained, miss. Thank you."

"You're welcome." Chiara pulled her hand from Vance's grasp. "I'm glad I could assist." Without warning, tears pooled. She blamed them on the stress of the move, the accident, the pressure of this new job. She drew a hard breath to collect herself and sidestepped the men's gazes. Fortunately, neither seemed to notice her distress as they walked toward the front door. Or, they were well-schooled in the art of politeness.

After ushering the officer out, Vance walked back and openly studied her. "Are you okay?"

She brushed a stray tear on her cheek. "Yes, of course."

"Sorry about your coat. Once you're settled, I'll have it cleaned."

She stared down at the blood stains, and a wave of emotion clogged her throat. "Thank you."

He paused. "Do you have another?"

"Coat? Yes. It's in my suitcase in my car." Along with everything else she owned.

*Keep cool. No more tears. No long-winded explanations. He's your employer and doesn't care about your traumatic day.*

Besides, she refused to crumble into an embarrassing meltdown in front of him.

She shook out her slacks, straightened her shoulders and held onto her determination.

A grandfather clock in the foyer chimed the hour. Eight o'clock.

"I'd like you to meet my sister, Gertrude," Vance said, "so you two can get to know each other. Afterward, I'll show you to the guest loft above the garage." He guided her to the living room where his sister waited in a wheelchair.

Gertrude was beautiful, with jet-black hair slicked into a ponytail and a sharp sprinkle of freckles across her cheeks. A flicker of a resemblance to Vance shone in her keen brown eyes.

She wore an ankle-length plaid skirt and V-neck yellow sweater.

Chiara smiled and acknowledged a greeting, then scanned the room. The vaulted ceiling added to the enormity of the space, painted in subdued gray tones. A fire burned in the grate, emitting a hint of pine.

And no Christmas decorations anywhere. Certainly not a tree, but not even a wreath over the massive fireplace, nor a grouping of glowing holiday candles on the mahogany buffet table. It was sad. She couldn't think of a room more suited for a joyous tree and shimmering gold-leaf garland.

A shiny-black grand piano was positioned beside the picture window. How Emma would have loved to run her fingers over the keys of such a magnificent instrument, Chiara thought. She'd been teaching herself how to play using YouTube videos.

Turning from the piano, Chiara focused on Gertrude. Once they started talking, she took an instant liking to the younger woman. She had a spark in her smile, a sense of mischievousness that reminded her of Emma.

"This wheelchair is temporary," Gertrude explained. "I had a bad fall from my horse in a riding accident. The doctor said I'll be recovering for a few more weeks, at least until Christmas."

So she said the word *Christmas* although they clearly didn't celebrate. Unless they preferred to wait until Christmas Eve to decorate as lots of people did.

In Kansas, Chiara's parents would have illuminated their house as if they were competing in a Christmas pageant by now. Their decorations went up on Thanksgiving night. A giant tree took up half the area in the narrow den, and their outdoor-lights display beckoned cars to stop and take photos.

Gertrude turned toward Vance. "How is Licorice? Did Joe—"

"Licorice is safely boarded in her stall. And Joe Brown is no concern of yours."

"Don't tell me what to do, big brother." Chiara caught the

look of stubbornness on Gertrude's face. "Joe's a remarkable guy. He's responsible and reliable and his affinity to horses matches mine. We share a common bond."

"He's an efficient manager. Too bad you don't share a common age." With an exasperated shake of his head, Vance grabbed his parka and shepherded Chiara out of the room.

"Thanks for taking the position," he said.

She extended a smile. "That was the fastest getting-to-know-you conversation I've ever had."

"I have a business meeting this evening and I'm already late." He tapped his watch. "So we're all set. My sister seems to like you. Officer Bennington likes you." He paused, his gaze softening. "And I like you."

"So, it's okay for me to live in the guest apartment?"

He pulled on his parka. "There's space for a small army on this ranch. It's only Gertrude and I and a household staff of two. Currently I'm tied up, which is why we advertised for extra help while my sister recovers."

"What do you do?" What a question, she scolded herself. Just look around.

She was gazing at him again, like she'd never seen a handsome guy before. But oh, with his sinewy muscles beneath his worn T and his movie-star smile, she couldn't deny the instant magnetism.

"I work." He zippered up his parka, and she regretted the loss of the view of his broad shoulders. "And then I work, work and work."

"And at other times?"

"Probably more work." He grinned, his smile crooked and appealing, and her heart did a flip-flop in her chest.

Chiara followed Vance past her parked car, across the gravel driveway to the garage, then up the exterior stairs to the guest quarters. He unlocked the door, and they entered the loft.

"Here it is." He spread out his hands, indicating curved stucco walls and slate tile flooring. In a whirlwind, he gave her an abridged tour of the eighteen-by-thirty-six-foot space, which was comprised of a bedroom, open-style kitchen, living room, and bathroom with a laundry nook.

"Wow, it's incredible. I never imagined anything as well-appointed." She unbuttoned her coat. "This apartment is the opposite of my former place in town."

"Which was?"

"Umm, in dire need of a thorough repainting for one thing. I considered painting the place myself."

"Well, please don't decide to repaint this apartment. You'll be busy enough keeping my chatty sister company. So here's the key." He set it on the coffee table.

"Thanks, Vance, and I'll say it before you do." She stood in the kitchen and held up a hand. "I'm not in Kansas anymore."

He laughed. "I saw on your application that you're originally from Kansas City."

"Yes, it's my home. That's why I can get away with that *Wizard of Oz* saying."

"That movie is all I know about Kansas. I was envisioning a dark-haired girl in pigtails wearing ruby-red shoes. You're wearing red boots."

"But, my name isn't Dorothy, and I'm a blonde," she countered.

"You know, you're a lot prettier than Dorothy." His dark eyes glinted as he closed the distance between them. "In fact, you're very beautiful."

She felt her cheeks heat as she gathered her thoughts into a protest.

"And do you want to know a secret?" he continued with a grin.

He was well-polished. A real charmer. She'd give him that.

"Do I have a choice?" she asked.

"I imagined you with curly blonde hair. And wearing a ruffled green blouse that matched your emerald eyes."

She took a step back and regarded him. "How did—"

"Your agency forwarded your profile picture along with your application."

Okay. She'd had the picture taken a year ago, her hair freshly styled, wearing pink lip gloss and her favorite pair of gold hoop earrings. Well, she certainly didn't look anything like that this evening, and, she assumed, he was quite disenchanted.

"Dorothy from Kansas," he said, smiling his heart-tripping grin again. "If you strolled into my foyer carrying a little dog named Toto ..."

She chuckled. "Chiara from Kansas—please."

"Chiara." He focused on her face with disconcerting intensity. "Your dimples turn up whenever you speak of your home. I suspect you miss Kansas?"

"Very much. My parents and sister live there and I'm returning for good after this job." She paused. She'd said too much. "Have you always lived in Virginia?"

He gestured toward the window and fields beyond. "Nowhere else, although my parents traveled all over the world. Nowadays, the ranch and my business keep me occupied." His smile turned grim and then faded altogether. "At any rate, I'm grateful someone can utilize these guest quarters. No one's ever here, unless a displaced cousin happens to call on us."

"Are you expecting guests for the holidays?"

"Considering my cousins haven't visited in years, and last I heard they migrated to Ireland, I safely assume no one will be here except you and me and Gertrude." He checked his watch. He did that a lot. "I'll get your suitcases, then I'm heading to the stable, then straight into town."

He left. Within minutes, he reappeared carrying her suitcases, strode through the apartment and placed them in the bedroom.

It was remarkable, she thought. All her material possessions fit into two suitcases, which was all she needed. All this commercialism at Christmastime, the buy, buy, buy mentality, was disheartening. The true meaning of Christmas could be found in ... Well, in Kansas, attending church services, watching holiday movies on TV, and baking cookies with her family.

"The refrigerator and pantry are stocked," he said. "I can phone Amanda to deliver dinner."

"No, I'm fine, really. I'll eat breakfast in the morning."

"What's your cell phone number?" When she told him, he sent her a quick text to confirm his. "Report to the house tomorrow morning at eight. I won't be around much these next few weeks."

"Because of work?"

His dark eyebrows lifted and he grinned. "Work, work, work. If you're missing anything while you're here, text me." He brushed a hand against hers as she walked him to the door.

"Sure. Thanks." Her cheeks warmed at his touch. What was she doing? She wasn't an enamored employee with a crush on her handsome employer. She'd only known him a little over an hour.

*You're here one month, remember? And then you're homeward bound.*

Yes, yes, she remembered. With a head shake, she shook off her attraction.

After Vance left, she devoted the next hour to unpacking, then showered with her favorite lemon body wash she'd brought with her. All the while, she couldn't stop thinking about Vance. He had touched her hand lightly, a fleeting,

31

spur-of-the-moment gesture. Yet his touch lit a strange sensation inside her.

After slipping into a pair of pink velour lounge pants and a cozy sweatshirt, she inspected her blood-stained coat draped over the chesterfield sofa. She'd forgotten to give it to Vance.

She set a kettle on the stove for tea and opened the container of leftover sugar cookies. She was thankful she'd brought them. After the exhausting day, she needed comfort food and a jolt of pure sugar.

On her first day off she'd drive into town for groceries, and purchase an evergreen tree and wreath to bring Christmas cheer to her cozy loft.

She plugged in her phone and switched on her favorite holiday radio station. A piano arrangement came on playing a buoyant "Jingle Bells."

A crunch of tires on the gravel driveway prompted her to peek out the window. It was a little after ten PM, and Mr. Dreamboat Employer was getting out of his SUV. She hurried to open the door as she heard him climb the outside stairs.

"My coat," she said. "We both forgot. It's on the couch."

He wiped his boots on the mat on the landing. "I'll get it." He walked past her into the apartment, wearing the same parka he'd worn earlier with the addition of scuffed work boots.

"Really, you didn't have to come back to—"

"Never turn down a man offering to help." He got to her coat before she did. From behind, his thick black hair was longer than she'd first realized and curled at his nape. She recognized the scent of fine leather again on his clothes, and the scent was oddly reassuring.

"How is your runaway horse?" she asked.

"Licorice? Spooked, but calm now." He hung her coat on

the doorknob, then reached inside his parka and brandished a bottle of sparkling water. "I was in a rush earlier and forgot proper protocol. My apologies. Welcome to Wellington Acres."

"Thank you."

A beat passed.

From the kitchen, the piano arrangement of "Jingle Bells" had morphed into a medley of "We Need A Little Christmas."

He was staring at her. Or rather, she was staring at him. Why hadn't she bothered to brush out her hair after her shower? When her hair dried naturally, it spun into a mass of curls.

He flicked a glance toward the kitchen, then her. "I love jazz piano music," he said.

"Me too. My sister plays piano. Or rather, she wants to learn how to play."

He rested an elbow on the back of the sofa, along the quilted leather upholstery. "I play."

"Piano? Really? I wondered when I saw the gorgeous Steinway in your living room."

This ruggedly handsome man had an artsy side she hadn't expected.

"So, we have something in common," he said. "The piano."

She pondered pointing out how much of a comparison stretch that was. He played a real piano, a glossy nine-foot concert grand. Her sister pretended her desk was a keyboard.

"Weren't you busy tonight?" Her gaze flicked toward the door. "What about your appointment in town?"

"I canceled it. I'll meet with my investors in the morning."

"So you'd like to come inside?"

"I am inside. If I'm invited, I'll stay."

"It's your apartment." She started for the kitchen while he tugged off his parka and placed it on a chair. She glanced over her shoulder. "How's your sister?"

"Sleeping." He followed her. "Since the concussion, she's susceptible to headaches and requires a lot of rest. Now she goes to bed at the time she used to go out partying."

"Thanks to the information the agency provided, I read up on her case."

"Then you know that because she's in her early twenties, the doctor confirmed she should recover quickly. Youth is a great healer."

Chiara looked up just in time to see an unexpected emotion pass across his face. Sadness? Contemplation? She couldn't identify it.

"I'm protective of my little sister," she offered into the silence. "Apparently so are you, and I understand completely."

She took a breath when he didn't respond. "I was brewing tea, although sparkling water sounds … refreshing." She reached for two glasses in the cupboard, then motioned toward the counter. "I brought the last batch of Christmas cookies I baked the other day. Do you want any?"

"Cookies?" He grinned. "Now I'm even happier I canceled my appointment tonight."

Why was he here? From what he'd said, he was beyond busy.

He flooded their glasses with water and brought them into the living room. She trailed with her container of cookies and set them on the coffee table.

They perched on either end of the deep-buttoned sofa, sinking into the smooth leather. She kept her hands on her lap, her feet on the floor.

Sitting on a sofa with a man. She hadn't done anything like that in ages.

"Tell me more about Kansas." He reached for a cookie, closed his eyes and chewed appreciatively.

"Well, I lived there all my life, until I moved to Virginia.

Our snowfalls around the holidays are lovely, and that's one of the things I miss most."

"And soon you're flying back."

"Finally."

He was quiet before grabbing another cookie. "These are heavenly."

"Thanks. It's a simple recipe, compliments of my mom's Christmas cookie collection."

"My family never celebrated Christmas."

"So you never attended church services?"

"Very rarely."

"You're a musician. At Christmas, the music is awe-inspiring, especially if there's a full choir and an organist."

He shrugged, and she couldn't tell if he didn't care or if he had learned not to care. And why had she asked him such personal questions, about religion and music?

"We just never attended," he said. "Too swamped with the ranch and my parents traveling far and wide."

"I'll be happy to bake one of my favorite cookie recipes with your sister and bring a little Christmas cheer into your lives. That is, if you're interested."

The melody from the other room had definitely inspired her.

He gazed at her for an interminable moment and then smiled. "I'm very interested."

A shiver of attraction raced through her. Quickly, she changed the subject. "And yes, to answer your earlier question, I love Kansas."

"I've never been."

"You need to go. People expect *The Wizard Of Oz* and tornadoes, but Kansas is so much more. Our motto is Ad Astra per Aspera."

"To the stars with difficulty." He translated the Latin. "But what does that really mean?"

"Honestly, I don't know." She chuckled. "What about you? What about your work?"

"Besides the ranch and ensuring my sister gets better, I'm developing a computer app."

"I applaud anyone who's skillful with computers. I can turn my laptop on and off. If anything goes wrong, I've got the Geek Squad on speed dial. What's your app about?"

He was quiet. The music coming from the kitchen had changed to a violin rendition of "O Little Town Of Bethlehem."

"It's a dating app," he finally replied.

"A dating app." She caught herself before she gaped. Certainly, he hadn't made the app for himself. With his good looks and easy charm, he probably had more dates in a month than she'd had in her twenty-five years. "Does your app have a name?"

"Vulcan."

"Vulcan?" She paused. "As in *Star Trek?*"

"In Roman mythology, Vulcan is sometimes referred to as cupid's father."

She quirked an eyebrow.

"Sometimes, not always." He smiled. "So we ran with that idea and our slogan will be 'An outer-space love,' and will feature a cherub aiming a bow and arrow toward the sky."

Really? *Really?* She couldn't imagine any woman subscribing to a dating app with that name and philosophy.

"What about the name Cupid's bow?" she asked.

"I like that." He shrugged. "Too late to change anything now, though."

Wisely, she grabbed her water and took a big gulp, keeping her thoughts to herself. "Oh, well, good luck."

"Thanks, I'll need it." He flashed her a smile, displaying even white teeth. "There's lots of competition in the computer world these days."

She sincerely doubted he needed luck with anything. He was much too self-assured. Competency fairly oozed from his strong shoulders.

"Enough about me." He picked up his glass. "What about you?"

"Most likely, you know more about me than I do, thanks to my agency's profile."

"Tell me anyway."

She wrapped her hands around her glass. "After years of course work and studying, I'm officially a licensed RN."

He chewed another cookie, swallowed a half glass of water. "Officer Bennington said you were exceptionally competent at the accident scene."

"I enjoy helping people. It's what I'm trained for and what I do best."

He shifted closer, lifted his glass to hers and clinked. "Cheers. To Kansas and helping people and Christmas cookies."

"And to your sister's quick recovery and to—to Vulcan."

"Absolutely." He set his glass on the table, then fixed his hands to his knees. "Thanks for a relaxing evening. Unfortunately, work beckons and I should go."

She accompanied him to the door and handed him her coat. "Thank you for the sparkling water."

"You're welcome." He shrugged into his parka. "I'll see you tomorrow."

"Don't you have appointments with investors, and the ranch, and—"

"If you recall," he said, grinning, "I live here. I'll make time. Maybe we can have dinner together."

Wait. No. She wasn't the type of woman to have a casual fling with her employer. She was leaving Virginia soon. Hadn't he listened when she told him about her intent to return to Kansas?

"Why?" she asked hesitantly.

"You do eat, don't you?"

"Yes, but—"

"So, we'll have dinner. Gertrude dines early, and I'm usually done working by seven."

"No, really, I'll be—"

"Chiara." He touched her arm. "You want to bring a little Christmas cheer into my life, remember?"

# CHAPTER 4

*V*ance kept his gaze on the enchanting woman sitting across from him in his living room. Chiara was perched on the edge of a silk-embroidered settee while Gertrude sat in her wheelchair. The two women leaned closer to each other, studying Gertrude's medical record, their serious conversation punctuated by bursts of laughter.

Speaking in a kind voice yet firmly, Chiara paged through the report, confirming all the doctor's instructions. She added at the end, "The doctor will determine when it's safe to begin light physical activity."

"Yes, yes, I know all that." Gertrude waved a hand dismissively. "But I'd do anything to get out of this wheelchair."

"You will. Your equilibrium is still shaky," Vance put in. He was comfortably seated in his wingback chair in front of the cheerful fire in the fireplace. He'd been checking emails on his tablet, but found his attention kept veering to Chiara.

Gertrude slumped back. "I miss seeing Joe and riding Licorice."

"There are two good reasons why you should stay right here in this house while you heal," he said.

Chiara opened her mouth, apparently to dispute him, and he held up a hand. "My sister has trouble setting boundaries, Chiara. One minute she'll be at the stable, the next she'll be riding her horse at a gallop around the widest curve. You've known Gertrude for a half hour. I've known her my entire life."

Chiara smiled at him. "You're right. I'm sorry to intrude."

He smiled back, his gaze shifting to his sister, then Chiara. She set the medical instructions aside and asked Gertrude about the book, *The Horse Whisperer*. Apparently, she'd seen the movie and loved it, although Gertrude was claiming the Robert Redford movie and the book were totally different.

Annoyed his cell phone had pinged a half dozen times, Vance checked the latest text from one of his tech developers.

*I said I'll be at the office by ten*, he replied.

He loosened his tie and stretched out his long legs. He intended to stay right where he was for as long as he could, sitting across from Chiara, admiring her lovely face and easy laugh.

The previous evening, he hadn't known what to expect when she showed up at his door with a police officer. He couldn't remember what she wore except for her blood-stained coat.

However, when she'd arrived a half hour ago, he'd caught his breath as he took her lightweight jacket.

"This is not warm enough for December," he'd said.

"All I have," she'd replied, shrugging.

"I'll take your other coat to the dry cleaners today."

"Yes. You told me last night. Thanks." She met his gaze. "Is anything wrong?"

"No. Why?"

"You're staring at me."

"You look lovely." She wore a slim-fitting black skirt and blue turtleneck sweater. That shapely figure. He'd be thinking about her all day while he met with his investors and programmers. Even more captivating than her slender form, her expressive green eyes fascinated him.

His sister had been waiting for Chiara since dawn, her new early-to-bed-early-to-rise schedule prompting her to drink a first cup of coffee with him before he left for the stable to begin chores. When he brought Chiara into the living room, Gertrude had asked her if she'd had breakfast. "We've got coffee and croissants."

"I ate, thanks," Chiara answered. "The loft is certainly well-equipped. Someone thought of everything—right down to bread, milk, and butter."

"All because of Vance. He's a planner," Gertrude said.

Chiara offered him a smile. "I'm a planner too."

"So we have something else in common."

Her smile widened.

She was a beautiful woman, and when she smiled, she was stunning. Her creamy skin glowed, and her curly blond hair framed her heart-shaped face.

Gertrude swept her hand toward the buffet table, where there was a coffee pot and porcelain cups, as well as a selection of croissants. "Coffee?"

"Thank you. I'd love some."

"I'll get it," Vance said. "Cream, sugar?"

"Just black."

Chiara accepted the cup and turned to Gertrude as Vance settled in his wingback chair with his tablet, intending to catch up on tech news while the women talked. But Chiara's first comment caught his attention.

"Tell me about your life before you were confined to a wheelchair."

"You mean last month?"

Chiara grinned. "Go as far back as you're comfortable."

Gertrude clasped her hands. "Brace yourself." She revealed her tumultuous teenage years and the older man she ran away with when she was eighteen. Chiara's expression was accepting, non-judgmental, but Vance was stunned his sister held nothing back.

"And now my excitement every day is trying to decide what to eat for lunch," Gertrude finished.

"All that will change as you get better." Chiara picked up the medical report and began going through Gertrude's injuries and what she needed to do to get better. Now the two women were talking books, Gertrude offering to loan Chiara *The Horse Whisperer* when she was done.

"What are you reading next?" Chiara asked.

Gertrude shrugged. "I've never been much of a reader. I mostly read mysteries. Can you recommend anything?"

"I like mysteries too. Have you read Agatha Christie's short story Christmas collection?"

"No, but I'd be willing to give it a try."

"I used to attend a book club in town with a former class-mate." Chiara finished her coffee and set her cup on the side table. "Why don't we create our own book club, and every day we'll discuss the chapters we've read."

"How fun!" Gertrude's smile was one of pure pleasure. "Finally, something to do in this big house until I can get to the stable."

"What's the name of the Agatha Christie book?" Vance interrupted. "When I go to town, I'll stop at the library."

"*The Adventure of the Christmas Pudding*," Chiara said. "Get two copies."

"You better write it down, Vance. Otherwise you'll

forget." Gertrude curved to Chiara, raising her eyebrows. "For such a brilliant man, he overlooks the littlest details. He says he can multitask, although it's been proven humans can't focus on more than one thing at a time."

"I'm right here." Vance's teasing voice roused a grin from both women. "And I can easily multitask."

As proof, he was focusing on Chiara while replying to his sister.

"Nobody can multitask. It's a myth," Gertrude replied. "But if you're happy being delusional, it's up to you."

Chiara kept her gaze on Gertrude and ignored Vance. "We can bake my mother's sugar cookies too. They're delicious."

"The same cookies I tasted last night?" Vance asked.

"The very same." Chiara's expression grew wistful. "My sister and I bake all sorts of cookies in Kansas."

"I've never been to Kansas," Gertrude said.

"It's wonderful." Chiara's voice had a catch to it, but when she looked at them both, she brightened. "But we weren't talking about Kansas, we were discussing cookies, and we can't have a book club without serving desserts."

"And wine?" Vance suggested.

Chiara regarded him with amusement. "Or tea."

"Wine is better."

For a beat, their laughing gazes held.

"Wine and homemade cookies are the perfect pairing," Gertrude said decidedly, then signaled to Vance to pour them all another round of coffee.

Compliant, he pushed to his feet. His sister's needs always came first.

"Gertrude, do you know if you have all the ingredients for cookies?" Chiara asked. "This recipe calls for several cups of sugar and flour."

"The kitchen is on your left." Gertrude pointed to the

foyer. "I'm not much of a cook, but Amanda can show you what's in the cupboards."

"I'll only be a minute." Chiara left for the kitchen.

"So, Vance." His sister gave him a deliberate, knowing smile as he passed her a fresh cup of coffee. "For a busy guy, you certainly slowed your pace this morning."

His own smile was bland. "I wanted to be sure Chiara was a good fit for you."

"And for you?"

Ignoring her, he walked over to the buffet table and chose a strawberry croissant.

Why was Gertrude always so preoccupied with his dating status? She seemed convinced that if she couldn't find happiness and true love, then surely he could. And she might be right … a few years down the road. Certainly not in the near future. Besides, he desired the kind of love and marriage that would last forever. And children, none of which had happened on his first go 'round.

He took a bite of croissant before turning back to her.

"Vance, you don't have to answer, but I saw the way you look at Chiara. You can't keep your eyes off her."

"Girl talk is so compelling," he joked. He took another bite of the croissant and glanced toward the foyer. "I'll take Chiara's coat to the dry cleaners today."

"Wow, you certainly mastered the art of changing the subject." When he didn't respond, Gertrude studied him. Her jaw was set, never a good sign. "If you married, your wife would help you with those types of errands."

"You're joking, right? I need a wife to bake me sugar cookies"—he gestured toward the kitchen—"and handle dry-cleaning duties?"

"You're my brother. I saw how happy you were when you were married."

"Yes, for the first five minutes, until I realized Shanna and I weren't suited and she couldn't be trusted."

"All happening years ago." Gertrude leaned forward. "And if it makes any difference, I'm back at Wellington Acres for good. For your own sake, ask someone else to shoulder some of the burdens of running our ranch."

"I can get everything done, and I've learned to rely on no one but myself."

"I'd like to begin dating again." Deeply, Gertrude inhaled. "Joe Brown is—"

Vance shook his head. "No."

As soon as he spoke, he caught the flicker of determination in Gertrude's eyes. He'd also seen the way her expression softened whenever Joe's name was mentioned.

He blew out a breath. Did he truly have the right to dictate who his sister should or shouldn't date? Of course not. It was just that she had made so many mistakes involving men, and he chose to protect her from making any more.

His practical mind argued that if she was finally settled, he could open himself up again. Somewhere inside, he realized his life had been empty for a long, long time.

Nope. Nope. He didn't have precious minutes to turn into a deep-thinking sort of guy. Days were busy and complicated enough, and he was already stretched in too many directions. He had no mental or emotional capacity left for another responsibility.

In his brief marriage, he'd learned that a woman could be an obligation as opposed to a life-long companion and partner.

Chiara, the primary topic of conversation, reentered the room.

"We're all set, Gertrude," she said. "Amanda showed me the ingredients and we can bake the cookies this afternoon."

Gertrude's eyes gleamed, her grin wide. He'd seen a similar expression years ago, when she turned twelve and their parents had gifted her with a sleek black horse for her birthday.

He voiced his remembrance aloud.

It was all the prompting Gertrude needed. She swiveled to Chiara and launched into a detailed description of her twelfth birthday, leading up to the excitement of realizing Licorice was truly hers.

Chiara walked over to the picture window, where the winter sun streamed in. She pushed back the heavy draperies, exposing a bright winter morning. In the distance was the stable.

"How many horses do you own?" she asked.

"A dozen, if you count the horses we board." Vance glanced at his wristwatch. He absolutely had to leave for town in five minutes to be on time for his investors meeting. But five minutes was five minutes. "Do you like horses?"

She turned and grinned. "I've never gotten close enough to one to say. Although my sister Emma will be over the moon when I tell her. She'll ask for all the details of each and every horse."

"I'll be tied up the next few days, but by this weekend I should be able to carve out some free time to take you down to the stable."

Another enchanting grin. "I'd like to see the property."

She was so pretty, so engaged in life. Certainly, she wasn't like the women he'd dated since his marriage ended. He'd been satisfied with brief connections. With Chiara, he wanted more than brief.

*Now why had that thought occurred to him?*

*And why was he staring at her again?*

"How old is Emma?" he asked.

A proud smile crossed Chiara's face. "Nine. And she loves

new adventures, although she sometimes plunges in head-long without thinking things through."

"Sounds familiar." Vance threw a pointed look at Gertrude.

Gertrude dismissed him with a shrug. "Nine years old is such a fun age," she said to Chiara. "Why doesn't Emma come for a visit while you're here?"

Chiara blinked. "Well, for one thing, she's in Kansas. Plus she has school and—"

"She can fly here on a weekend."

"No really, I couldn't afford—"

"We insist." Gertrude half-rose. "And I wouldn't invite her if I expected you to pay the plane fare."

"I can't accept. I'm sorry."

It struck Vance that Chiara was too proud to consent to anything she considered charity.

"This is a working ranch," he put in. "Emma can help me in the stable."

"That way," Gertrude said, pushing her wheelchair to the window, "she can get to know Licorice and Peppermint and the other horses. And there's an indoor riding ring we hardly ever use. We even have an old sleigh."

At Chiara's uplifted eyebrows, Vance explained, "Years ago, when our grandparents were alive, part of our acreage was a Christmas tree farm. They offered sleigh rides, and they even had a pavilion set up where they served food."

"And yet there's no sign of Christmas anywhere," Chiara said softly.

"No. We've never celebrated Christmas."

"Until now." Gertrude extended her arms and enveloped Chiara in a bear hug. "Thank you for coming," she whispered. "We're going to be good friends, I just know it." She leaned back. "And as your friend, I would like your sister to come visit."

Chiara hesitated and then said she would talk to her parents about it.

Vance smiled and took one more look at his watch. Saying he had to go, he strode into the foyer. Chiara's enthusiasm for a book club and holiday baking, accompanied by her firm recommendation to his sister to adhere to the doctor's orders, gave him a sense of encouragement. Gertrude would experience a day filled with laughter, and he could get back to work with a peace of mind he hadn't felt in quite a while.

And if he'd stayed longer than he'd intended, it was only to be certain Chiara worked out, he rationalized. After all, she was the new caregiver for his sister, the most important person in his life.

But somehow he knew it was more. There was a pull, an appeal that drew him to her. It was more than her friendliness, her sweet charm, her quiet grace. Sure, that was some of it, but the simple truth was, he was attracted to her.

He also appreciated that, just as he was devoted to Gertrude, Chiara's green eyes had glowed with love whenever she mentioned her sister, Emma.

He'd been surprised when Gertrude had extended an invitation for Emma to visit, and even more surprised when Chiara said she'd talk to her parents about it.

It would be wonderful to have a child in the house, Vance thought.

He had always wanted children, although it wasn't in God's plans for him.

He grabbed Chiara's stained coat, started to open the door, and then strode back into the living room at the conclusion of one of Gertrude's long-winded stories, this time about how horseback riding was a true sport and how extensive competition training was.

"What was the name of that library book again?" he asked. Yes, so okay, his sister was right. He'd forgotten.

Gertrude gave a hoot of laughter.

"It's *A Christmas Carol*," Chiara, said, "and the main character is Ebenezer Scrooge." She winked at him. "Just kidding."

# CHAPTER 5

*O*n a late afternoon three days later, the scents of vanilla and spices welcomed Vance as he walked into the kitchen. Chiara had brought small touches of Christmas to the room, trimming the glass sugar bowl and creamer with greenery and red berries. She'd even tied a velvet ribbon to the polished nickel globe hanging from the ceiling.

In fact, there was a touch of Christmas in his home wherever he looked. A fresh pine wreath strung with clear lights covered the entryway door, magically appearing the day after Chiara arrived. Groupings of red candles, circled by preserved leaves, sat on the stone fireplace's mantel. There was also a majestic Christmas tree in the living room that Chiara had picked out, with Gertrude's Facetiming guidance, at a farm near them. It had been delivered and set up while he was writing computer code in town, and the tree shimmered with silver tinsel and gold and blue bulbs.

And music, always music. At the moment, the Vienna Boys Choir was singing "O Christmas Tree" in German, the music coming from her cell phone propped on a shelf.

The combination of familiar melodies and festive colors, the blends of cloves and cinnamon, filled his heart with a sentiment he couldn't describe.

Chiara and Gertrude sat at the kitchen table, chortling, their heads bent over a printed recipe. "—and you can see where my mother made some alterations," Chiara was saying. Smiling, she glanced up at him. "Hi, Vance."

"Good to see everyone so cheerful," he said.

Their laughter was contagious, and he chuckled along with them. The comfortable warmth of the kitchen made his body relax.

"Chiara, here's your coat." He lifted her cream-colored coat, wrapped in a thin clear-coated plastic dry-cleaners bag. "You'll be pleased to know the blood stains came out."

"Thank you." She gazed across the table at him. "We haven't seen much of you lately. Have you been extra busy?"

Had she missed him? he wondered. He had certainly missed her. He thought about her when he was in meetings, when he was at the stable, when he was in his SUV, his mind always drifting to the same question: How would it feel to kiss her?

She certainly was a temptation, although he knew he should resist. He wasn't ready for a commitment, and Chiara wasn't the sort of woman a man could kiss and walk away from. In his experience, people always let him down. True love didn't exist, at least not for him.

He tugged off his coat. His silk tie and suit jacket came next. It was good to be home.

"I've been tied up in endless meetings," he said. He hung the dry-cleaners bag by the door, then rested his arm on the back of Chiara's chair.

"Always hectic, big brother," Gertrude said. He'd been so preoccupied with Chiara, he'd neglected to say hello to his sister.

"And how are your headaches today, Gertrude?" he asked. "You look well."

"Better and better, thanks. Chiara is keeping me busy between my naps." Gertrude held up a hand. "And before you ask, I'm following the doctor's orders to a tee. Chiara is a diligent nurse."

"Excellent." Vance steepled his fingers and blew out a sigh. The beta testing for his dating app was going well, the ranch might actually turn a profit this month, and his sister was absorbed and happy.

He opened his mouth to ask if the women needed baking assistance, but they were managing well without him—discussing using less sugar, the baking time for chocolate chip cookies, and the benefits of whole wheat versus white flour.

During the next fifteen minutes, he attempted to make small talk but got very little response.

Finally, Gertrude drummed her fingers on the table. "Vance, can't you see we're busy?"

Chiara smiled up at him. "We didn't mean to ignore you. I made wassail."

That smile. He loved her entrancing smile.

"I thought I smelled cinnamon and apples along with all those other wonderful smells," he said.

"Do you want some?" She nodded to a pan simmering on the stove.

"Sure. It's cold in those horse stalls." He rubbed his hands together. The kitchen certainly wasn't cold with the oven blasting, but at least he had her attention.

Getting up, she took a mug from the glass-fronted cabinet and ladled him a steaming cup.

He snatched a handful of cookies from the mound piled high on a gold-speckled platter. "Not that I don't love sugar," he said between mouthfuls, "but what will we do with all these cookies?"

"We'll freeze a couple dozen for Christmas," Chiara said, "and I'll take some back to my apartment. The rest I'll distribute to the homeless shelter when I'm there on Sunday."

She volunteered at a homeless center too. He was impressed, because, well, everything about her was impressive.

"Did you eat dinner yet?" she asked.

"Nothing since breakfast. What about you two?"

"We made tomato soup and toasted cheese sandwiches," Gertrude said.

He touched Chiara's hand. "There's a Christmas-tree-lighting ceremony tonight in the town center. Would you ladies like to accompany me?"

"Vance, we've lived here all our lives and we've never gone to a tree-lighting ceremony," Gertrude said.

"Is that a yes, Gertrude?"

"Actually, it's a no. Amanda and I are watching *A Holiday Engagement* tonight on television. The movie is a romance and I've never seen it. And be honest, Vance." Laughter flickered in her dark eyes. "You would prefer to take only Chiara so you can be alone with her."

He laughed—as usual, his sister was right—but Chiara's alarmed gaze shot to his face.

Trying to keep his voice normal, he said, "When a man wants a woman's company, there's no reason to pretend otherwise. Chiara, will you join me at the tree-lighting ceremony in town this evening?" He hoped he didn't betray how much it meant to him if she agreed.

Stillness reigned for a beat, cut short by the rhythmic ticking of the wall clock.

"Well, there's one more batch of cookies left to bake," Chiara said. "What time is the tree lighting?"

"Eight o'clock."

She glanced at the clock. "I should get back to the loft. I planned to do some reading."

"Can't your reading wait one more day? I'm sure Agatha Christie won't mind. Besides, the tree-lighting is only once a year."

"When you put it that way ..." A grin broke across her face. "Actually, I've never seen it in all the time I've lived here."

"As I passed by the town square, food trucks were lining up. We can grab a bite to eat there too." He refilled his mug with more wassail and turned to Gertrude. "You'll be okay?"

"I'm twenty-two years old, and Amanda is here." She slid the mound of cookies toward herself and grabbed a few. "You can just leave these here."

* * *

TWO HOURS LATER, Chiara and Vance were buckled in his SUV with the windows rolled up and the defroster on high. Night fell quickly in December, and the winter air bit through Chiara's freshly cleaned coat. For warmth, she also wore her patent-leather boots and a heavy sweater, and she wished she had thought to wrap a scarf around her neck. On impulse, she had pulled her blonde curls straight up and back, tying her hair at the crown with a red velvet ribbon, the same color as her sweater and boots. After all, it was Christmastime.

Vance wore his usual graphite gray parka and work boots. A white T-shirt and navy sweater peeked from his neckline. He'd gone to the stable beforehand, then showered, changing his stable clothes and mucking boots for a pair of laced-up chukkas and clean pair of jeans.

She glanced at him admiringly. Those dark wash jeans fit his muscular legs to perfection.

He started driving down the long driveway of Wellington Acres. In the distance, a full moon and sprinkling of stars played off the glossy surface of the pond. With temperatures below freezing, the pond was beginning to ice over. Vast fields took on the appearance of rutted brown in the moonlight, the pastures enclosed by visible fencing.

"Do you bring the horses in at night?" she asked.

"It depends on the horse because each is different. Joe and I monitor them every day. If their winter coat isn't coming through as much as we think it ought, then we'll bring them into the stable."

"So some horses stay outside?"

"Yes, and we rug them."

At her questioning glance, he explained, "A horse blanket. It keeps the horse protected from the elements and wind."

"Do horses get cold?"

"If they're in a shelter, they can tolerate temperatures of up to minus forty degrees. Between eighteen and fifty-nine degrees is most comfortable, though."

"You know a lot about horses. And computers. And Gertrude said you're brilliant at finance." Chiara tried to keep her tone matter-of-fact, but he looked so handsome, so well-built and strong, it was hard to keep the awe from her voice. "That's quite a bit of knowledge for one man."

"Thanks," he drawled in teasing amusement. "You're pretty incredible yourself." He paused and studied her for a moment. "You know, exchanging compliments always go better with a—" He slowed the SUV, the headlights sweeping over the expansive pasture land.

Then he put it in park and bent his head.

Surely he wouldn't kiss her before they were even out of his driveway, she thought. Surely she should draw away, not shift closer and raise her head in blatant invitation.

A horse's whinny interrupted them, and they both looked up to see a white horse had trotted close to the fence, not far from Chiara's window.

Vance drew back and grinned at the horse. "Hello, Peppermint."

Chiara turned to peer out the window. "I saw that horse the day I arrived."

"She's an older mare and should be foaling sometime this spring." He shut off the engine. "Do you want to meet her?"

"Sure, although I've never been up close to a horse before."

He came around to open the door for her, then laced his fingers with hers as if it was the most natural thing in the world. Together, their boots crunched on frozen ground as they approached the fence. Overhead, the full moon sailed in a bright clear sky.

The promise of new life, the hope of the holiday, and holding hands with this handsome man who took her breath away filled her with happiness.

"Is it okay to pet a pregnant horse?" she asked as they approached the fence.

*Wow, now that was a genius question.*

"I wouldn't advise it," Vance said, "unless you want to turn into a pony."

She laughed out loud. There was something about him, the way his grin disarmed her coupled with his wry sense of humor. She didn't understand why her heart fluttered every time he looked at her.

Or maybe she did.

"Peppermint likes to have her ears rubbed," he instructed. "Don't be afraid to stroke her strongly."

The horse held her head high, her ears forward. She nickered softly while Chiara stroked her, then sniffed Vance's coat pocket, investigating.

"She loves peppermints," he explained. He fished a round candy out of his pocket and offered it to the horse. Gently, he stroked her muzzle, whispering to Peppermint as he fed her the candy.

Chiara's heart melted at the sight of his gentleness with the pregnant mare. How could she resist a man who was so kindhearted around animals?

"Thus her name is Peppermint," Vance was saying. "Not the most ingenious name in the world, but it fits." He popped a candy into his mouth, then offered Chiara one, which she accepted.

Back in his SUV, they buckled their seat belts, and he switched on the heated seats.

Chiara snuggled into the warm leather and glanced at his profile. Well-defined nose and chin, sharp cheekbones, a dark stubble on his jaw. Yes, an extraordinarily attractive man, like a young Clint Eastwood.

As they neared the main road and the metal gate opened, a bald, stocky man was leading a black horse to the stable. He waved as they passed.

"Licorice?" Chiara asked. "Gertrude's horse?"

"Yes."

"She's beautiful. And I know the man." She waved as they passed. "He's Joe Brown."

"Yes, Joe's the ranch manager."

"From what Gertrude has said, he's trustworthy and very dependable."

Gertrude had said plenty more, including how she believed she was in love with Joe. Chiara didn't share that part with Vance.

"My sister's biased opinion." Vance's features tightened.

"But yes, Joe is outstanding at what he's paid exceedingly well to do."

Chiara felt a flicker of defensiveness. And although she attempted to overlook the family discord, Joe Brown obviously caused dissension between Gertrude and Vance. She stayed silent, preferring not to get in the middle of a family feud.

"So, how is work going? I mean, computer work," she asked, neatly navigating around the Joe Brown issue.

"I've designed the computer app and algorithms, identified the target group, and developed the prototype. Now the web developers are integrating appropriate analytics tools."

Her gaze widened. "You lost me at 'target group.'"

"Technical stuff." He flicked on his left blinker and eased onto the main highway to Turning Point. "We're well into beta testing. Care to volunteer?"

"No, no. I'm not good at relationships. I don't date much."

"Why would someone like you not date much?"

"What does that mean?" Her tone sharpened. "Someone like me?"

"Someone smart and beautiful and ... Are you dating anyone at all?"

"No, I'm not interested. Okay, I was, which is the reason why I moved here, but it was a huge mistake and I broke it off. I met the guy through an online dating service, by the way."

"What happened to you would never have happened with my app." He grinned. "I came up with the idea because I was tired of hearing about crude photos and distasteful comments. My app is for smart professionals."

"You're very enthusiastic when you talk about it." She offered an encouraging smile. "However, my perception of a dating app is tainted because of what happened to me." She blew out a breath. "However, three years later, I'm finally able to move back to Kansas City."

"Why?" Briefly, he angled toward her. "Are you going back for a Kansas City relationship?"

"I'm going back home. I told you. And I don't date much."

This conversation was a subject she didn't wish to discuss any longer. She switched on the radio, found her favorite oldies station, and experimented with just sitting back and surrendering to the prospect of a delightful evening.

He slowed when they entered the town and eased into a parking space a couple blocks from the square.

"I can drop you off if you don't want to walk," he offered.

"I don't mind. After all those cookies I ate today, a little walking is just the thing."

He parked, got out, and had her door open before she finished unbuckling her seat belt. He had that southern gentleman's character, standing when she entered a room, holding doors, waiting for her to finish speaking while he attentively listened.

"Thanks," she murmured, and stepped outside. The air was brisk, the assurance of snow in every breath she took.

But no. This was Virginia. It hardly ever snowed in Virginia.

Vance took her hand. His fingers were long, his grip firm yet gentle, his palm warm against her skin. It was odd, walking with him like this, like a typical man and woman on a date.

But no, this wasn't a date. It was a tree-lighting ceremony in *his* home town of Turning Point.

Sounds of Christmas rang through the streets. Children giggled and shouted as they raced and twirled; a gathering of teenage carolers sang an impromptu rendition of "The Twelve Days of Christmas." In front of the grocery store, a

Salvation Army worker rang his bell, and Vance reached into his wallet to leave a sizable donation.

And the sights—multicolored lights strung along bare tree branches, shop windows adorned in silver stars and colorful garland. Art galleries occupied a side street, selling images of Turning Point at the turn of the century.

And the smells were enticing and irresistible. Hickory logs burned in outdoor wood pits, sweet breads and mince tarts—among many other delectable treats—were being served hot and fresh from a long line of food trucks.

When they approached the town square, the poignant melody of "Silent Night" brought memories of the first time she'd heard the song at a concert in Kansas City. She'd been five years old, and she had cried at the peaceful, soul-touching lyrics.

"The wonder of Christmas," her mother had murmured, taking Chiara's hand.

"Vance, wait. It's my favorite carol." Chiara paused, closing her eyes, inhaling, taking it all in. And tears welled again, just like when she was five. Why had she never perused this enchanting little town and its Yuletide atmosphere? Why had she never been aware of the goodness emanating from the kind residents greeting her with a cheerful smile?

When she opened her eyes, Vance was studying her, her lips, her face.

"This community brings Christmas to life," he said quietly. "I've never taken the time to appreciate it."

He echoed her thoughts, and she agreed. She was appreciating the picturesque town in a whole new way, perhaps because she was seeing it with different eyes and with Vance beside her.

"Should we buy something to eat?" He edged toward a fudge stand displaying creamy chocolate and maple fudge.

Nearby, a food truck enticed customers with hamburgers sizzling on an outdoor grill.

"No, I'll wait for a cup of hot chocolate," she said. "What about you?"

"I'll grab hot chocolate and a pretzel farther down."

"You haven't eaten dinner."

A slow flame lit his dark gaze. "I have all I need."

Her heart gave a peculiar lurch. She wanted to tell him she felt the same, that in this moment, all was right in the world. Her thoughts scrambled, and she recognized the tell-tale warmth on her cheeks, betraying her emotions. Suddenly shy and unable to meet Vance's gaze, she focused on the rustic tavern located across the square, tiny white lights twinkling all around its exterior.

A thin man wearing glasses called out Vance's name.

Vance paused. "And there's one of my brilliant tech developers." He nodded toward the man signaling him, and let go of her hand. "I'll only be a minute."

They'd been holding hands, all this time.

As he walked off, Chiara heard a woman call her name.

She pivoted, delighted to see Adeline, her friend from the nursing agency. Adeline and Chiara were the same age and had shared the challenges of attending school while working. Despite Adeline's unconventional looks—this week, her shaggy hair was dyed a vivid shade of purple—she'd graduated at the top of the class. She was a voracious reader, thus the book club, although the rest of her life was a mystery. Some said she was a transplant from California, others mentioned Canada. At any rate, Adeline loved Turning Point and had declared it was the closest she'd ever come to a storybook town.

"I haven't seen you since we graduated," Adeline said. "Are you still volunteering at the homeless shelter? I'm there every Sunday." She raised her eyebrows, plucked to thin, arching lines, at Vance, who was talking intently with the tech.

"Yes, I missed a few weeks," Chiara said. "I've been busy moving, but I'll volunteer again. I'm working all month at Wellington Acres." She took a step nearer the fudge stand. "It's a ranch a little way out of town."

"The fancy place on the hill with the black metal gate and horse engravings? I always admired that property."

"It's just as beautiful on the inside. My position is live-in, and I'm staying in a loft apartment above the garage. It's a big rent savings for me this month."

"And who's the gorgeous guy you're with?"

"Vance Thatcher. He's my employer."

"Oh really?"

"His sister is my patient. Why are you grinning at me like that?"

"I just don't remember ever holding hands with any of my employers." Adeline shrugged. "Of course, if they were that drop-dead handsome … Oh my. Take a look at him."

That was all she seemed to do, Chiara thought. Look at him, think about him. And yet, he was the textbook example of the wrong man for her. He was her rich boss who lived in Virginia, a state she couldn't wait to get out of.

Or not? Sometimes she thought about staying, but that was ridiculous. Her heart belonged in Kansas.

She noted Adeline was studying her. "Before you ask," she said, "we're just friends."

"Is he single?"

"Yes."

"Uh huh. And last I checked, so are you. Is he the reason you haven't attended book club? We meet there every Friday night at seven o'clock, rain or shine." Adeline pointed to the Turning Point Hotel.

"I told you, I've been busy," Chiara reminded with a laughing look. "So, what are you reading?"

"Currently nothing." Adeline chuckled. "Right now, we're using the book club as an excuse to enjoy a night out with the girls. And there's a good band the hotel has hired called The Crestfallen, so we can indulge in a glass of wine and a whole lot of dancing."

"Sounds fun." Chiara grinned. "For now, I've created my own book club with Vance's sister."

"How old is she?"

"In her twenties. We get along great."

"Chiara, do you still want hot chocolate?" Vance had returned. "The stand is around the bend."

Chiara introduced the two of them, agreed to the hot chocolate, and Vance grabbed her hand and led her away as Chiara called good-bye.

"Don't worry about me, you two," Adeline called after them, giving Chiara a deliberate wink. "I only drink hot chocolate on cold winter nights when there's a tree-lighting ceremony. In the meantime, enjoy your evening."

Chiara could detect a delighted matchmaker from a mile away. Her mother had set up numerous blind dates for her, all for naught. Vance hadn't invited Adeline to join them and Adeline clearly took that as a good sign. She was like every other woman, tickled by the prospect Chiara had met a boyfriend.

Except Vance wasn't Chiara's boyfriend.

And wasn't it ironic he was launching a dating app?

Him, the buttoned-up executive by day, and rancher by night. A man who confused her at every turn because she never knew for certain when he was joking about his feelings and when he was serious.

And her, a woman who'd never experienced true love from a man and felt she was navigating unfamiliar terrain.

Especially when her only serious relationship had been with a man she met through an online dating service.

That had been disastrous, and she couldn't see the point of online meet-ups. Wasn't it easier for singles to connect with other singles at social events like this one? When they met face-to-face, people recognized that the other person was a genuine human.

"There's quite a crowd here tonight," Vance was saying. He paid for a pretzel at one of the food trucks and then stacked his plate with four thick slices of maple fudge.

They waited in line for hot chocolate, then wended through the crush of people to a spot where they had a perfect view of the Christmas tree.

They savored and munched and shared, leaning against an ancient oak tree, waiting for the ceremony to begin.

And they talked. About his life in Virginia, about her life in Kansas.

Eventually, the eighteen-foot-tall Christmas tree was lit amidst jubilant applause and a resident brass band performing "O Christmas Tree."

A gust of cold wind prompted her to shiver, and Vance put his arm around her. She snuggled into his warm hug, gladdened by the steady beating of his heart.

Nearly an hour later, when the ceremony was long over and the crowd had diminished to a trickle, when the band members were loading up their instruments and most of the food vendors were shutting down, they stayed in the square. It had a cozy, hometown atmosphere, a sense of timelessness.

Chiara sighed as she looked around once more. "Beautiful," she murmured.

One arm still firmly wrapped around her shoulders, he bent his head and kissed her forehead. "My thoughts exactly."

Her breath caught at the gentle caress. With effort, she

focused on making conversation. "The town is presenting an entire month of holiday festivities," she said.

"They always do." His arm tightened when she stirred. "And a parade."

"I've never seen any of that." She leaned her head back and gazed up at him. "And it's my fault, always making excuses for how busy I am."

"Me too."

She didn't want the magic of the night to end, the flutters in her chest to subside. "Vance, thank you for bringing me here tonight. I loved it."

"So did I." Gentleness and desire smoldered in his dark eyes. Slowly, his lips grazed her temple, and then glided lower. "You are beautiful," he whispered, his soft breath warming her cheek. Both his arms encircled her, and his mouth moved over hers.

She molded closer to his muscular body. His lips tasted of chocolate and maple fudge and peppermint.

And he tasted delicious.

# CHAPTER 6

*a*nother week went by, and Vance attended church services with her. The first time in ages, he declared, and she was heartened he was reestablishing a relationship with God.

The pastor's message was simple. God wasn't always going to give you something new. Sometimes the best thing God gave you was something you already had.

So true, she thought.

Vance clasped her hand and locked gazes with her. There was that connection again as if the words of the pastor had really spoken to him, in the same way they had resonated to her.

He seemed always in tune with her, with her thoughts, with her feelings.

Today, he wore a charcoal gray suit and black wool over-coat. Tall and handsome, he sang all the traditional hymns in his bass voice, belting the chorus of "Greensleeves" with enthusiasm. Her heart filled with gratitude, for the man, for God, for the charming town. Sure, she intended to move on, move away, although lately she couldn't remember why.

After service, Vance accompanied her to the homeless shelter on the next block. That was another thing she liked about Turning Point—everything was within walking distance. In Kansas City, where the population was over two million, people drove everywhere.

"Text me if you get done earlier than planned," Vance said as he left her. "In the meantime, I'll miss you." He drew her into a cuddle. His mouth hovered so close, his breath blended with hers.

She hesitated.

"This is the part where you're supposed to tell me you'll miss me too," he said.

"Vance, I'll see you again in less than three hours."

"And?"

She chuckled, knowing she should be truthful. "And I'll miss you."

His eyes glinted with an emotion she couldn't read. "Good."

With seeming reluctance, he released her. She stepped into the shelter, and he walked to his office around the corner.

Sitting in a volunteer planning meeting an hour later, after she distributed the sugar cookies she'd baked, she was thrown a curveball when Adeline slated her as the coordinator for the shelter's annual Christmas party. Complete with Santa Claus, Adeline declared. Which meant they had to find a man willing to play Santa.

After a few minutes of discussion, they decided on designating someone to play one of Santa's elves instead. There was an elf costume in the back room that hadn't been used for years.

Chiara pondered about asking Vance once she looked over the costume and determined it would fit him with minor alterations. However, he was over six feet tall and lean and certainly didn't claim a traditional elf physique. He already sported the hint of a beard, though, and a set of pointy ears, a pointy hat, and padding beneath a green velvet suit could work wonders. In addition, Chiara thought, Wellington Acres could host the shelter's Christmas party in the unused pavilion. She imagined a gingerbread event for the children, using graham crackers and white frosting and colorful candies. Renate, one of the volunteers at the center, had given her the instructions, which were easy enough for everyone to make their own. In addition, Santa's elf could tote a bag of candy canes to give to each child.

And there was a pond at Wellington Acres. Perhaps the kids could ice skate. The weather had turned cold, but as she mulled the idea, she quickly nixed it. Ice skating on a frozen pond could be dangerous if the ice cracked. The pond water was very deep.

"How does the Christmas party sound, Vance?" she asked after explaining the details to him.

He'd picked her up at the shelter, coming inside to introduce himself to the staff, talking and reading with the children, and then assisting with cleanup. To Chiara's and the director's delight, he contributed a substantial donation.

An hour passed before they left.

Dusk had darkened the sky, ever sooner these days as the shortest day of the year approached. Streams of multi-colored Christmas lights stretched across the roofs of homes and businesses.

He held her hand as they crossed the street to the other side of the square.

"I've never hosted a gingerbread house party," Vance said as they stepped up onto the brick sidewalk. "Or really any party."

"But you'll consider it? Someone suggested we should

start putting aside milk containers for the gingerbread houses."

"Good. I drink a lot of milk."

"A pint-size container is best. We'll also need canned frosting and candy and—"

His hand tightened around hers. "If making gingerbread houses brings a mile-wide smile to your face, I'll agree to just about anything."

His words sent little chills of excitement skittering up her spine. She struggled for a sharp, witty response but couldn't think of anything except *thank you.*

They continued their stroll, window-shopping as they progressed. Kiosks selling hot dogs and poinsettias and post-cards of the town lined both sides of the square. Conversations from holiday shoppers weaved in between good-natured laughter, and children played near the impressive fountain in the center of the village green.

Never a town with factories, Turning Point had been founded by pioneers in the late 1700's. The colonial charm had been preserved to keep the character intact.

"How goes the development of your algorithms and coding and whatever else you tech guys do?" Chiara asked.

"Encouraging." He gestured to a stately brick building. "I'd take you to see my office, but several techies are working out last-minute details and I'd rather not disturb them."

Vance fascinated her on so many levels. Not only was he content wearing jeans and work boots while shoveling out a horse stable, he was equally as comfortable in an office sporting a crisp white shirt and silk tie, or honing his computer tech skills.

She paused when they came to a quaint store called Char-lie's Unique Gifts.

Chiara peered in the window, noting the local wares

ranging from pottery to hand-made jewelry to sparkling scented candles.

"I'd like to stop in for a few minutes and browse," she said.

Vance nodded. "I should buy a gift for Gertrude. I've never bought her a holiday gift before, because we've never celebrated Christmas."

"Are you looking for anything special?" The pony-tailed shopkeeper, wearing jeans and a long-sleeved neon-green T-shirt, welcomed them from behind the cash register. Then he smiled at Chiara, staring appreciatively. "I'm Charlie, gorgeous. Who are you?"

"My name is Chiara."

"Very pleased to meet you, Chiara." He pushed up the sleeves of his shirt. His right arm displayed a colorful tattoo of the moon and stars.

"You own the store?" Vance asked. "I've never shopped in here before."

"Yes, going on five years," Charlie replied. His gold earring glinted in the fluorescent lighting.

"How about jewelry for her, Vance?" Chiara picked up a flowered necklace. "Although I imagine Gertrude's not a bling type of woman. She's more of a tomboy."

"That she is," Vance agreed, turning to the shopkeeper. "Do you have anything with horses?"

"There's a horse book in the back of the shop." Charlie meandered through the cluttered store to a dusty bin of books, poked through the pile, then pulled out a hardcover book entitled, *How To Think Like A Horse.* "How's this? And we gift wrap at no extra charge."

"My sister doesn't need that book," Vance said. "She probably wrote it."

With a chuckle, Chiara wandered over to a mix-and-match display table. "Vance, look at this." She held up a bronze sculpture of a woman hugging a horse. It was called

"Mutual Affection." "It's perfect. Your sister has such a strong bond with Licorice."

Vance agreed and Charlie wrapped the gift in an old-fashioned reindeer-print wrapping paper and tied it with a burlap string. He stamped a gold label on top that read "Charlie's Unique Gifts."

"Advertising," he joked with a half shrug, and handed the wrapped gift to Vance.

As they were leaving the shop, Chiara dawdled over a large Christmas snow globe on a display shelf. The globe portrayed Turning Point's town square, complete with miniaturized shops and the Turning Point Hotel.

Vance watched as she reached for the globe and ran her fingers over the polished edges. "It's heavy!" she exclaimed as she picked it up. Vigorously shaking it, the white particles and silver glitter churned and whirled. "And it's musical." She wound the shimmering gold base and the globe played "Silent Night." She listened, smiling all the while, the melody chiming to the sound of carillon bells. With a reluctant sigh, she placed the globe back on the display stand.

"Your favorite carol," Vance remarked, holding the shop door open for her as they exited. "And I'm surprised Charlie didn't wrap the globe and gift it to you for walking into his store."

She laughed. "Don't be ridiculous. He was just being friendly."

"A little too friendly, if you ask me."

They walked for a while in silence, her hand entwined in his.

"You remembered my favorite carol?" she asked. "Why would you remember something like that about me?"

"You know why."

Right there in the middle of the square, he drew her into his arms and kissed her.

She hesitated for a moment, then wound her hands around his nape. His jet-black hair was thick and silky, his chest warm and hard. "Vance, we shouldn't," she whispered. "We're in full view of the entire town."

"Are we?" He threw a glance over his shoulder, then kissed her again. "No one is concerned with us. They're busy doing last-minute shopping."

She grinned and yielded to the tenderness of his kisses.

Infinite minutes later, he lifted his head. "My app should be ready by next week," he said. "And then I'll have more time to spend with you."

"Then you'll just need to deal with the ranch, and running the estate, and ..." Her voice trailed off. Wow, that hadn't come out right. *Just?* The man practically worked around the clock.

"Thank you for being a perfect nurse," he said. "You've enabled me to concentrate on my app, and I've never seen Gertrude so happy. I feared she was going to go stir-crazy because she can't go to the stable."

"We went soon after I arrived. Didn't she tell you?"

"No." He stepped back. "Was Joe there?"

"Yes, of course. He brought his truck up to the house so Gertrude didn't have to contend with the wheelchair, although she rarely uses it anymore. From what I've observed, she's recovered from the concussion and her ankle is healing nicely."

Vance was silent as he guided her to his SUV, helped her in and then slid into the driver's seat. She felt the heat of his body, the solid strength of his arm as it brushed against hers.

"The weatherman is forecasting a cold front and freezing rain this evening," he said, as he turned his key in the ignition.

So, the conversation about Joe was finished, she thought.

"Then it's best we get back before the weather turns," she said aloud.

"I meant to ask how you recognized Joe in the pasture on the night of the tree lighting." Vance kept his gaze on the windshield. His fingers tightened around the steering wheel. "Now I know why."

*So the conversation regarding Joe wasn't finished.*

Vance seemed entirely put off whenever Joe was mentioned. However, Vance was her employer, so she couldn't not tell him that Gertrude had gone to the stable. And besides, there was nothing to hide. It wasn't like Gertrude and Joe were doing anything wrong. They were simply in love. Sure, there was an age difference, but so what?

She settled into the luxurious leather seat as they headed out of town and didn't respond to his comment about how she'd recognized Joe. Instead, she madly searched for another subject.

"Gertrude booked Emma's flight into Richmond," she finally said. "I haven't seen you long enough to go over all the details."

"That will change, remember?"

She hoped that was true. She hoped to spend as much time with him as possible before returning to Kansas.

"So, is it okay about Emma?" she asked. "I realize you're paying for her flight."

"I'm more than happy to pay and can't wait to meet her. So yes, everything's okay and I'm delighted. I've always wanted children."

She pondered his remark, said casually despite the emotion in his voice. Sometimes, she mused, people could be more open when they didn't actually face each other.

"Emma can stay a week," she continued. "School's out and Christmas vacation started in Kansas."

"Good. Hungry?"

"Sure." *Well, that was easy.*

"I stopped at Pisano's before I picked you up at the shelter. Two large pepperoni and pepper pizzas are in the backseat."

She laughed and swung around. "I thought I smelled something spicy. If the pizza has been sitting a while, though, it will be cold."

"There's a microwave in your apartment. We can eat there. All right?"

"You think of everything."

He shrugged, his grin boyish. "I'm a planner."

"So you said. Just like me." She liked the idea of spending the rest of the day with him. In fact, she liked everything about him.

"Should we stop at the main house and offer one of the pizzas to Gertrude and Amanda?" she suggested. "We can't possibly eat two."

His boyish grin stayed in place. "Of course, we can."

"We? Speak for yourself. Between cookies and pizza, I'm going to gain twenty pounds between now and New Year's."

"You're gorgeous, Chiara, inside and out." His tone softened. "And you're very considerate to think about Gertrude and Amanda, but Gertrude texted me earlier. They decided on a light supper and are watching Christmas romantic movies on the Hallmark channel."

She chuckled. "My favorite channel."

"So, would you prefer to eat pizza with me or watch movies with them?"

What a question. Should she live vicariously through romance movies on television, or experience a real-life romance with a man who made her pulse race every time he smiled at her?

That was easy. She opted for real life.

# CHAPTER 7

*A* half hour later, Vance followed Chiara up the exterior stairs to her apartment.

"Besides the gigantic Christmas tree Gertrude and I decorated for your home a few days ago," she said, "I also splurged on a tree for myself."

"I assume you didn't scrimp on the size, judging by mine," he said wryly. "The one at the house takes up more space than my grand piano."

"A small tree in a vaulted room would look out of place. And did you notice how splendidly it's decorated? All those gold and blue bulbs were Gertrude's idea. She's extraordinarily creative."

"I'm surprised she doesn't sing "O Christmas Tree" every time she passes the tree. She's certainly welcomed the Yuletide spirit."

"It's the music and the cookies and the ornaments."

They had reached the top of the stairs and Vance stopped her from opening the door.

"It's you," he said.

She shifted. "Vance, I've only been here a short while."

He gazed down at her radiant face and kissed her temple, her lips. "It's you."

She looked uncomfortable, and he broke eye contact. Why did she seem to hold back from him when he expressed his affection? He pressed his lips tight and stepped inside with her.

"Remember," she was saying, "mine isn't nearly as large as your eight-foot spruce because—"

He halted in midstep and laughed. A miniature pine perched on the coffee table, trimmed with hot-pink ornaments and gold tinsel.

"Ta-dah!" Not even bothering to take off her coat, she fairly skipped to one corner of the room and switched on tiny white lights strung inside a rustic bird cage. "Gertrude and I found this in an unused room in your house."

He couldn't contain his grin. "You have a flair for bringing your fun style into limited spaces."

"It's an acquired skill from living in cramped apartments. I'm a Christmas lover, so as long as I have the scent of pine and can bask in a holiday glow of lights, I'm good."

"You're more than good, Chiara." She was special and resourceful, imparting a zest for life he'd forgotten amidst all his work. He set the pizza boxes on the kitchen counter and pulled her into his arms.

Her gaze shifted from the miniature tree to him. "Are you complimenting me because I picked the smallest tree in the grocery store?"

Her soft laugh reminded him of shimmering Christmas bells.

"I'm complimenting you because you are exquisite." He lifted her lustrous hair and nuzzled her neck. Her fragrance was light and lemony, reminding him of carefree days and endless weekends.

He couldn't resist her. His lips traveled to her chin, her mouth. He kissed her exhaustively, insistently, and she molded herself to him, pressing nearer.

When the kiss ended, she rested her head against his chest.

"Should we continue, or should we eat our cold pizza?" he whispered.

Her laughing gaze found his. "We probably should take our coats off before we decide what's next."

He preferred kissing her over pizza. Actually, he preferred kissing her over anything, but he kept the thought to himself. He felt like a sixteen-year-old caught in the exhilaration of a first love, unable to stop staring at her.

She beamed up at him, nodding, as if she read his thoughts.

But then she whirled into the kitchen, effectively cooling the ardor between them.

After pizza and sugar cookies, she fixed mugs of hot chocolate and carried them on a tray to the living room. Vance sat on the sofa, appreciating the twinkling lights from the birdcage.

"I love the way everything in here smells," he said.

"Like chlorine bleach?" She laughed as she set the tray on the coffee table. "I cleaned my entire apartment before church this morning."

"I smell pine and chocolate." And lemon from her hair.

She settled beside him, and he brought her nearer. Lazily, he twirled a lock of her curly blonde hair.

"Tell me more about Kansas," he murmured.

She kicked out a breath. "Well, Kansas City was the framework of my childhood. My sanctuary. Whenever life got rough, I talked with my parents and they supported me."

He reflected on his own upbringing. He'd never had a meaningful conversation with his parents. They were always more interested in people and activities outside the home, not in their children.

"How about you?" she asked. "You've lived your entire life right here, in a radius of a few miles. Haven't you ever wished to explore the world?"

"Sure, although the ranch and my sister come first."

"I suppose if I lived here, I wouldn't want to leave, either." Sighing, she looked around the small apartment. "Your gorgeous home reminds me of a castle, and the fifteen-foot-tall entry gate and all that fencing is like a moat keeping intruders out."

Or a fort trapping him inside. A place where he was unable to escape. He was solely responsible for taking care of his headstrong sister as well as maintaining the property's legacy.

He attempted a smile, although he knew it wavered.

"It's the least I could do for my grandparents," he said, "two people I grew to admire. They had died by the time I made my appearance in the world. My father told me his parents worked hard to buy the estate and then to maintain it."

All through his childhood, he'd heard stories about his grandparents' struggles and their commitment to the ranch. And although his parents had preached the "nose to the grindstone" mantra, they hadn't followed suit.

"Your grandparents must have been remarkable," Chiara said.

Her quiet observation made him feel she genuinely cared about him, his story, and Wellington Acres. Having her here, spending so many delightful hours with her, negated much of his frustration toward his parents and his endless responsibilities. She was humorous and fun to be around, but it was more than that. It was her loyalty and kind heart.

"If there's anything I can do to help you with your work …" Smirking, she put up a hand in warning. "Except I won't sacrifice myself to be your beta dating experiment."

He laughed and brought her closer. He'd never encourage her to use his app, because he didn't want her to date anyone but him. He wanted to have endless conversations with her, long, lazy afternoons like this one, leisurely dinners with stimulating conversation and laughter.

*Hold on*, his logical mind warned. None of this had been his intention when he hired her.

He stopped his mind from considering logic, preferring to focus on the delight coursing through him whenever he was with her. Curled up together on the sofa, she burrowed nearer as he kissed her. Along with her other attributes he added affectionate, empathetic, and vivacious. Innately, he knew she'd never bring him down, that she would always support him.

"I love this ranch," he said quietly. *And with Chiara by his side …*

"I know you do." She smoothed her hand across the stubble on his chin. A fleeting caress, yet so intimate. "And Gertrude loves the ranch too. She's a born horsewoman."

"When she was younger, she pushed against any restrictions to the max," he said. "Finally, at twenty-two, she's settling down. She's even mentioned going back to college and completing her degree." He still remembered with painful clarity the night she ran off with the motorcycle guy, the finality of her shouted good-bye and the slam of the front door.

Chiara leaned back and subjected him to a lengthy scrutiny. "Yes, she mentioned majoring in equestrian studies at a small college a few towns over, the same school you went to. Truly, you should be proud of her."

"Now if only she can keep her head on straight and avoid getting entangled with the next available guy who shows up at our doorstep."

"Like Joe?"

"Exactly. I think—"

Chiara's frown made him pause. "Vance, you may not like this, but Gertrude and Joe get along well, and he's more than just 'the next available guy.' He cares a great deal about her."

Vance thrust a hand through his hair. "A fifteen-year age discrepancy is considerable. At thirty-seven, Joe's five years older than I am. Her daredevil impulses landed her in trouble throughout her adolescence, and she capped them off by quitting college and wasting two years of her life roaming the country with a wannabe rock star."

"She's home now, older and more mature. Let go and trust her to make her own decisions."

"Leaving me to clean up after her latest failure."

Just as he had when his parents practically bankrupted the ranch.

"No. She's an adult and understands there are consequences to her actions, although I wouldn't worry." Her green eyes radiated faith in his sister. "Gertrude is perceptive and exhibits good judgment."

"I appreciate your eternal optimism but—"

"Did you miss her when she took off with the motorcycle guy?" She must have seen the hurt in his expression, because she touched his arm and quickly said, "Oh, Vance, of course you did."

He reached for his hot chocolate, now barely warm. He drank a mouthful, then set it back down. "I missed her desperately," he finally said.

It had been such a familiar feeling. As a child, he had missed his parents, feeling rejected and abandoned when they disappeared for months, leaving him and Gertrude with a nanny. The same sense of desertion when his wife left him and blown all the wind from his sails. Whenever he opened his heart to someone, they crushed it.

Chiara remained quiet for a full minute, the silence broken by sleet tinkling against the window.

She grasped her mug and sipped. "Vance, Gertrude mentioned you were once married."

"Yes, to a woman named Shanna," he said with a grim smile. "And you were in a failed relationship too."

"But Kevin and I weren't married, and I haven't dated anyone since."

That laid to rest something he'd been wondering. She was selective, and evidently didn't take advantage of men. Surely, with her understated beauty and empathy, there were droves of guys who wanted to date her.

"Do you care to talk about your marriage?" She set her mug on the table and avoided his gaze.

He rubbed his forehead. "Presumably as much as you'd like to reminisce about Kevin."

"Is it okay if I ask you some personal questions?" Despite her wobbly smile, her determination was clear. "Gertrude alluded to your ex-wife, but said the actual story should come from you."

*Why not?* He spread out his arms, realizing he wanted to be absolutely honest with her. "I'm easy. Ask away."

"Well ..." She nibbled her lower lip. "How long were you married?"

"Slightly over a year."

"What happened?"

"She was unfaithful."

He stated the words flatly. Clearly at a loss for what to say, Chiara hesitated. "There was no chance of saving the marriage by seeing a counselor?"

"No. In hindsight, our marriage began falling apart soon

after our wedding vows. We were young, in our early twenties, and I suppose that was part of the reason. And I was so fixated on the ranch, I didn't notice Shanna's disinterest. Of course, the same can be said for me, because I was hardly ever around."

"Vance, I'm sorry. Truly. The loss and the betrayal—"

"Don't be." His arms enveloped her, tightening possessively. "I'm well over it."

Unfaithfulness and busted pride? He'd recovered. Now he understood that for him, love bolted whenever it came within his grasp. Weren't his parents, his ex-wife, his sister, all proof of that? An exit was normal, people came and went.

He drew back and gazed at her. His precious Chiara, so radiant, always with a smile.

*No, no, no.* He must hold back his emotions. He *would* hold back, because love led to heartache. He could not face picking up the fragments of his shattered heart again.

Better not to become any more involved, no matter how delightful this courtship.

Except it wasn't a courtship, because Chiara openly counted the days until she left Virginia. And not for one minute did he doubt she would take off.

Of course, he would never detain her. But when she looked up at him with her soft green eyes, his practical mind lost the battle to his impractical heart.

He blew out a breath and gazed down her, relishing the exquisite feel of her in his arms.

*Chiara, I love you.*

The words came to his mind without fanfare, a sudden swelling of his emotions.

*Impossible.* He'd only known her a short while. Love took time.

Or did it?

*Stop overthinking. Since when was there a set timeline for relationships?*

He tipped his head back and sighed. A romance when he least expected. But he'd experience it for what it was.

*Love.*

# CHAPTER 8

*T*he next Friday after lunch, Chiara noticed that Gertrude seemed more lighthearted than usual. As she walked from one end of the living room to the other—part of her physical therapy for her ankle—she kept peering out the window and remarking on the unseasonably cold weather.

"Let's get our hair done this afternoon," she finally suggested. "I have a date tonight."

"With Joe?" Chiara looked up from Gertrude's medical file, where she'd been making notes about her patient's progress.

"Who else?" Gertrude's gaze shifted to Chiara. "He's picking me up for dinner. We're trying a new restaurant in a town a few miles away. And before you ask, Vance knows. I may not have always been honest with my brother before, but I am now."

Chiara touched her riotous curls. She had gotten up late that morning, since Vance had been at her apartment until after midnight the night before. He'd brought takeout

Chinese, and they'd eaten sesame chicken and fried rice while watching *It's A Wonderful Life* on television. She'd been surprised Vance had never seen the movie which she considered a Christmas classic, and she'd been pleased when he announced it was now one of his favorite movies.

In her hurry to report to the cabin by eight a.m., she had let her hair dry naturally after her hasty shower.

"I haven't been to a salon in ages," she admitted.

Gertrude eyed Chiara's hair. "Platinum-blonde highlights and a trim would bring out your green eyes. And then we'll get our nails polished too. I prefer shiny red nails for the holidays."

Gertrude had welcomed Christmas with a zeal that Chiara had never imagined, perhaps because she'd missed so many Christmases as a child. Not only had Gertrude assigned an Advent wreath to the mantle, she'd also sprayed a basket of pinecones a gleaming silver and arranged them in the foyer. To top off the holiday decor, she'd hung oversized snowflakes from the dining room chandelier and set glass candlesticks with a variety of red candles on the eight-foot-long table.

"Different heights create interest," she'd explained every step to Chiara.

Definitely, Gertrude had a creative edge in addition to her boisterous manner.

"I'll drive you into town for an appointment," Chiara said, in an effort to fulfill her commitment as Gertrude's caregiver. "Although I don't intend to color my hair."

"It's more fun if we go together," Gertrude insisted. "Vance is in Richmond drumming up more investors for his app, and tonight he's hanging out with his computer friends."

Chiara glanced at her watch. "We won't be able to book an appointment on such late notice."

"I phoned the salon this morning." Gertrude's smile was positively mischievous. "And don't use the excuse that you can't afford it, because it's my treat."

Reluctant to dampen Gertrude's enthusiasm, Chiara agreed.

An hour later, the women walked into Cut and Curl, a trendy salon in Turning Point. They settled into side-by-side high-backed chairs.

Sally, Chiara's stylist, fingered the blonde curls. "Do you like the length?"

"Yes, so just a trim, please," Chiara cautioned when Sally brought out her sharp scissors.

"And lighter-blonde highlights around her face," Gertrude chirped.

"I can't."

"It'll be an exciting change," Gertrude urged. "And I've decided on caramel highlights. So nod your head and agree because we're doing this together."

Having little choice, Chiara reluctantly granted her stylist the go-ahead.

While their foil-wrapped hair processed, the women sat in a corner of the salon nibbling chocolate-coated truffles, compliments of the specialty candy shop next door.

"So," Gertrude asked, resting her chin in her hands. "How are things with Vance?"

"He's well. Very well." Chiara took a bite of her truffle, savoring the rich chocolate.

"Uh-huh. I see him every morning," Gertrude said. "I want to know how *you* feel about him."

"I respect him. He's remarkably ambitious." Chiara mustered her sunniest smile.

Still, she would be leaving soon. And because of the ache forming in her chest, she couldn't control the catch in her voice.

Gertrude subjected Chiara to a studied analysis. "You realize he's keen on you."

"We're just great friends. Our relationship will end when I fly back to Kansas. He's never encouraged me to stay."

"And he won't." Gertrude snatched a spare towel to mop a glob of hair dye off her arm. "He has a considerable amount of pride. I suppose it's because people have left him flat—our parents, his wife, and me, although I came back."

"He told me about his wife."

"Then you must've had a lot to talk about."

"He didn't say much. Knowing him, I assume he was a wonderful husband."

"He was. And he's a dutiful brother." Gertrude went for another truffle, sending the towel sliding to the floor. "Vance shows his love in a thousand ways, although he'll never say the words out loud. Look at everything he's sacrificed—shouldering the burdens of the ranch, putting up with my antics. Always remember you can count on him."

It was true, Chiara thought. He was a man of his word, treating people with respect. He was responsible, level-headed, and loyal.

She viewed Gertrude's reflection in the mirror and saw her affection for her brother radiating on her freckled face.

"He'll never say 'I love you,'" Gertrude went on, "because he's closed off that part of himself. He's afraid to connect. But as his sister I know he's a man who loves and loves deeply."

"Our relationship can't develop." Chiara hesitated, trying to remain nonchalant. "My home is in Kansas."

Or was it? More often than not, especially of late, she questioned her decision. And now, the thought of Vance holding back, afraid to utter words of love because he might be hurt again, melted her heart.

* * *

AFTER THEIR TWO-HOUR hair and nail appointment, the women returned to the ranch. The last rays of the sun scattered across endless pastures as the day disappeared into early darkness.

"Ladies, you look stunning!" Amanda exclaimed as they walked in. She called for them to twirl and show off their new hairstyles.

When Chiara had looked in the mirror at the salon's unveiling, she'd done a double-take. Sally had styled her hair into a wavy bob, and the platinum highlights framed her face. Her self-confidence rose the longer she stared, and she felt pretty and rejuvenated.

Gertrude's ebony hair floated in cascading waves, her caramel highlights creating an ombre effect at the tips of her waterfall braids.

"I assume you two are planning something special tonight," Amanda declared.

"Joe's picking me up at six o'clock." Gertrude glanced at the grandfather clock. "Umm, Chiara, would you like to come with us?"

Cheerfully ignoring the reluctance in Gertrude's voice, Chiara replied that she had other plans. Certainly, she wouldn't intrude on their date. And she could rest and catch up on her reading.

Then she recalled Adeline's book club. It was held every Friday evening, rain or shine, and she had enjoyed it the few times she attended. That sounded much more fun than staying home alone, especially since she didn't expect Vance to return from Richmond until after she'd gone to bed.

Decision made a couple hours later, she donned a black sequined skirt and cozy red turtleneck to match her fingernails. She spent extra time adding a vivid red lip color, along with swipes of mascara to her long lashes.

Self-assured and confident, she shrugged on her ivory coat, got into her Ford Escort and started to town.

\* \* \*

AT TEN O'CLOCK THAT EVENING, Vance was perched on a bar stool at the Turning Point Hotel with some of the tech geeks who had built his dating app. A local band, The Crestfallen, had just begun their second set. The band featured both a guitarist and keyboardist, and he focused on the keyboard player's ability.

They opened with a Billy Joel classic, and Vance was immediately impressed. He really should hone his piano playing, he thought. He'd taken lessons for nearly ten years and was losing his skills because he hardly ever practiced.

He tapped his foot to the beat and sipped his non-alcoholic beer. After nursing Gertrude through one too many hangovers, he rarely drank anymore.

A rock classic by Journey followed Billy Joel.

No Christmas music tonight, Vance mused, leaning back on his stool.

Earlier, he'd texted Chiara, asking how her day had gone. He was glad she and Gertrude had enjoyed an afternoon at the salon, and encouraged her plan to stay in that night and get some reading done. He made a mental note to bring her to hear the band; they were booked every Friday through New Year's at the hotel. He considered FaceTiming her now so she could listen with him, but he didn't want to interrupt her reading.

Since she had told him she wasn't going out, Vance didn't recognize at first the blonde bombshell sitting with her back to him, chatting and laughing at a table with several other women. When he saw one woman's purple hair and recognized her as Chiara's friend from the tree-lighting ceremony, he took a closer look at the blonde.

She was talking to a man with long hair tied back in a ponytail. She kept shaking her head no as the man gestured to the dance floor. He was persistent, though, and the woman finally stood up, confirming that she was Chiara, dressed in a tight-fitting red turtleneck and a black skirt that skimmed sleekly over her hips, drawing the attention of every man there.

As they stepped onto the dance floor, Vance recognized the guy. Charlie, the owner of Charlie's Unique Gifts. The man with a tattoo of the moon and planets on his arm who had taken a decided interest in Chiara.

Vance debated storming over. What was she doing, dancing with someone else? He watched the way Charlie smiled at her and how she smiled back, appearing to be having a marvelous time.

The tempo shifted to a slower song—"Have I Told You Lately?" by Rod Stewart.

Not only was the keyboardist excellent, Vance granted, but so was the vocalist.

However, the primary target of his thoughts, Chiara Johnson, was dancing way too close to another man.

*His Chiara.*

Instinctively, he pushed the thought aside. He had no claim on her, although he'd just admitted he was jealous.

He and Chiara were only friends, he told himself. She was an admirable nurse and outstanding in her care for Gertrude. His sister couldn't stop talking about her.

He couldn't stop thinking about her.

But nothing would come of it for she planned to return to her beloved Kansas very, very soon.

Vance shoved to his feet, made excuses to his friends, and paid the tab. If they gave him speculative looks as he stalked out of the hotel, he didn't care.

He just couldn't bear to watch Chiara in another man's arms.

# CHAPTER 9

"*V*ance, she's here!" Chiara called as she and Emma stepped into the foyer. They stamped their boots on the entry rug. Snow was falling, a dusting of white powder that outlined the pine trees along the entrance. "Come out of your study to meet her."

On the drive from the Richmond airport to the ranch, Emma was her chatty self—possibly because the attendants had let her have as many sodas and bags of candy as she wanted.

Emma's flights included one stopover between Kansas City and Richmond. Because the airline classified her as an 'unaccompanied minor,' she required special supervision.

As Chiara hung their coats on the rack in the foyer, Emma peeked into the living room. "Mr. Vance and Miss Gertrude have a piano *and* horses? They're so lucky!"

"Yes, so it will be hard for you to choose which to do first." Chiara laughed.

"And there's a pond so we can ice skate."

"The weather hasn't been cold enough for the ice to

freeze properly. You'll have to wait for when you go back to Kansas."

In a quick mood change, Emma sighed. "I wish you were coming with me."

"Remember I told you I'd return by New Year's to build our gingerbread house? I'm committed here at the ranch until then."

In truth, she could leave sooner. Between her good health, youthfulness, and diligent attention to physical therapy, Gertrude was almost fully healed. So, Chiara had booked herself a ticket back with Emma, because it had become clear that Gertrude didn't need her anymore. She hadn't yet shared the news with Emma, or anyone, for that matter. She was waiting, although she didn't understand why she waited.

Every day Gertrude went down to the stable to see Licorice. And Joe, Chiara presumed. At her doctor's appointment a few days earlier, the doctor's only advice had been that Gertrude stay off horses for another month.

"You've allowed your brain and ankle time to heal," he concluded. "Excellent recovery."

As she reported the doctor's prognosis to Vance when she and Gertrude returned to the ranch, Chiara told him she was uncomfortable accepting her full salary. He insisted he would keep paying her. Trying another tack, she suggested she leave Wellington Acres early, for she obviously wasn't needed anymore. She could fly back to Kansas with Emma and celebrate Christmas with her family, something she'd dreamed about for three years.

Vance was silent at first. She held her breath, half hoping he'd voice an adamant no, that she had signed a contract to be Gertrude's nurse through the end of December and that was that.

He did nothing of the sort. "The decision is yours and I'll pay your salary either way," he flatly stated. "Although your gingerbread house event for the homeless shelter is scheduled on Christmas Eve."

"Yes, but it's in the morning and Emma's flight leaves at four o'clock. I can do both."

Vance shrugged with apparent indifference. "The decision is yours. Although that sounds like a lot to do in one day."

She hesitated, and so did he. She hid her hope behind a facade that she trusted was as imperturbable as his.

Instead of disagreeing, she tapped a finger on her lip. With all the goings-on the day of the event, packing her belongings would be difficult. Better to honor her contract and stay until New Year's, in case she required a reference from him for a future job in Kansas.

Sure, it was too late to turn in the plane ticket. Perhaps Gertrude could use it at a later date to fly out to Kansas to visit Chiara and Emma.

At least, that was what her sensible mind rationalized when she told him her decision. Her heart, however, leapt elatedly when his expression softened and he smiled. She'd be able to spend the last few precious days with him. Perhaps he'd devote more time to her, because his elusiveness this past week had been shattering.

She planned a Christmas feast, intending to remain useful. When she asked Vance whether he preferred ham or turkey, he elected for a turkey dinner with all the trimmings. For a moment, his chilly reserve of the past week had thawed, only to swiftly return.

The object of her musings strode from his study. "So, this is the famous Emma," he teased.

Emma giggled. "Hi, Mr. Vance. I saw your horses as we entered the driveway. Miss Gertrude is visiting Mr. Joe near the stable, in case you're wondering where she is. Do you have any ponies?"

He chuckled. "In a few months, Peppermint is having a foal."

"Is she the white horse?"

"Yes."

"Can I come back to see her pony?"

He grasped her small hands in his large ones. "Emma Johnson, you can visit Wellington Acres any time. That's an open, forever invitation."

A lump rose in Chiara's throat as she pictured Emma enraptured by a playful, newborn foal. The estate would be beautiful in the spring, the sun warming the air, mountain bluebirds hovering near their nests, the little stream she'd discovered rushing with water.

"And Licorice is Miss Gertrude's black horse?" Emma asked.

"Yes, she's owned Licorice since she was twelve years old."

"I'll be twelve in three years and I want a pony." Enthusiastically, Emma jumped up and down, her blue-green eyes sparkling. "Do you think I'll get one?"

Vance knelt to be at Emma's height. "I heard."

Loudly, Emma whispered in his ear, "I told Santa."

Chiara caught Vance's gaze and smiled. Briefly, he nodded and looked away.

What had happened to their easy camaraderie? Her eyes burned with sharp tears, hurt by his indifference.

Emma balanced on her tiptoes. "Mr. Vance, did you know I flew here by myself? Mom and Dad forced me to have supervision although I didn't need any."

"I'm sure you didn't." He grinned. "So how do you like flying in an airplane?"

"I love it, and I wasn't afraid, even though it was my first time." She swiveled and grabbed Chiara's hand. "C'mon, you promised I could see the horses!"

"Aren't you tired?" she appealed, as Emma towed her

toward their coats. "We can go to my garage apartment and unpack."

"Nope, I want to pet the horses."

And so the following days passed in a blur of activity. By the time they all gathered in the dining room for dinner, Gertrude insisting that Chiara and Emma eat with her and not in Chiara's apartment, Chiara was pleasantly worn out. Gertrude and Emma had become fast friends, noisily chatting about horses and how they both planned to tour exotic places. Their mutual zest for adventure and disregard of any hazards created a strong bond between them. Chiara loved the sound of their enthusiastic laughter ringing throughout the house, but the best part of the meals was that Vance joined them. It was the only time she saw him, and she didn't know if he was kept even busier than usual with the launch of his dating app coming ever closer, or if he was avoiding her.

So, she was surprised when, four evenings before the gingerbread house event, Vance invited Chiara to dine at Pointers, a restaurant they'd favored, both agreeing the intimate atmosphere and friendly wait staff were unsurpassed.

She quickly accepted the invitation, looking forward to seeing him alone. She prayed this would lead to a tender reconciliation.

She decided on dressy wool slacks and a red-sequined knit sweater, adding a shimmery cubic zirconia necklace and matching earrings.

Vance held open the door at the restaurant, and she grinned as she walked past the four-foot-high nutcrackers that flanked the entrance. The noble nutcrackers' arms were lifted, directing customers inside. In the dining room, a guitarist nimbly strummed a holiday carol. Chiara's boots clicked against the wide plank floors as she and Vance were led to a table near the central fireplace, where lively flames crackled.

A waiter in pressed black pants and a long-sleeved white shirt filled their water glasses and handed them menus.

"What looks appetizing?" Vance asked, perusing the entrées.

The menu changed nightly, but could be depended on to include pork roast, beef tips, and mashed potatoes smothered in thick brown gravy.

"Everything, as usual." She took a long look at him. His nearness kindled a fire in her belly, a yearning so intense she almost felt faint. He'd been so indulgent with Emma, patient and wonderfully kind. If he broached the subject of his current lack of interest in her, she would fling herself into his arms and beg for …

Beg for what? Forgiveness?

She ached to spend every last minute with him before she left, and he was preventing her from doing that by avoiding her.

Unwilling to think about that, she studied the menu and chose pork roast and a side of macaroni and cheese. Vance ordered steak and scalloped potatoes.

With a sigh and silently counting calories, she closed the menu.

"I'm going to miss this place," she said quietly. As soon as she spoke, she admonished herself. She hadn't intended to voice her thoughts aloud.

Quickly, she glanced at him. Wanting him. Wanting more. He stared at her before she looked away. She knew he'd caught the wistfulness in her sigh.

I'll miss you most, she thought.

He claimed her hand across the table. "You don't have to leave Turning Point, Chiara." His voice was deep, his expression thoughtful. Her senses were alive to everything about him—his strong callused hands, his chiseled features, his impressive frame. She loved how his chestnut-colored cashmere sweater brought out the serious glint in his dark eyes.

"Don't I?" Her throat clogged with an unexpected sob. "Lately, I've seen you only at dinner. You'll hardly miss me."

He let go of her hand. "I assumed you intended to spend your last days here with Charlie."

"Charlie?" She frowned. "Charlie who?"

"The shop owner in town. He's obviously interested in you."

Her mind scrambled for a response. "I haven't seen him since you purchased Gertrude's Christmas gift."

"Haven't you?" His gaze rested momentarily on her face before shifting to his water glass. "What about the other night at the Turning Point Hotel?"

"How would you know? Wait a minute." She pushed her chair back and glared at him. "Were you spying on me while I was at my book club?"

"That's an odd book club. I didn't see a book anywhere in sight."

She narrowed her gaze. "Where were you?"

"I was sitting at the bar with my tech developers."

"I didn't see you." Confused, she shook her head. "Why didn't you come over to my table?"

"You were too busy dancing with Charlie. You know, the guy who wears an earring and is fond of tattoos?" He gave an indifferent shrug.

The full import of his remark gave her pause. He had watched her dance with another man and he'd been jealous. *He'd been jealous.* She swallowed, profoundly touched, and pulled her chair back close to the table. Now she'd figured out why he'd been acting so distant; because he cared. If only he'd admit his feelings.

She tilted her chin and forced him to meet her gaze.

"Charlie and I danced twice, and I left soon afterward. And you know what else?" She lay her hand on his arm. "The entire night I thought only about you."

In the flickering firelight, a smile crossed Vance's handsome face. "And I considered FaceTiming you so you could listen to the band with me."

"They were good, weren't they? They're playing every Friday night until New Year's."

Which meant one more Friday before she left for Kansas.

As always, Vance read her thoughts. "And then you fly away."

To avoid looking at him, she scanned the room—the guitarist quietly plucking, the other patrons eating and talking.

The past several nights she'd lain awake, contemplating what to do. She could easily get a full-time nursing position in Richmond. The thriving city was less than an hour commute from Turning Point.

If only the implacably polite man within a hand's grasp would urge her to stay, instead of watching her with an indecipherable expression.

But he didn't, effectively dashing her fantasy, and the meal pushed on.

For dessert, the holiday menu included peppermint chip ice cream and milk and cookies for Santa Claus. They ordered both, cookies for Vance and ice cream for Chiara. The cookies were scrumptious, salted grahams with chunks of candied ginger, served with ice-cold chocolate milk. Chiara opted for hot tea with lemon and a heaping bowl of ice cream, and didn't refuse when Vance offered her a bite of his cookie.

"Do I detect a hint of rum?" she teased.

A smirk tugged at the corners of his mouth. "Rum in salted grahams makes them extra special."

"Uh-huh." She laid down her spoon, realizing she'd devoured her entire helping.

"Should I order another round of desserts?" he joked.

She pressed her lips together and shook her head, too full to answer.

This was a decisive moment. They'd enjoyed dinner at their favorite restaurant, they were alone, and they were poised on the edge of their future.

And the silence between them beat on.

She groped for a subject matter to break the quiet. "Experts say a nine-year-old is on the cusp of adolescence."

"Emma is at a wondrous age," he said. "She's intelligent and fun-loving."

"And chock-full of activity. Thank you for your understanding when she's around the horses. If it were up to her, she'd live at the stable. Every morning after breakfast she races down there, and she's taken a liking to the chestnut mare."

"Ariel?"

"Yes. And Joe's given her a couple riding lessons."

He nodded. "I've seen her. She's got a good seat already."

A rush of pride went through her. "She keeps talking about returning to see the foal."

"She's welcome any time."

"Thanks."

Hypnotic embers in the fireplace cast a reddish radiance, and she inhaled the welcoming smoky scent. Every day at Wellington Acres filled her with contentment. Each hour flew by with alarming swiftness.

On mornings when Vance worked from home, she stole glances at him whenever she passed his study. He was either engrossed in a phone conversation or staying at his computer. She always longed to slip into the room and rub his shoulders, or smooth her hand over his cheek with its ever-present dark stubble.

She had learned this was his isolated world, where he ran the estate and developed his computer app, his ideas far-sighted and perceptive. And the work too often filled up his life.

"I intended to spend more time with Emma," he said.

"You've been buried in work."

"Unfortunately, my last investor meeting resulted in a snag."

"I assumed you were on track for your December thirty-first deadline."

He set his napkin on his lap and cupped his hands around his glass. "One of the investors voted against the name Vulcan. He thinks women will equate the name with logic and reason and that will deter them from using the app. Women prefer romantic love."

She nodded. "That's because of the *Star Trek*, Mr. Spock inference." Despite the fact she agreed with the investor, she refrained from telling Vance.

"Anyway, I need a name before the launch, so we might be delayed. And of course, it will be years before I see a profit." He shrugged. "Still, I like developing a product that might benefit society."

Typical Vance, constantly thinking of others, although, as his sister had stated, he was unable to express his feelings aloud. Case in point, he hadn't confronted her about dancing with Charlie. He'd simply withdrawn.

"Maybe outer space is too far to fly to meet the perfect partner," she said.

And maybe God had placed everything she was looking for right in front of her. All she had to do was reach out and grasp it.

Imperceptibly, Vance nodded. Surely, he hadn't read her thoughts again.

Whether he was grooming horses in the stable or making small talk with a goat in the pasture, his manner was caring, his voice compassionate. Besides, what woman could resist a guy who loved animals?

Even around Joe, Vance had mellowed. Slowly, he was accepting that Gertrude and Joe cared for each other, and Chiara had encouraged Vance's tolerance.

After a lengthy silence, he finished his last salted graham cookie and said, "You know, these are almost as good as your Christmas cookies."

When her eyebrows raised, he clarified, "Notice I said *almost*."

He signaled for the check, and after he paid they walked to the lobby to retrieve their coats. The entry was deserted as most of the other patrons had left. While they waited for their coats, Chiara remembered one thing they needed to talk about. His elf costume.

"About your elf costume ..." she began.

"I'm an elf?"

She plunked her hands on her hips. "Yes, as you well know."

He nodded. "What I know is that you volunteered me and told me about it later. So, I'm one of Santa's helpers?"

She smirked. "That's the plan. And I'm telling the children at the shelter that you're Santa's favorite elf."

He helped her on with her coat, then enveloped her in his arms. His strong chest was warm and solid beneath her cheek.

"What do you want for Christmas?" he asked softly.

*You.* The thought came unbidden, and she looked around, half-fearing she'd blurted her wish out loud. She blew out a breath and evaded his stare as well as his question. "Back to your costume. The tailor called and said he's done with the alterations, and you can pick it up anytime."

"Sure." He drew her hand through the crook of his arm, and quickly ushered her to his SUV. Sometime during dinner, it had started to rain. She hadn't even noticed. But then, she had found that when she was with Vance, she noticed only him and nothing else. It was a little disconcerting.

He switched on the heater, and the interior of the SUV quickly warmed. The wipers began their rhythmic flapping in an attempt to chase off the droplets.

"I like the sound of raindrops." She settled back, loving the heated seat. "However, snow for Christmas is better."

"The weatherman forecasts a white Christmas because a cold front is moving in again."

"Emma will be gone by then, although she's loved being here. I reminded her she'll see at least a foot of snow in Kansas. Speaking of Emma, I almost forgot to give this to you." Chiara fished a piece of paper from her purse and handed it to Vance.

At the quizzical lift of his dark eyebrows, she explained, "The note's from Emma. She knows you're one of Santa's elves at the Christmas party and figured you had a direct line to Santa."

He unfolded the paper and read the hand-written note aloud. "'Dear Santa, I have been 80% good this year.'"

He grinned at Chiara. "Eighty percent?"

"An excellent percentage for my sister. Keep reading."

"'Here's my Christmas list: A hair straightener. A piano. And a pony.'"

"Put a check mark by the hair straightener from me. As far as the piano goes ... perhaps someday. A pony? Well, that's impossible."

"Why do you say that?" He folded the note and slipped it into his pocket.

"Unlike you, my head isn't in outer space."

He threw her an accusing look, his gaze flat. "What's that supposed to mean?"

"I apologize. I was joking." Their misunderstanding had been resolved, and she wouldn't provoke another disagreement. "It's coming from my own frustration because I can't provide Emma with pianos or ponies."

The twinkle was back. "Well there's an excellent reason why you can't."

"Which is?"

He caught her hands in his and kissed her lightly on the lips. "You're not one of Santa's favorite elves."

# CHAPTER 10

For the next three days, Vance sent Chiara and Emma a little gift. She had mentioned she adored the truffles from the specialty candy shop in town, and two chocolate-coated truffles wrapped in red and green foil waited alongside the Richmond newspaper each morning outside her apartment. Did he know she'd been searching the online classified ads for a nursing position?

Accompanying the truffles was a note.

"From Santa's favorite elf," he wrote in his bold hand-writing on stationery embossed with the initials WA— Wellington Acres. "Can't wait to see you tonight."

In any case, this was Vance, showing how much he cared in the only way he expressed himself, through gifts and thoughtfulness.

Christmas Eve morning dawned cold and clear, the temperatures hovering in the midthirties. Snow was fore-casted for later in the evening, and anticipation was in the air for a white Christmas.

They had strung red and green steamers from the ceiling of the outdoor pavilion, and Chiara and Vance had covered oblong tables with green tablecloths. They'd saved thirty milk cartons, the number of children expected, and Emma and Gertrude had rinsed the cartons and let them dry.

Boxes of graham crackers and white canned frosting were set out, and Amanda lined up a half dozen muffin tins filled with assorted candy to decorate the houses.

The party was a great success, and Chiara breathed a satisfied sigh when it ended at noon. The children were on a sugar high, giggling and running in circles while playing tag. Emma made new friends, and had pointed out the horses in the nearest pasture to them. Peppermint was her natural welcoming self, whinnying and letting the little hands pat her.

As parents left with their children, Emma told Chiara she was going to go say good-bye to Licorice.

"Is Gertrude there?" Chiara called after her sister as Emma headed for the stable with a spring in her step.

"She and Joe are always there," Emma shouted over her shoulder.

True.

"Be back here in fifteen minutes," Chiara said. "You need to finish packing and we're leaving for the airport in an hour."

She turned to Vance as he approached, and was startled when he took her in his arms and kissed her.

She closed her eyes, yielding to his kiss before realizing that not everyone had left yet. She swiftly stepped back. "Vance," she whispered, "there are children here."

"I'm well aware." He yanked off his green pointed hat. "I just handed out a million candy canes."

"Umm, your math is a little off. Thirty children and their mothers attended, not a million. And you were wonderful with everyone."

"Because I'm Santa's favorite elf?"

"Because you're the handsomest elf ever." She ran her fingers along the faux white fur at the neckline of his soft green jacket. "Nice touch with the red pants and striped knee socks, but I'm not crazy about the upturned toes on your green booties. However, at least they match the jacket."

Grinning, he tucked her arm through his and led her to the pavilion. "I have a surprise for you. I was hoping you'd sit on my lap when I handed out candy canes and I planned to give it to you then."

"Another truffle?" She rolled her eyes.

"Miss Johnson, this is a special gift meant only for you."

The heart-touching tenderness in his voice sent a quiver of anticipation up her spine.

"I can't wait." Very lightly, she leaned against him. "Although can we postpone our celebration until later?"

His hand dropped to her waist, and he pulled her nearer. "Tonight is Christmas Eve. My gift can wait a few more hours."

She sensed his reluctance to release her as she playfully danced away. She intended to assist with cleanup while the remaining mothers rounded up their children for the ride back to town.

A while later, when the last child had departed clutching a candy cane and a gingerbread house, Chiara glanced at her watch. Emma had been gone a long time. Vance, who had changed out of his elf costume and into his familiar jeans, parka, and boots, was collapsing one of the tables, and she asked him if he'd seen the girl.

"Didn't she go to the stable to say good-bye to the horses?" He straightened. "How long has she been gone?"

Chiara calculated the time. "At least thirty minutes. What's taking her so long? I told her to be back here in fifteen minutes." She pulled out her phone and sent Gertrude a text. *Is Emma with you?*

*No,* Gertrude responded instantly.

*Where's Licorice?*

*With Joe and me. I saw Emma walking toward the pond.*

*How long ago?*

*Twenty minutes.*

Chiara's phone slipped from her fingers and she quickly retrieved it.

*Deep water, barely crusted. The ice wasn't safe.*

She started running. Surely Emma was old enough to know better than to venture too close to water that had scarcely iced over.

Vance took off after her. "Chiara, where are you going?" he shouted.

"The pond!"

He grabbed her hand, and she shook him off. He was slowing her down.

"Isn't Emma at the stable?"

Frozen terror. She couldn't breathe, couldn't respond with more than a negative shake of her head. *Not Emma. Please, no.*

"Emma!" she screamed. Blood pounded in her ears. On the day she arrived at Wellington Acres, Emma had asked to ice skate. If anything happened to her dear sister, she couldn't bear the loss. Why hadn't she kept closer track of the time instead of focusing on Vance?

Her heart skipped several beats when she spotted Emma standing by the pond, gazing longingly at the mirrored surface.

"Emma, what are you doing? Can't you listen to simple instructions?" Chiara knew she was lashing out, but Emma was too adventurous for her own good. "Why must you constantly overstep your boundaries?"

"She's safe." Vance halted beside them, catching his breath, speaking calmly. "See, Chiara? Everything's fine."

Although it wasn't fine because whenever she was with Vance, she noticed only him and forgot about the rest of the world.

"Emma's too young, she doesn't understand the dangers …" Chiara pivoted, facing him. "If she had fallen through the ice, no one would have been there to grab her. She could've died."

He put his hands on her forearms. "But she didn't."

Chiara winced and pulled away. With her arm around Emma's shoulders, she marched the girl to her apartment on legs threatening to collapse beneath her.

She couldn't do this any longer, stay at this ranch where she didn't belong. She needed to be in Kansas with her family where life was familiar and safe. Her decision to stick around until New Year's had been a mistake. Gertrude didn't need her, and her relationship with Vance had reached its end.

Who had she been trying to fool, believing he'd profess his feelings, hoping for more than he could give? Yes, she loved him, but he didn't love her back. The truth had strode quietly beside her and she had refused to acknowledge it, letting her love blind her to reality.

He had followed her and Emma, and she glanced at him, recalling what she had witnessed the day before. She had heard a plinking sound coming from the living room and peeked inside. Emma had sat at the shiny black piano, looking confident, swinging her feet on the piano bench. Both hands on the keys, she had picked out the melody for "Away in a Manger." Vance stood behind her, encouraging, humming as she played, reaching over her shoulder and indicating the next key.

Neither of them had been aware Chiara watched from the doorway.

At the end of the Christmas carol, he applauded and high-fived Emma, promising to give her a piano lesson whenever she visited.

Remembering that moment, Chiara's chest squeezed. If she never again visited Wellington Acres, Emma would be beyond disappointed. So perhaps … perhaps …

Maybe she and Vance could continue their relationship. If she moved back to Kansas, Vance could fly out for weekend visits. They'd talk nightly on the phone.

*No, no.* Everyone knew long-distance relationships didn't work. Besides, she hadn't come to Wellington Acres looking for a man. She'd come for a job, and the generous salary had allowed her to pay off her last tuition bill. She should be thankful.

Emma raced up the stairs to the apartment, hightailing it inside to finish packing. Chiara faced Vance on the landing.

"I'll see you when you return from the airport," he said. "Several inches of snow are predicted for later this evening, so drive carefully. Gertrude and Joe will attend midnight church services with us, but that's assuming the roads are plowed."

"Vance, I'm not going."

"To church? I told you—"

She shook her head and stared at him, trying to memorize his handsome features because she'd never see him again. "I'm not attending Christmas Eve celebrations in Turning Point."

"Why not?"

"I've decided to leave this afternoon with Emma. I'd bought an extra plane ticket a while back. I planned to fly back to Kansas." She blew out a sigh. "And then I decided not to."

"Why this change of heart? You never told me …" He paused, then stared at her. "Because of what happened? She's a kid, Chiara, but she's smart and responsible. So she lost track of time. We all do."

And that was the problem. With him, time, place, and emotions became a whirlwind of confusion.

"I need to pack and I'm already late." She turned and stepped inside.

He followed.

For a split-second, he was silent.

"Chiara, you're being irrational." He covered her hand with both of his. "Let's talk about this."

She jerked away and wouldn't meet his gaze for fear of changing her mind.

"We both know we can't be together," she said. "I'll leave the key under the door mat."

She wavered, and then she didn't.

"Good-bye, Vance." With a decided shove, she forced him onto the landing and slammed the door behind him. Then, to be extra sure he couldn't persuade her, she locked it.

* * *

TWO HOURS LATER, Vance rugged Peppermint and led her into the stall. A cold wind gusted outside, creaking the bare tree branches. Snow had begun to fall, thicker by the minute, hushing the pastures and hugging the distant log home in a snowy blanket.

Chiara would have loved the snowfall. She had said snow was one of the things she missed most about Kansas. And now she was gone.

He had texted her a number of times since her Ford Escort had raced down the driveway.

*How are you?* Was the first one. He'd cringed as soon as he'd sent it. Did that sound like he expected an answer?

It didn't matter. She hadn't responded.

*Are you at the airport?* came next.

No response.

*I'm waiting.* Wow, had that ever come out wrong.

And so on. His one-sided texts continued with no acknowledgement.

He confirmed the time on his watch. She and Emma would have boarded by now.

On his phone, he Googled the next flight to Kansas City and booked the first departure available, frustrated that it was two days later. He'd surprise her, as soon as he found her address. He surmised she'd given it to Gertrude during one of their many cozy conversations.

Done with the plane reservation, he checked his texts again. Nothing from Chiara.

"Can't you send me a courteous reply, so I know you're all right?" he asked the chilled stable. "I won't give up, Chiara."

Didn't she know he loved her?

Unconsciously, he took a step back.

How would she know that? He'd never told her.

He felt the seconds tick by and his heart plummeted. Each tick was another moment without her.

At first when she said she was leaving—when she dumped him—he'd been angry. She hadn't given him a good reason. And then she'd shoved, actually *shoved,* him from her apartment, *his* apartment, before locking the door. Talk about a double-edged sword. For the first time in his life, he'd embraced Christmas, and she had rejected him on Christmas Eve.

Where had they gone wrong? They got along so well together. She understood him, laughed at his jokes. And she was fun, a pleasure to be around, and sweet. So sweet.

*I'll be happy to bake one of my favorite cookie recipes with your sister and bring a little Christmas cheer into your lives. That is, if you're interested.*

And he had hesitated to tell her. Sure, he'd acknowledged his interest and smiled, but he had never said the words.

I love you.

Because he was afraid.

No, that couldn't be … Yes, it was. His heart couldn't risk another rejection. Ironic, because by protecting his heart, he had lost her, the woman of his heart. And she was all that mattered.

He stood at the entrance to the stable, peering toward his home. Gertrude had switched on the colorful Christmas lights and smoke billowed from the brick chimney. He hadn't told her yet that Chiara had left since the women got along famously, and Gertrude was looking forward to a real Christmas dinner with the ones she loved. A soreness gathered in his lungs, and he breathed in deeply. Already, the ranch was so lonely.

Wishing to escape the sadness, he wandered back into the stable, walking from stall to stall, speaking quietly to the horses. Once a source of such joy, the stable now felt empty and cold.

He remembered the way Chiara curled up to him when they watched Christmas movies, or shared earnest exchanges over mugs of hot chocolate. Her upturned face, her laughter, how she melted into his arms when he kissed her. Certainly, neither denied their attraction to each other.

He heard the sound of car tires skidding into the driveway as headlights swept across the snow.

He hastened from the stable. Now who would be out driving in—

His heartbeat raced as he recognized the car. He was beside it before Chiara shut the engine.

"Vance?" She pushed the door open and bounded from the car, throwing her arms around his neck. "I'm sorry."

"Why? Is Emma okay?"

"Yes, she's on her way to Kansas and will text me when she lands."

Snow was falling harder, covering Chiara's blonde hair in thick wet flakes. She was here. She'd come back to him.

"Let's get inside." Grabbing her hand, he hurried her into the stable. He pulled her close, inhaling raw air and a lemony scent and the woman he cherished.

She nestled into his embrace. "Vance, I—"

He pressed a finger to her lips. "Chiara, I need to say something, first. Words I haven't spoken in years." He didn't stop to think, or analyze. His feelings were too deep. "I love you."

Her green eyes welled with tears. "And I love you."

"I should've told you long before you left."

"You're telling me now. That's all that matters."

"You didn't answer my texts."

A grin brightened her beautiful face. "Well, for one thing, the roads were slick, and I was gripping the steering wheel with both hands. And Vance, I was so afraid."

"I was afraid too."

"Afraid of what, a snowflake?"

He grinned, then kissed her softly, sweetly. "I was afraid of losing my heart, and losing you," he whispered against her lips. "In fact, I was terrified. Trouble is, I had already lost it to a beautiful nurse from Kansas wearing ruby-red—"

"Don't start quoting from *The Wizard of Oz*," she warned.

"I won't." *Yet.*

He cuddled her, his fingers caressing her damp blonde curls. Still, she shivered in the frigid air. They should return to the house. But first …

Though reluctant to release her, he went into the wash stall. Beneath an assortment of horse hooks was a wire-mounted shelf. A neatly wrapped gift sat on top.

"I have a Christmas gift for you," he said.

"It's not horse shampoo, is it?"

He chuckled. "Nope. I love the scent of your lemon shampoo." He sobered and handed her the large heavy box, gift wrapped in reindeer print and tied with burlap string.

She studied the label on top. "Charlie's Unique Gifts? I thought you didn't like Charlie."

"I never said that. I just didn't like him dancing with you. However, I was forced to patronize his store because of the … uniqueness."

She sat on a bale of hay, untied the string and opened the box. Inside was the snow globe depicting Turning Point's town square. As she wound the base, the sweet, peaceful melody of "Silent Night" chimed softly.

"Vance, it's beautiful," she breathed. "And so thoughtful." She looked up at him. "I'm sorry for what I did, bolting on you like that, not giving you a chance."

"When you didn't respond, I booked the next flight available to Kansas in a couple of days. I was frustrated because I didn't want to miss spending Christmas day with you, so I planned to keep calling the airline."

"Do you know where I live?" She frowned and looked around the stalls as if one of the horses might answer.

"I was working on that."

She gave a sardonic shake of her head, then laughed.

Gazing down at her, he said softly, "I love you, Chiara. I was hiding from my fears. I'm not hiding anymore."

"And I love you. I love you very much."

He tipped up her chin. "Will you marry me?"

Tears glistened and flowed freely down her cheeks. "Yes, yes." Her hands glided around his nape.

Gently, he wiped the wetness away. "I understand you want to return to Kansas, but we'll make it work. Maybe Joe can run the ranch, and I can work on new apps anywhere."

"Vance." She placed her hand on his jaw. "I'm happy here

at Wellington Acres with you. I'd like to get married in Kansas, though."

"A spring wedding?"

"After the new foal is born." She tilted her head to the side to regard Peppermint in her stall, then smiled. "I'll ask Gertrude to help me plan the wedding. We'll have to go out to Kansas for a visit first so my parents can meet you."

"I hope they love me as much as I love their daughter." He lowered his head, bringing his lips closer to hers. "Why don't we leave in a couple of days? I booked one ticket, and the airline said there were seats available, so I can book another. Since we're spending Christmas Eve and Christmas Day with Gertrude and Joe, we can spend the rest of the holiday with your family."

She tilted her head so that her lips were within a hairsbreadth of his. "I promised Emma I'd fly back to Kansas for New Year's to build a gingerbread house, anyway, so this will be a wonderful surprise. Especially since I told her I was going with her, then changed my mind."

"How did she take the news?"

"She encouraged me to drive back to the ranch so I could be with you." Chiara laughed. "Besides, she likes being fussed over on the plane as an unaccompanied minor. She was already picking out a soft drink as I left."

Peppermint interrupted with a whinny, then poked her nose through the stall, sniffing in Vance's pocket for candy.

"I only have three left, girl." He pressed a candy into his palm and gave it to her. Then he offered one to Chiara and took the last peppermint for himself.

"There's no place like home, right?" His arms went around Chiara and he winked. "I couldn't resist."

"There's no place like home for the holidays," she modified, then she kissed him, her body softening against his.

"Wherever my loved ones are is home to me, because that's where my heart is."

He wholeheartedly agreed, and then he savored the exquisite taste of her sweet peppermint kisses.

**THE END**

# "RECIPE" FOR GINGERBREAD HOUSE

Collect milk cartons ahead of time. (Pint size is recommended)

Rinse the cartons and let them dry.

**Ingredients:**

Graham crackers (plain or cinnamon)

White canned frosting

Candy (any kind is fine)

Paper plates

Milk cartons

**Directions:**

Attach the graham crackers to the milk carton house with frosting, then attach the house to the paper plate with frosting. Decorate with candy as desired. Please note: These houses are not meant to last a long time.

**Additional tips:**

Place the candy in muffin tins for easier visibility.

Use craft sticks to spread the frosting on the houses and when adding candy.

If pint containers are not available, use whipped cream or coffee cream containers. Also, you can use up your old Halloween candy for decorations.

Enjoy this fun craft with your little ones!

# A NOTE FROM JOSIE

Dear Friends,

Thank you for reading *Sweet Peppermint Kisses*. I wanted to write a holiday romance in a picturesque location and set *Sweet Peppermint Kisses* in the fictional small town of Turning Point, Virginia.

The heroine, Chiara Johnson, is a wonderful caregiver. I've always admired the dedication and compassion of anyone in the nursing profession.

The hero, Vance Thatcher, runs a horse ranch. He is responsible and loyal and level-headed. In my research, I also learned a great deal about dating apps!

Set against the backdrop of horses and peppermint candy, it is my hope that this book helped you celebrate the joyous Christmas holiday along with me and my characters.

Sweet Peppermint Kisses is available in ebook, Paperback, Large Print Paperback, Hardcover, and Audiobook.

If you loved this sweet holiday romance as much as I loved writing it, please help other people find *Sweet Peppermint Kisses* by posting your amazing review.

With sincere appreciation for your support,
Josie Riviera
P.S. And remember, "There's no place like home."
My Spotify Play List for Sweet Peppermint Kisses is here.

USA TODAY BESTSELLING AUTHOR

# JOSIE RIVIERA

## a Chocolate-Box Christmas

# PRAISE AND AWARDS

**USA TODAY bestselling author**

**#1 Bestseller 90 minute short romance**
**#1 Bestseller Single Authors Short Stories**
**#1 Bestseller Contemporary Short Stories**

# 5 STAR READER REVIEWS

**Amazon Review by J. Barr**
    5.0 out of 5 stars
    "Fun Christmas read, enjoyed it."

**Amazon Review by Teresa**
    5.0 out of 5 stars
    "Short and sweet romance. Love happens when you least expect it."

# CHAPTER 1

*M*aise Anderson stood at the entrance to the women's shelter in her new hometown, her gaze fastened on the front door. The weather was a typical mid-December afternoon in California, but she was accustomed to cooler temperatures.

However, this wasn't about winter. This was about chocolate.

Under normal circumstances, she would have admired the magnificent landscape surrounding the town of Bloomingfield—the imposing snow-capped mountains, the towering ponderosa pines—but she couldn't, because all she focused on was reaching for the metal door handle and turning it.

With a nervous inhale, she gave herself a stern reminder.

*You can accomplish this simple assignment. Candy is a sweet holiday treat. Besides, everyone loves chocolate.*

Maybe. Maybe not.

She hadn't eaten chocolate in over two years because of a nasty bout of food poisoning.

Nonetheless, she hadn't gotten sick because of the chocolate, she rationalized, as she recalled that particular dining assignment. Most likely, she'd gotten sick because of her entrée.

She flicked a glance toward the leaden sky, grimacing when a brisk wind blew misty rain across her face. A chill rose up her neck and she shivered.

She tucked her small umbrella under her arm and pressed her lips together.

Outwardly, she passed for the ideal food critic. Her shoulder-length chestnut hair was pulled into a classic chignon, her beige leather pumps sported a sensible heel, and her camel-colored blazer was tasteful and practical. She'd opted for tailored navy-blue slacks, topped with an emerald-green turtleneck sweater, holiday looking but conservative. She'd kept her makeup to a minimum—muted red lipstick, a light rosy blush, and mascara to highlight her green eyes.

Confidence and expertise on the outside. Foreboding and anxiety on the inside.

She blew out a whoosh of air, straightened her shoulders, and pushed open the door to the shelter. "Here we go," she said under her breath. "I can withstand anything for an hour."

"Happy holidays, Miss Anderson." The mayor, Ed Johnson, a thin man but with a wide grin to make up for it, hailed her as she stepped inside. They'd met at a Hometown Holiday event at the County Museum the previous weekend. "There's a cold front coming in. I'm pleased you agreed to judge our annual fund-raiser."

"I'm happy to participate," she lied. In reality, she had no choice. Her boss, the editor of *Bloomingfield Daily Dispatch*, had given her the assignment with a gruff, "There's no food budget for this affair. Take a couple of pictures with your phone camera, sample the weirdest piece of chocolate you can find, and follow up with a full-of-praise article."

Such was the job of a food-writer reporter. No extravagant feast or fancy sushi. Just pure, sweet chocolate.

At the thought, her stomach roiled.

"Are you settling into your role as our town's newest food critic?" Ed asked.

"Yes." She tempered her voice to sound calm and professional. "There's a wealth of fine restaurants here."

"You're originally from Anchorage, Alaska, correct?" He accepted her blazer as she shrugged it off, hanging it on a coat rack and placing her umbrella beneath it. "California's weather must feel quite warm compared to the frozen north."

"Anchorage winters are certainly memorable." She smiled, well remembering the freezing temperatures and shortened daytime hours that descended on the city from September to May.

"My wife saved your piece in the newspaper about preparing a week's worth of meals ahead of time. She prefers to eat out, but she actually cooked and froze five dinners." Ed reached for a piece of peanut butter fudge on a side table and popped it into his mouth.

"I'm glad my article was helpful." Maise followed him into the dining hall. Eight tables were set up, each covered with a red velvet tablecloth and laden with silver-plated chocolate displays. The entrants, men and women of all ages, stood behind their respective tables and eyed the mayor, then Maise, nervously.

An undecorated Scotch pine soared in the corner of the large room. Beneath the tree, gaily wrapped packages donated by the community were earmarked for the children. The previous day, Ed explained, the shelter had held a Christmas caroling party. Today, most of the women were out job hunting while their children attended school.

Though Maise tried to maintain a semblance of composure, the scents of sweet and bittersweet chocolate filled the air, and she choked back the nausea in her throat.

"Smell that?" Ed inhaled deeply and smacked his lips. "Peppermint fudge, my favorite. This fund-raiser is a chocoholic's dream."

*Or nightmare.*

She extended a gamely smile, sending a stern command to her queasy stomach to settle.

"All the candies are handmade from the local shops and restaurants," Ed continued. "From my experience, all women love chocolate, so you must have jumped at this assignment."

Jump? Umm, no. Actually, she'd cringed.

But she couldn't refuse. She'd been on the job less than a month and had finally settled into her comfortable second-floor apartment at the edge of town. She had no intention of moving back to Alaska and hoped to make Bloomingfield her permanent home.

In Anchorage, her five older brothers had doted on her, while she'd been suffocated by controlling parents who constantly argued. She'd moved away, much to her brothers' dismay, but she wanted to prove to herself that she could manage her life independently.

"Well, I didn't really jump," she said.

"Watching the waistline, right? If I was paid to eat out, I'd gain a pound a week."

She fumbled to say more, but he'd turned to welcome the two other judges. The man and woman, who appeared to be in their early sixties, regarded Maise with smug superiority.

Maise understood that she was in a competitive business, and the unspoken truth that came with it. In food journalism, as in most professions, it was necessary to prove oneself in order to establish a distinguished reputation.

A cheerful rendition of "Rudolph the Red-Nosed Reindeer," sung by Gene Autry, played on repeat, and Ed sang along for a few measures. She grinned as he enhanced his singing with a little dance.

When the song began another loop, Ed led the judges to the tables.

"Here are the eight hopeful candymakers." He exchanged a grin with the woman behind the first table, then motioned to an adjacent counter. "Judges, if you want water or coffee in between bites, it's here."

Coffee. Her favorite beverage. Maise regarded the steaming foam cups set on the counter and whispered an appreciative thank you.

As they went down the line of tables, Ed presented the judges to the candymakers, and Maise realized that she already knew two entrants from her recent assignments. Both were restaurateurs, and both acknowledged her. But the other six entrants were strangers. As she tried to remember all the names Ed recited, she paused at the last table. A tall, lean man with a strong, square jawline and solemn demeanor was being introduced.

He was startlingly handsome, with piercing blue eyes and dark curly hair.

"This serious guy is Ben Elliot." Ed surveyed Ben's table, the glass apothecary jars bursting with peanut butter brittle, and the red bento boxes labeled Bean-to-Bar Chocolate. "Everything looks good, Ben."

"Thanks." Ben gave a quiet sigh and tossed aside a cardboard bento box he'd been trying to put together.

The mayor and judges started back to the first table, but Maise lingered. "Aren't you happy you're here, Mr. Elliot?" she asked. "You don't look as thrilled as the other candymakers."

"Like you, I couldn't be more delighted to be here." He met her gaze, and a lazy smile swept across his face. He'd obviously been watching her and had noticed her apprehensive scan of the displays.

She pulled a notepad and pen from her tote bag and flashed him a polite smile. "And what exactly is bean-to-bar chocolate?"

"Why? Is this an interrogation?"

She frowned. "Isn't this a chocolate contest? I'm a judge and—"

"I don't believe the contest has started yet." He glanced at his watch. "Would you like to try a chocolate-covered almond while you wait?"

"No. No, thank you." She angled away from him. She knew her complexion had gone pale at the mention of chocolate. Nevertheless, his admiring stare roved over her face, then glided down her body to her feet, which were shifting restlessly.

"And your name is—" he inquired.

"Maise Anderson. The mayor just introduced me."

"Right." His lips quirked. "You're a bit nervous this afternoon, Miss Anderson. Brand-new on the job, I take it? I read your recent critique in the newspaper about The Pasta Junction, an established restaurant in town. Apparently you don't like pasta?"

"Pasta is my favorite food."

"Really? You certainly didn't mince words in the article. What were some phrases you used …? Oh yes, the sun-dried tomatoes were too dry, and the pasta stuck together."

She stiffened. "I give my honest opinion, without malice. Most restaurants want feedback so that they can get better."

"You recommended that The Pasta Junction add pizza to their menu."

"Because they serve Italian cuisine, I assumed pizza might be offered, perhaps for lunch, if not for dinner."

"I can assure you that pizza hasn't been added. My sister, Julie, owns that restaurant." He regarded Maise in impassive silence. "If she wanted to sell pizza, she'd open a corner pizzeria, not an upscale Italian restaurant that's been in business for ten years."

Maise kept her posture strong, although inwardly her chest felt like it was caving in. She truly wanted diners to discover new restaurants because of her articles. "I realize the word 'critic' may have a negative connotation, but I write honestly and fairly."

"Let's not forget that it's all through your perspective and therefore colored by your opinion. It's up to the reader whether to agree or disagree with you."

Curtly, she nodded. "Correct." She kept her gaze steady and her chin high. Her self-assurance came partly because he'd laced his voice with a teasing tone, and partly because of his good-natured grin.

"Mr. Elliot, please tell your sister that the antipasto was delicious and I look forward to visiting her restaurant again."

"Ben."

She tipped her head. "Excuse me?"

"My name is Ben. May I call you by your first name, Maise?"

"Of course. There's no need for formality." She met his stare. "Rest assured, Ben, I strive to judge restaurants impartially. Surely you must realize my critiques can't be all fluff."

"An impartial food judge." Mayor Ed had returned and gazed at her with a gratified grin. "You're exactly what our little town needs to put it on the map. I read about your writing expertise in Anchorage, a city five times the size of Bloomingfield. Your stellar review of The Moose's Pad helped launch that restaurant. Diners wouldn't have discovered it otherwise."

She winced, remembering the nasty emails she'd received. "Not everyone agreed with my review."

"Apparently enough people did. Your article was picked up by several major newspapers."

Which had been the problem. In a big city, she'd been expected to write ten to twenty posts a week, plus restaurant reviews, plus handle the social media that came with it. After her article exploded, the workload had doubled.

A thoughtful, well-reported piece took time, and she'd begun to burn out. A small town like Bloomingfield was just what she needed to decompress. She'd still do what she loved, but at a slower pace.

Nevertheless, Ed was a skillful politician, strategically spinning the conversation in order to praise her, and the realization made Maise grin.

Ben grinned at the same time, and they shared a chuckle. Belatedly realizing that he might be flirting with her, she took a guarded step backward. He stood only a few feet away, casually dressed in dark pants and a white polo shirt, and became far more handsome the longer she stared at him. His blue eyes were bringing unexpected changes to her heartbeat.

And there it was. An unanticipated magnetism. An attraction that drew her wholly by surprise.

Mayor Ed tossed a piece of peppermint fudge into his mouth and chewed while he spoke. "Ben Elliot is the owner of Bloomingfield Candy Shop."

"All that?" Maise looked directly at Ben.

"All that and more," Ben quipped, then met the mayor's gaze. "Correction, Ed. I'm the co-owner."

"The man behind the scenes. Don't let his unassuming manner fool you, Maise. This guy is our very own small-town hero."

Why, she wanted to ask, but Ed was ushering her back to the coffee table, where the other judges waited.

He addressed the three of them. "Folks, the directions

are simple. Sample the candies and write down your thoughts and criticisms. You can visit the tables in whichever order you choose. Give the candy a score between one and ten—ten being the most delicious." He eyed the sturdy wooden clock hung on a bare wall. "It's two o'clock, everyone is here and we'll begin. By three o'clock, you should be finished. Bring your comments and scores to me. Ready?"

"Ready!" Maise forced an upbeat tone and made her way to the first table while the other judges dispersed.

"This is a pepper truffle," the wiry ginger-haired candymaker said, quickly enlightening her. He handed her a piece set on a red lace napkin. "Try it."

"You mean a *peppermint* truffle?"

He gave her a knowing look and didn't reply.

She took a deep breath and sampled a bite. Immediately, her eyes watered. She'd expected something sweet with a cooling aftertaste. This candy wasn't sweet. It was flaming hot.

"No, I mean pepper," the man replied. "It's made with red pepper flakes and a dash of pepper oil. A light tang to chocolate candy gives it a punch, wouldn't you agree? It packs a hint of unexpected spicy heat."

Jerkily, Maise bobbed her head, although she wanted to point out that the heat level was more than a hint. While he went on to describe the process of tempering chocolate, she grabbed some water from the counter and greedily drank. Then she switched to a cup of black coffee and sipped appreciatively.

"I worked in France as an assistant chocolatier before opening my own shop," he said. "No doubt a person like you is aware that candy making requires a special skill."

She nodded as she jotted notes on her notepad. "Anything else?"

"Don't get water in the chocolate while you're heating it, because the process will be ruined."

"Thank you." Her stomach rebelled, and she eyed the other seven tables. She snapped a picture and stepped unsteadily to table number two.

She hoped the dark lemon crème candy, charmingly showcased on a linen napkin, might soothe her stomach. It didn't. Maise thanked the chocolatier, took a quick picture, and moved on.

At table three, a blond woman presented Maise with a piece of white chocolate shaped like a candy bar.

"What are the red specks?" Maise asked.

"Strawberries and rose petals, and the petals are edible," the woman replied. "Taste it."

Maise inhaled, then nibbled. "Delicious," she assured. The woman didn't seem to notice Maise's shudder while she explained the difference between pure white chocolate and dark chocolate.

"Did you know that white chocolate is simply cocoa butter and sugar?" the woman quizzed.

"I know now." Maise thanked her, then swiveled to the counter, pondering if she should grab another cup of coffee. The caffeine rush seemed to help her to carry on.

She did, and it helped again.

That is, until she tried the candy at the next four tables.

It was a struggle, and she knew that the fixed, objective expression on her face was slowly disintegrating.

By the time she neared Ben's table, she only had one thought. How could she get out of there? Wildly, her gaze searched for the exit, and she peered at the clock on the wall.

Only a few more minutes. Would it really matter if she skipped his table? He probably wouldn't even notice.

She started toward Mayor Ed, intending to leave. She'd hand in her notes and give Ben's chocolate a score of …

"Hello, Miss Maise. Or is it Mrs.?" Ben called out to her.

Her lips parted, and she spun to regard him.

*That* was his greeting? *That* was his question?

She squinted against the sickness in her throat and treated his remark with dull courtesy. "I'm not married."

She'd been engaged when she lived in Alaska, but had decided to break it off. Now, in her early thirties, love didn't come easy for her. Perhaps because she was commitment shy after her argumentative parents had finally divorced once Maise and her brothers had gone off to college.

"Good." He lifted a dark eyebrow. "Were you going somewhere and trying to skip me?"

She stepped to his table, heat flooding her face. "No, I … Well, yes." She sighed. "It's been a long day." She braced herself for his reprimand.

Instead, he offered a simple, tender smile. "Sorry. I've watched you since you walked in, and I wanted to chat."

So he had been watching her. Her cheeks warmed, and a thrill of excitement heightened her senses as he openly admired her.

"Then you have more than one intrusive question?" she asked.

Her reproof brought a smile to his lips. "Many more."

"May I ask a question too?"

"About me? Sure. I'm an open book."

"Are you married?"

"Divorced. Two years ago," he said quietly. "And a bachelor at thirty-five."

She hung back. *So he was single too.*

"I'm glad you're here," he went on. "Our town prides itself on its good taste." Ben laughed at his pun and Maise's heart did a surprising leap. He threw her totally off-balance, and the composure she'd desperately tried to maintain tumbled a notch.

"I was thrilled by the newspaper's generous job offer," she said.

"All this opportunity in one small California town." Again, she was taken aback by his fine features. His thick hair was a tad too long, those deep-set eyes a vivid blue, and he sported the physique of a well-toned athlete.

Maise stalled and took a sip of her coffee. "Will you explain your candy-making process, Ben?"

He shuffled his feet. "What would you like to know?"

"All the other contestants expounded on their delicious candy. I assumed you would do the same."

"I don't want to oversell my product."

"I find that remarkably refreshing and humble." With laughing relentlessness, she continued, "But I'm still interested."

"Would you like a piece of our shop's signature chocolate coffee fudge?" His gaze drifted to her lips, then to the cup she'd set on the corner of the table. His deep tone had a persuasive gentle quality. "I've noticed that you like coffee. Isn't that your second cup?"

"My third, if you count this morning." She pulled her gaze from his and stared at the cup, anything to delay eating another bite of candy.

She took another sip of coffee, and the most surprising thing happened. Here, amidst all this chocolate, her nausea seemed to dissipate, and she began to relax.

Was it the coffee? Or the man standing a few feet away, his gaze riveted on her?

Shakily, she chuckled. "I'll jot down your comments." Noting that his head drooped ever-so-slightly, she asked, "That is, if it's okay?"

"Of course." He avoided eye contact, or maybe she was imagining it.

"Good." She poised her pen on the notepad. "Can you begin by explaining your candy-making process?"

BEN FELT HIS MUSCLES TENSE. He wanted to answer her, but he couldn't follow through if her questions became too exacting.

"For instance," she was saying, "what are the exact ingredients in your signature chocolate coffee fudge?"

"Let me think about it." He swallowed hard, trying to remember what Gee, an excellent employee who had given his sister the recipe, had told him numerous times.

"Still thinking?" Maise prodded after a lengthy beat. Her enchanting features, a clear, porcelain complexion with a smattering of freckles, a pert, upturned nose, and her full pink lips holding a hint of a smile, made him hesitate.

Was she on to him?

Absolutely not. How could she be? They'd only just met.

He glanced at her profile as she scribbled on the notepad —the profile he'd admired ever since she entered the room. Her tall, slender figure was model-like, and her huge green eyes—enhanced by full black lashes and a touch of mischief —were magnificent.

*A touch of mischief.*

"What are you writing?" he asked, finally breaking the silence. "I haven't said anything."

"I'm writing my grocery list."

Her reply made him laugh.

"I'm still waiting," she reminded, pen poised on the notepad.

He wet his lips and combed through his mind for any details that might be helpful. "Well, our secret ingredient is … coffee."

"In coffee fudge, I wouldn't call coffee a secret

ingredient."

"And marshmallows," he hastened to assure her. Gee had mentioned marshmallows in the recipe, hadn't she?

"Chocolate too, I suppose?"

"Yes, yes, of course." Ignoring Maise's furrowed eyebrows, he placed a chunk of fudge on a white lacy napkin and presented it to her. "The final test is in the tasting, don't you agree?"

She lowered her gaze and muttered something that sounded like, "I'm finally beginning to feel better, and I can't eat another piece of chocolate."

But she didn't look sick.

He reached across the table and lightly touched her arm. "The candy from Bloomingfield Candy Shop is the best. I genuinely believe that to be true."

"Which is through your perspective and therefore colored by your opinion?" She echoed his earlier remark. "Please clarify so that my readers will understand."

"Because our ... chocolate chips are ... sweet."

Her face glowed with laughter. "You mean semisweet?"

He squirmed. "Yes, yes, that's it." With an apologetic grin, he lifted the candy toward her. "Take a bite."

There was something about her over-bright smile that made him suspicious.

"You don't like chocolate, do you?"

A rosy blush stole up her cheeks, and she bent her head, shoving a wayward strand of thick chestnut hair behind her ear.

"You don't like chocolate?" he repeated. Desperately, he struggled to keep his features straight.

"Not today."

He crossed his arms. "A food critic judging a chocolate candy event who doesn't like chocolate."

"I said not today."

"What about tomorrow?"

She fumbled with her bag, her movements both graceful and endearingly awkward. "Two years ago, I had a bout of food poisoning after eating stinkhead and then topped the meal with chocolate for dessert. The memory stuck with me."

"What on earth is stinkhead?"

"It's the mushy fermented head of a king salmon and a delicacy in Alaska. I wrote a review of my experience in the Anchorage newspaper, minus the food-poisoning incident."

Despite her professional tone, her voice quivered. He had the uneasy feeling that he had somehow hit a nerve.

"So, the article wasn't a success?"

"That's putting it mildly." She bit on her lower lip and looked down at her hands.

"Look, I'm sorry about what I said earlier. Your review of my sister's restaurant has actually brought in more diners."

"Apology accepted." Slowly, the embarrassment drained from Maise's face.

Across the room, Mayor Ed was conversing with the other judges.

"Enough about me." Maise plunked her hands on her slim hips. "Let's have a heart-to-heart about you, Mr. Chocolatier. Admit that you have no idea what you're talking about."

"You discovered my secret." He chuckled with relief. "What I know about chocolate could fit into a peanut butter cup. I'm just the businessman who owns the shop. My sister, Sally, makes all the candy. I'm covering for her today, as her daughter is home sick. She's a single parent."

"So you have two sisters? Julie owns The Pasta Junction, and Sally runs Bloomingfield Candy Shop?"

"And a third, Katie, who is a lawyer." Ruefully, he shrugged. "I'm besieged by females."

Maise laughed. "In Alaska, I was surrounded by five brothers."

"So why did you leave?"

"Many reasons. You listened to one of them."

"I'd like to hear the others." Because he wanted to get to know her better.

"I started to lose my readership and credibility," she replied, "after patrons complained that a restaurant I wrote a glowing review for served sub-par food."

He heard the disheartened tone in her voice. "Don't take it to heart." He smiled as Gene Autry began singing again about knowing Dasher and Dancer and Prancer and Vixen.

"This song has been in the same loop at least nineteen times."

"Twenty by my count," Maise said.

"Are you feeling any better? Will you try a taste of my shop's signature chocolate?"

Hesitantly, she accepted his offering, then closed her eyes as she took a bite. Her eyes popped open. "Ben, this is delicious."

"It's my favorite."

"Mmm. I forgot how much I love the combination of coffee and chocolate."

"So, Bloomingfield Candy Shop gets a perfect score?"

"Are you trying to sway me? I'm the judge, you're the contestant." She wrote a number on her notepad, then leaned over the table and whispered, "Is there any way I can make a clean getaway?"

He nodded toward the exit and gave a cheerful wave to Ed, who eyed them warily.

"Thanks." Maise snatched another piece of coffee chocolate fudge, then stepped toward Ed. She handed him her notes, grabbed her blazer and umbrella, and studiously avoided Ben's gaze as she departed.

Still, he laughed when he saw that she'd finished his chocolate.

# CHAPTER 2

*C*hristmas Eve came a week later. As usual, Maise hadn't completed her shopping, because buying for five adult brothers and her parents was more than difficult.

It was impossible.

She parked her Volkswagen at the curb of Main Street and stepped out of the car, smoothing her red-and white-striped dress. California weather was mild, almost balmy, and she loved it.

She peered around. Hopefully, a few shops were open, and she'd know the right gift when she came upon it.

A sign in the window of Bloomingfield Candy Shop caught her attention.

*Winner of the Women's Shelter Annual Fund-raiser for best candy. Come in for a free taste of flavor-rich fudge.*

The shop's red canopied entrance welcomed her as she entered, and she admired the tin pails and decorative boxes tied with exquisite satin bows. The scents of high-quality handmade chocolates combined with the aromas of butter, vanilla, and sugar. Truly, this shop was a chocolate lovers dream.

She'd pondered her conversation with Ben that day at the shelter. At first, she'd thought he was just schmoozing her to win her vote. But no, he'd been sincere. And besides, his candy had deserved to win.

"Maise!" A handsome, familiar man behind the counter greeted her as she stood at the end of a long line. When it was her turn, he quickly filled her order for seven boxes of chocolate.

"Do you ship to Alaska?" she asked.

"We ship all over the world."

"Can you put a rush on it? It's for my five brothers and my divorced parents who live separately."

"Chocolate is sent two-day air, so it won't be overexposed to the elements. However, your family won't receive the candy in time for Christmas."

"I always run behind. I'll call them on Christmas Day and explain."

Ben added a complimentary cup of hot chocolate and an extra box of signature fudge to her order and placed them on the counter.

"I'll help you drink the hot chocolate," he replied as she raised her eyebrows. "I wasn't supposed to be here tonight, but wanted to lend a hand because of the last-minute rush. My sister left a few minutes ago to be with her child. You just missed her."

"It's Christmas Eve and completely understandable."

He gazed at her for a long moment. Around them, the shop began closing down, and he bid his employees a joyful holiday.

He raised the cup of hot chocolate to her. "Merry Christmas, Maise."

"Merry Christmas, Ben."

"What are you doing this evening?"

"I'm attending a church service at the little chapel in

town, then will order a pizza and going home."

"I'll accompany you." His infectious smile made her immediately agree. "But I planned to make a stop at a military service family's home. I'm a volunteer for the USO."

"Is that part of your small-town hero story?"

He nodded.

"I'm fascinated." She swallowed a sip of hot chocolate, then put the cup aside on the counter. "What do you do for the USO?"

"Anything and everything. I'm dedicated to our service members. But mostly, I provide a listening ear."

"Can I visit them with you?"

"I'd like that very much." He took an easy breath and placed her candy in a bag. "Afterward, we can dine at a distinguished Italian restaurant."

"And what's the name of this distinguished restaurant?"

"The Pasta Junction." He caught her hand and led her out the door. "My sister's restaurant stays open late on Christmas Eve."

Maise grinned. "Does she offer pizza?"

"Nope. But I have it on excellent authority that she serves a delicious antipasto."

**THE END**

# A NOTE FROM JOSIE

Dear Friends,

Thank you for reading *A Chocolate-Box Christmas.*

I wanted to write a holiday romance centering around chocolate.

If you loved this sweet romance as much as I loved writing it, please help other people find *A Chocolate-Box Christmas* by posting your review.

*A Chocolate-Box Christmas* is available in ebook, paperback, audiobook, and Large Print paperback.

Josie Riviera

My Spotify Play List for A Chocolate-Box Christmas is here.

Want more of the Chocolate-Box Series? Click here.

# RECIPE FOR CHOCOLATE COFFEE FUDGE

From Gee's Kitchen

<u>Ingredients</u>
- ¼ cup freeze dried coffee granules (Can use decaf)
- 2/3 cup canned evaporated milk
- ½ cup (1 stick) butter
- 2 ounces baking bar chocolate – broken
- 1 ½ cups white granulated sugar
- 2 cups mini marshmallows
- 1 cup real chocolate chips (semisweet)
- ½ teaspoon vanilla extract

Prepare a rectangle cake pan lined with parchment paper or aluminum foil with enough overhang that you can lift fudge out for cutting. For thicker fudge use an 8 inch x 8 inch pan.

**Large pot (or use a wok)**

Place milk and coffee in pot over medium heat, stirring to dissolve the coffee

Now add the butter, sugar, and baking chocolate with the pot on medium high heat and stir occasionally while they melt adding the marshmallows next. Bring contents to a boil and boil for 5 minutes stirring constantly.

Remove the pot from the heat and add the chocolate chips stirring to dissolve. Add the vanilla extract (it will bubble) stirring till glossy.

Pour into prepared pan and smooth top. Let set on a flat surface for an hour and then refrigerate.

Remove from refrigerator, lift up paper/foil and place on a cutting board. Cut into squares.

Store in an airtight container.

Don't forget to sample the crumbs.

Enjoy!

# HOLLY'S
## Gift

### SMALL-TOWN
### CHRISTMAS WISHES
### SERIES

USA TODAY BESTSELLING AUTHOR
# JOSIE RIVIERA

# PRAISE AND AWARDS

**USA TODAY bestselling author**

**#1 Amazon Bestseller Religious Short Stories**

**#1 Amazon New Release Asian American Literature**

**#1 Amazon New Release Religious Short Stories**

# 5 STAR REVIEWS

**Review from InD'Tale Magazine:**

Holly's Gift

"Holly Kim is a piano teacher who is missing a student. She enters a homeless shelter searching for the student. She finds the building inspector, Tim Stewart, closing the place down due to unsafe wiring—just in time for Christmas. He swears he's just doing his job, but Holly is convinced he is simply a bad man. Tim has known bad people, bad times, and homelessness in his life. And he knows God pretty much stays away from all that. Until he runs into Holly's steady faith, and as it slowly erodes his tough outer shell, he might catch himself praying for a Christmas miracle too...and Holly's gift.

This is a standalone novella, fifth in a series. It's a clean, sweet Christmas romance. This is a story that has such strong bones! Readers seeking a wholesome Christmas romance to enjoy any time of the year will be satisfied with a visit to Snowflake Colorado and Holly's Gift."

### Amazon Review by Mary F.
#### 5.0 out of 5 stars

"This Christmas story is a beautiful tale of how love can take you by surprise. Author Josie Riviera has once again drawn me into one of her wonderful stories."

### Amazon Review by Dotty:
#### 5.0 out of 5 stars

"Josie Rivera is an amazing author who writes clean books filled with inspiration."

### Amazon Review by Deutsche
#### 5.0 out of 5 stars

"A holiday inspired series with a unique believable premise, delightful small town Colorado setting, diverse relatable characters, often gut wrenching dilemmas, twist and turn plot and satisfying resolution. Each holiday novella is a stand alone. Josie Riviera is a talented writer addressing contemporary issue of homelessness and homeless shelters, especially in small communities."

# CHAPTER 1

*H*olly Kim's piano student was always dependable. Well, nearly always. But the wintry weather in Snowflake, Colorado, might have delayed her.

At least, that's what Holly assumed as she peered at her watch for the tenth time in ten minutes.

Rather than remain at her piano bench in her cozy living room, Holly took up a position by the window of her first floor apartment and surveyed the drifting snow covering the tree branches. Dusk edged the gray sky with a pink blush before the sun set, and murky clouds emerged. With less than four weeks remaining until Christmas, the forecast called for freezing temperatures.

And this Thursday was no exception.

She opened the French door separating her living room from the kitchen, then prepared a cup of tea while she waited for Jasmine.

"We prefer a white Christmas season, right, Butter-scotch?" Holly expressed her sentiments aloud to the calico cat sitting in a laundry basket in her well-scrubbed kitchen.

She'd rescued him from an animal shelter when he was a young adult. He'd been missing half an ear and crawling with fleas, but she'd nursed Butterscotch back to health.

The cat looked up from licking its white paws, but only for an instant. Apparently, paw licking took precedence over Holly's concerns.

As the water in her teapot heated, Holly's thoughts circled back to Jasmine. The child hadn't shown up for her piano lesson the previous week, either. And prior to that, Holly had had to cancel two weeks' worth of lessons for all of her students in November, as she had traveled to North Carolina to help take care of her aunt. She'd emailed all her students to notify them. So, for Jasmine, there had been no lesson in a month.

Holly knew that Emily Webster, Jasmine's mother, drove the eleven-year-old girl from their home in Snowflake to Holly's home in Pine Cone Valley every Thursday, then waited outside in her pick-up truck. She also knew that Emily was a single parent.

Despite being unfamiliar with specific aspects of the family situation, Holly had suspected for a number of months that things in the home weren't right. Jasmine and Emily seemed isolated from any other family and friends. And Jasmine, a diligent student who loved playing the piano and had taken lessons for two years, had seemed distracted and listless all Fall.

"Is anything wrong?" Holly had asked Jasmine in late September. As a professional teacher, she chose not to pry into a personal situation, even though she'd developed a genuine bond with the girl.

"Nope," came Jasmine's typical close-mouthed reply. "Everything's fine."

Yet, when it came time to pay her October tuition, Jasmine declared that she'd forgotten the check.

"Tell your mother not to worry about payment," Holly said. "I'm happy to teach you at no charge. You're a promising student, and I expect you'll become a fine pianist."

On the few instances when Holly had spoken with Emily, a withdrawn woman wearing shapeless clothes, she'd seemed rushed and hadn't met Holly's gaze. Jasmine was an only child, she'd explained.

After pouring boiling water into a ceramic mug, Holly lifted the window blinds and peered out onto her small garden. More snow, collecting quicker now.

Earlier that day, she'd baked Chinese Christmas cookies which had cooled on wire trays on her granite countertop all afternoon.

She plated a cookie, placed an herbal tea bag into her mug to brew, then flicked a glance at her watch again.

With a sigh, she stepped into the living room. She placed her mug on a garden stool she used as a side table, nibbled at the cookie, then sat at her spinet piano. A Chopin nocturne she'd memorized in college flowed easily, and her fingertips glided over the keys. The music was hauntingly beautiful, and Holly paused after the opening measures.

Each time she played a chord, she thought of Jasmine. When she finished, she gathered up the holiday sheet music she'd intended to teach her, which included a duet arrangement of "Silent Night." Unexpectedly, tears gathered in her eyes.

The living room was quiet. Too quiet. The clock on the mantel heralded the seconds with a near-silent tick.

Quiet. Something she'd avoided for weeks. Times like this.

Time to think.

About life. About sorrow. About the death of a friend.

Because of her sad thoughts, Holly picked up her cell

phone and rang her aunt Clementine in North Carolina to bolster her spirits.

In her sixties, plump and with age spots on her fragile skin, Holly surmised that Aunt Clementine would be either at her preferred vantage point—sitting on the front porch swing watching the neighbors' activities—or caring for her rescue dogs.

Her aunt answered immediately. "Holly, I recognized your caller ID. Hang on a second—" Her warmhearted voice was invariably a comfort to Holly, as was the recognizable barking of Angel, one of the current rescues, a pint-sized, skinny cocker spaniel with intelligent eyes and soft brown fur.

"Has Angel gained any weight since I left?" Holly asked.

"All she does is eat, and the vet told me that her health has done a complete about-face."

Holly recalled with crystal clarity the two weeks she'd spent with her aunt in November while Clementine had convalesced from hip surgery, and Angel's face-to-face doggy kisses and demands for belly rubs.

As if on cue, a dog barked.

"Is this a good time to talk?" Holly asked. "I'm waiting for a student and hoping she'll still show up."

Holly visualized her aunt wrapping a crocheted shawl around her shoulders, then busying herself with filling Angel's water bowl. "Anything in particular you'd like to discuss?"

"The loss of my wonderful friend."

"Charity Hart." Her aunt paused. "I'm sorry you weren't able to attend her funeral because you stayed to help me."

"I wanted you to get back on your feet." Holly said.

Aunt Clementine was a caring, giving person, much like Charity. However, unlike Charity, who'd longed for a husband and children, Aunt Clementine was a confirmed spinster.

"Besides, I love spending time in the Carolinas." Holly injected a note of levity into an otherwise somber conversation and subsequently failed when her voice caught. In the preceding days, she'd sought to suppress the high school memories, and now they were flashing before her eyes.

"I can't believe she's gone," Holly said. "Charity never uttered a bad word about anyone. When we first met, I was a little skittish after hearing about her reputation."

"Good or bad?"

"The best." Holly took another bite of her cookie, relishing the crunch of chow mein noodles and peanuts. "She cultivated relationships with everybody and wasn't focused on other people's opinions. Her giving came from her sweet heart. She did the right thing, all day, every day."

"Did she always live in Snowflake?"

"She left to attend college in Denver." Holly cradled the phone on her shoulder as she drank her tea. "But after her diagnosis, she chose to live with her mother."

*And then, two weeks before Thanksgiving, Charity died.*

"Don't cry for me," she'd told her mother, told her friends. "God is faithful."

"You mentioned she left no husband or children?" Aunt Clementine asked.

"She said she'd know when God placed the right man in her life."

Unlike herself, Holly thought, since she'd done the marriage part and failed miserably. Jim, her ex, was cruel and interested only in himself. He'd committed infidelity, left her and initiated the divorce. She'd been broken, fighting a loneliness so deep that she'd turned inward while she desperately tried to maintain an outward composure.

Marrying him had proved that she wasn't cut out for dating and men and happily-ever-after.

Awash with uncomfortable remembrances, she swept Jim from her mind and focused on the loss of her friend.

"Charity was a servant of God," her aunt said.

Holly nodded into the phone. "We attended Bible club together and studied scripture at our youth group. We'd sit in the front row and take notes."

"I imagine you heeded the pastor's words in respectful silence."

"Well, with a little giggling now and then," she admitted.

They were young then. Now, in their early thirties, they were still young.

"Is Pastor Tom still the pastor at Snowflake Chapel?"

"He is," Holly said, "along with the associate pastor, Manuel Cruz, and his wife, Alma. Whenever I'm the substitute pianist, I see them." Otherwise, she attended her local church in Pine Cone Valley.

At the same moment that she spoke, Holly stood and wandered to the enormous picture window overlooking the street. Outside, the ground shimmered a glistening, icy silver.

It had been a late afternoon much like this one when she'd first met Charity. In turn, Charity had introduced Holly to her friends—Caro, Taye, Sara, Nate, and Mia. They all became instant comrades for they shared a common denominator: They were all Christians. Over the years, they'd remained friends, though some had moved away.

"Holly, are you still there?" her aunt asked.

"Sorry, Aunt Clementine. I was thinking. You may not remember, but during Christmas winter break of my senior year, several of us decided to gift a special person with something we had chosen."

"And who was your special person?"

"It was a secret, which made the activity more delightful and memorable."

"Who did you choose, dear?" her aunt repeated.

"I chose you." Holly smiled, assuming she could divulge her secret after all these years. "You lived in Snowflake at the time, not far from my parents."

Her aunt chuckled.

"I bought you a picture album and filled it with photos of our family," Holly continued, "so you could recall our fun times."

*Secret Angels,* Charity had declared.

"I wondered who delivered that photo album wrapped in red polka-dot paper and tied with twine. The doorbell rang, but when I opened the door, no one stood there."

Holly giggled. "And now you know."

"I suspected, but was never certain. That album was filled with many precious images, and your mother and I were as close as two sisters could be."

Holly fingered the sterling silver charm bracelet she always wore, a beloved memory of her mother's thoughtfulness. Each charm signified important events in Holly's life—a piano, a flag of South Korea, and her graduation.

"Equally important was the gift of your time and interest," her aunt went on. "I can't tell you how much I appreciate your kindness."

"Nothing's changed. You were like a mother to me after my parents died."

Holly experienced another rush of sadness for another loss. Her adoptive parents had died while serving as missionaries overseas, and it wasn't supposed to happen that way. They were compassionate citizens, trying to help others.

As usual, her aunt was spot on. Time with loved ones was the most precious gift.

*Time.*

She should have made time to visit Charity when she got sick, Holly thought. But by the time she'd come home to Colorado, Charity had passed.

Truly, it was better to give than to receive. And Charity had offered Holly a precious gift—the gift of an irreplaceable friendship.

*Walk with the wise and become wise, for a companion of fools suffers harm.* Holly's favorite Scripture verse, Proverbs 13:20, came to mind. Such accurate words—the guardrails that kept her on a straight path that she largely attributed to Charity.

"I didn't keep in touch with her as much as I should have, Aunt Clementine."

"Life gets in the way sometimes. But you mentioned that Charity had moved to Denver."

"Still, we lived in the same state. We relied on social media to stay connected." Holly readied for the pep talk she assumed her aunt was about to offer.

"I understand all about young people and social media," came her aunt's response. "Everyone is connected nowadays."

Though in reality, were they? What was better than a face-to-face chat with an extraordinary friend or loved one?

"We're all busy," Charity had assured Holly when they'd video chatted one chilly evening. "The main thing is we are serving the Lord. God granted us his mercy and forgives our sins every single day. So praise him every single day."

*Every single day.*

But that's where the similarity ended. Yes, they were both Christians, but unlike Holly, Charity had lived up to her name and continued her charitable giving. Whereas, Holly had not.

"Thanks for chatting with me, Aunt Clementine." Holly peered at the wooden clock perched on the fireplace mantel. "I'm going to call my student. I tried last week when Jasmine missed her lesson, but wasn't able to reach her and left a message. She's my last lesson for tonight."

"Good luck. I love you, dear," Aunt Clementine said.

"I love you too. I'll phone again soon."

Holly clicked off and walked over to her desk by the piano. The certified letter from Green and Sons Law Firm lay open, the first page exactly where she had left it.

In Charity's handwriting, she'd added a note along with the letter:

"Dear Holly, please use this $1500 check to give someone special a wonderful Christmas. Remember all those fun times in high school? Create that magic again. For me."

Consequently, Holly had phoned Don, the lawyer at the firm, who confirmed that each of their friends had received the same amount of money.

In their conversation, Don reminded Holly that if she didn't wish to disperse her check, she had the option to refuse and the firm would donate the money to a worthy cause.

So far, Holly had done nothing except for that quick call to the lawyer's office saying she'd received the check while staying in North Carolina with her aunt. Since returning, she'd let the check sit on her desk and neglected it, as if acknowledging the letter would make her friend's death absolute.

Should she keep it? Because she certainly had no charitable cause in mind.

Another glance at her watch confirmed that Jasmine was now thirty minutes late.

*The girl wasn't just late. She wasn't going to show up.*

With a worried frown, Holly scrolled through her student contacts and tapped in the number Jasmine had given her when the girl first enrolled for lessons.

"This number is not in service," came the recorded message. "Please check the number and dial again."

Odd, because the number had been in service the previous week.

Holly took a deep pained breath. She should have known something was wrong. *She should have known.*

She doubled through her contacts until she found Jasmine's address.

"I'll drive into Snowflake," she announced to Butterscotch as she headed for the kitchen. She gulped a last mouthful of tea and set her mug in the stainless steel sink.

In the foyer, she surveyed herself in the mirror and tamed her straight black hair into a semblance of a style. She'd worn navy slacks, a white chenille sweater, and brown leather loafers for teaching. Now she switched her loafers for knee-high boots and drew on a crimson-red wool coat, a knitted green beanie, and gloves.

Her stomach churned as worst-case scenarios raced through her mind. Suppose something had happened to Jasmine and her mother?

Holly expelled a breath, grabbed her car keys and rushed out the door into a bitter cold evening.

# CHAPTER 2

*U*nder fifty minutes later, Holly reached Snowflake. As always, her windshield wipers carved out a clear spot for her to peep through, and she handled her four-wheel-drive Jeep with proficiency. Fortunately, the weather had calmed by the time she arrived, and only a thin layer of slush coated the roads and walkways. She'd adhered to the speed limits, although she preferred to drive fast, with the adventurous assertiveness and bold disregard of peril that was uniquely part of her parents' legacy. Similarly, they'd loved watching NASCAR on television.

However, she reserved her stock-car racing passion for when she visited Aunt Clementine in North Carolina, and attended live events.

She typed Jasmine's address into her phone's GPS and soon discovered there was no such address.

Disconnected phone number. Fake street address.

Holly envisioned Jasmine's round angelic face, her blond curls arranged into two pigtails. Whenever Holly complimented her piano playing, the girl would blush to the roots of her hair.

Well, the address might be fake, but the wonderfully artistic child was real.

So, where was she?

Holly clutched the neckline of her coat and took a deep breath to calm herself.

"Snowflake Homeless Shelter," she said aloud. She'd volunteered at the shelter with friends from church and knew it was located near Blue Spruce Plaza. It had been set up for single mothers and families who needed emergency, temporary shelter.

She brushed the snow off her Jeep with the foam brush she kept in the glove compartment, then hopped back inside. As she drove closer to the town center, she admired the stores festively adorned for Christmas. Lampposts on Main Street were graced with red satin bows and wreaths, and white lights twinkled from boutiques and mom-and-pop shops.

She hung a left and pulled to the curb of the homeless shelter a few minutes later.

Her boots clicked on the shoveled concrete sidewalk as she walked to the entrance. A pavilion was piled with plastic garbage bags crammed with personal possessions and damaged, street-worn luggage. She opted for the wheelchair ramp and shook snow from her coat sleeves.

When she entered the shelter, turmoil greeted her. The smell of cheap industrial cleaner made her hang back. Women, many holding young children, were grouped near an enclosure where an employee worked. A woman in a wheelchair waited silently in the hallway, and a handful of orange tabby kittens looped through the crowd.

At the far end of the lobby rose an undecorated five-foot Scotch pine.

Two men, a slightly hunched, heavyset man with gray

hair and a tall good-looking man she guessed to be in his thirties, hardly spared her a second look. Nonetheless, they seemed the most official, so she waited for them to acknowledge her.

"Stand in line over there, miss," the heavyset man said to her. "You'll get a ticket for some clothing and a bed, and a list of shelter rules."

Holly shook her head. "Sir, I'm not here for—"

"Apologies if you're hungry," he said with a harried glance. "Ask a staff member to unlock the refrigerator. We have bottled water, tuna, or peanut butter and jelly sandwiches."

"I've eaten dinner, thanks," Holly replied. "I'm looking for someone."

"You'll be able to find that someone real soon." He glared at the younger man, his blue gaze sparking. "All the residents have been asked to leave."

"Why?" She stepped back. "It's freezing cold out there."

"I've lived here all my life, miss, and am conscious about a Colorado winter and the danger it presents. Nonetheless, tell that to Tim, our hotshot inspector. He thinks we're in the middle of July." Lou stroked his stringy white mustache and scowled.

"Lou, I'm not the bad guy here." Tim seemed to hold his irritation in check with an apologetic exhale. Absentmindedly, he pushed a lock of wavy-brown hair off his forehead and granted Holly a slight smile.

She didn't expect to be attracted to a man in a place like this, with its utter chaos and people swarming everywhere.

But she was.

A glimmer of concern in his deep brown eyes gave her pause. Self-consciously, she worried her knitted beanie with her gloved hands. She'd yanked it off when she'd entered the building and consequently assumed her hair was a staticky mess, the ends sticking straight out in all directions. Adding to her disheveled appearance, she knew any lip gloss she'd applied that morning had faded.

And still, he regarded her with interest.

"Hello," he said.

"Hi." She looped the straps of her purse over her shoulder and offered a faint smile.

Normally, she was unimpressed by extraordinarily handsome men. In her experience, they were oftentimes hollow and superficial, or, like her ex-husband, self-absorbed. But this man threw her totally off balance, because his voice sounded soothing in the disorder that surrounded them.

He towered over her, his muscular shoulders impeding everything but her view of him.

And for some reason, he looked vaguely familiar.

"I told you, Tim," Lou was saying. "All the permits, including the electricity, should be in order."

Tim shook his head. "I'm forced to execute city regulations. You realize that. If this problem isn't taken care of it could lead to a fire hazard."

"I can't turn all these homeless people away. Where are they supposed to go?" Lou pivoted and pointed to the Scotch pine in the corner. "What about the tree-trimming party? The children are looking forward to decorating for Christmas."

"Fortunately, you have the weekend. While everyone is decorating, begin making arrangements at the hotels here in town," Tim responded. "There's the Blue Jay Motel and Rocky Mountain Bed and Breakfast."

"For thirty single women and their children?" Lou asked harshly. "The bed and breakfast has six rooms."

"I know the owner, Theresa Rose."

"So do I, and she's usually fully booked," Lou countered. "I suppose you expect the motel to accommodate everyone?"

"Of course not." Tim tapped a forefinger on his lower lip. "How about the Snowflake Inn?"

Lou cast a long-suffering scowl. "All eight suites?"

"There's the Blue Spruce Apartments."

"You mean the Blue Spruce *rented* apartments?"

Tim reacted as if he'd been punched in the stomach. He leaned over and made a pleading gesture with his hands.

"I'm sorry," he said to Lou, although his expression was set.

"Make way," an EMT shouted, steering a gurney into the hallway.

Holly hustled to the side to let them through.

"What's going on?" she asked the woman in the wheelchair. Her boots were hardly worn, and Holly surmised they'd been donated.

"Lou had to call for an ambulance a little bit ago. Old lady Alley fell off her bunk bed again." The woman put a fistful of coins into the vending machine and tugged out a bag of chips. She grinned, displaying a row of missing teeth. "She's a longer term resident and claimed the top bunk in a semiprivate room. Last time this happened, she split her head on the concrete floor." She wheeled to the window and gawked at the ambulance stationed at the curb, its blinking lights steadily flashing through the shelter's windows.

Holly trained her attention back to the two men.

"Who will pay for all these rooms?" Lou pointed a gnarled finger at Tim.

"Look, I don't want to quarrel. If there was something I could do, I would do it," Tim shot back. "But as it stands now, the shelter needs to close."

"Impossible."

"It won't be forever, just until we get this problem sorted. That's the best I can do."

"Then your best isn't good enough."

"I wish I could offer more," Tim replied in a chillingly polite manner. "But I can't."

# CHAPTER 3

$\mathcal{T}$imothy Stewart watched Lou stalk down the hallway. Again and again, he'd deflected Lou's questions because he didn't have an answer. He'd expected to sway Lou's animosity by explaining the residents' safety and the city of Snowflake's concerns.

It had been to no avail.

"I'm phoning Mayor Hardy," Lou muttered over his shoulder, half to himself.

"I said I was sorry twice now," Tim replied loudly, but not loudly enough, since Lou didn't swing around.

For the second time, Tim regarded the beautiful Asian woman standing near the vending machine. Too stressed to do anything else, he shoved his hands into his jean pockets. "I'm truly sorry about this," he said to no one in particular.

Apparently overhearing him, she nodded. "Now that's another apology."

He pushed his hair back with a shaking hand. "Do you need something, miss ...?" He heard the impatience in his tone, which he blamed on fatigue and the pressure of a wearying day.

"No, I assume *you're* certainly not the one who can help."

*Great. Just great. More blame.*

Lou's words continued to hammer into Tim's brain. Even his best wasn't good enough.

He stretched a wool cap over his ears, conscious that the woman was staring at him. Her dark almond-shaped eyes were magnificent, her cheekbones prominent.

And she was extremely attractive.

He shook his head. She was certainly a complication he didn't need.

In order to avoid her stare, his gaze flitted to the window. The ambulance threw on the siren and sped away.

People were hurt all the time, physically and emotionally. Which hurt worst?

With no other place to look, he met her stare. "Lou is a friend," he explained.

Why he suddenly felt that he should clarify anything to anyone, especially a stranger, was beyond him.

"Right. I can see you are best buddies." Ruefully, she shook her head. Her mouth held the hint of a smile.

Debating whether to grin or scowl, he summed up his indecision by offering a rueful shrug.

He was supposed to have clocked out of work two hours ago, yet he'd stayed, unsuccessfully trying to fix the shelter's electric problem. He was an inspector, not an electrician, he'd finally reminded himself when, frustrated, he'd given up.

And now, as a result for his concern, he was being chastised by an attractive homeless woman.

"Were you waiting for a bed, miss?" Tim gestured to the line by the glass enclosure, all impatient to be checked in. Viewing the foyer, he noted a woman in a wheelchair munching on a bag of chips.

Holiday stockings were piled high on a table against a wall, along with a miniature Christmas card village. A kitten wound around his legs, and he picked it up to stroke the velvety fur.

"Your friend already asked me." The attractive woman said, as her gaze met his. "I don't need a bed or a meal. I'm searching for a mother and her daughter."

For a lengthy moment, Tim truly assessed her, and consequently, two things hit him at once.

First, she had a wonderful smile, and second, her soft, gorgeous eyes were brimming with … bemusement.

Since gazing at her was infinitely better than worrying about the homeless shelter and a decision he couldn't control, he preferred to gaze at her. There was a vivaciousness about her, the way her silky straight black hair hung loose around her face. And her profile, the pert, turned-up nose, her shoulders rigidly set, were all adorable.

He doubted she'd appreciate his observations.

"May I ask your age?" he inquired, then cringed at his audacity for asking such a question.

She flashed a smile. "I'm almost thirty-three. Why?"

"You don't look a day over twenty-one."

"My birthday is January first." She flavored her response with levity. "So, I'll look older in a month."

He grinned. "A New Year's baby?"

"I am, yes."

She didn't appear to be the average shelter resident, but because of his past, he knew well how appearances were deceiving. His mother hadn't looked like she lived in a homeless shelter, either. And she'd made certain that she and Tim were always clean and tidy.

"Who might have information concerning this woman and her daughter?" the woman asked.

"Speak to Lou." Tim shifted. "He pretty much runs things around here."

"Lou is facing bigger problems these days." She gazed out

the window where a few women stood and Tim followed her gaze. To fight off the cold, the women shivered and clutched thin coats to their shoulders.

"Right." With an exasperated sigh, Tim set down the kitten. "Bigger problems."

"Finding rooms for all these people in one weekend is a big undertaking."

"I'm well aware of the situation." As a result of him creating it, although he'd only been following orders. "What I meant was, why are you looking for this mother and daughter?"

"Because I want to help them."

"Is this a good Christmas deed or something?" he asked. "The shelter is already supported by generous private donations."

"Hmm. If you look around, we can both agree the donations apparently aren't generous enough."

"The contributions are reliable and support the day-to-day expenses." He ignored her killing frown. Apparently his explanation wasn't helping the situation. "Though rewiring a place this old will cost thousands of dollars."

"How about prayer?" she asked.

"How about it?"

"Prayer will help."

He lifted an eyebrow. "How about money? Money will really help."

"You sound like a cynic. Some call it an escape so that they don't get wounded."

"So now you're analyzing me?"

"Hardly. I'm just stating a fact." She surveyed the people waiting. "All I'm suggesting is to have faith too."

Faith. God. When was the last time anyone had mentioned either to him? Probably his grandmother when he was a child. But it was more comfortable believing in nothing, and that was the way he intended to keep things.

Consequently, he was never hurt. He'd learned early on that if he relied only on himself, at least he could depend on someone.

She was evidently waiting for a reply, so he extended his right hand. "I'm Tim."

"I gathered."

"Tim Stewart." His hand was still outstretched, yet she wavered. He pressed his lips together. "And you are?"

"Holly. Holly Kim."

"You're Asian?"

She smiled. "Yes."

"Chinese?"

"Korean. We have a rounder face."

The way she watched him, with gentleness in her strikingly expressive eyes, caused him to stand still. His mother had never looked at him with such consideration. Similarly, neither had his girlfriend of the past six months.

"You live here in Snowflake?" he inquired.

A blink of a hesitation before Holly responded. "I live in Pine Cone Valley."

"About an hour away, right?"

"Under an hour, depending on how fast you drive."

"I can't imagine someone like you would ever buck the speed limit." He shot her a look of amusement. "You don't seem the type."

"And what type is that, Tim?"

A biased stereotype. He expected a blue-eyed blond wearing a tight skirt to drive fast cars, not a demure Asian woman. Noting Holly's scowl, he wisely didn't express his sentiments aloud.

"I meant—I'm a type." He congratulated himself for shifting the topic so effortlessly.

"Oh, really. What type is that?"

"I suppose I *am* a cynic when it comes to faith and religion." He offered a contrite head shake, then zipped up his navy-blue quilted parka. "But for the record, I don't have the patience for God."

"Did God take too long to answer your prayers?"

"I don't know. He's never answered any."

"Perhaps faith will produce patience so that you can trust again."

"For instance, you mean trust in God?" he countered. "Or trust in others?"

"Both."

"Right." His shrug meant just the opposite. *Wrong.*

He had sent endless prayers to heaven throughout his adolescence, asking God to change his family's situation. Instead, Tim and his mother had slept beneath bridges when the shelters in Denver were full. Free weekly newspapers served as their blankets.

Of course that was when they weren't joy riding on country roads with her so-called buddies who were forever intent on partying. If the scene involved booze, his mother was the first to arrive, oftentimes with Tim in tow.

"I understand," Holly said.

His gaze narrowed on her smile. He had the edgy feeling that she was one of those people who might try to convert him to her way of thinking. An evangelist—someone who fancied Gospel preaching and spreading the Good Word.

"Well? Is there a way I can locate them?" Behind her beautiful face was a determination that caught him off guard.

"All the women and children are housed down the hall," he said even as his radar went up. Once, his mother had mistakenly depended on individuals who claimed they wanted to help her and her son. "Call the shelter later. Or, if you wait, things should quiet in an hour."

Her shoulders stiffened. He hadn't meant to sound curt, but the day had been long and disheartening.

"Call who?" she asked.

"The shelter, miss—"

"Holly," she reminded him.

"Holly, I'm one of two building inspectors in Snowflake. I don't work here. Their exact hours are posted somewhere."

"I assume they welcome visitors day and night." She rubbed the middle of her forehead. "So the shelter really must close?"

"Yes." He steered them to an out of the way corner. "I don't make the rules, I just enforce them."

"No need to get defensive, Mr. ..."

*Had he been defensive?* He exhaled. *Yeah, probably.*

"Tim. Tim Stewart," he said. Was he really that forgettable? Who else walked away from a promising acting career?

*Someone who was disillusioned.*

He'd certainly felt that way when he was young—invisible in a sea of high school students as he and his mother moved from place to place. Ten schools in as many years, and being the new kid wasn't fun, especially as he entered adolescence.

"What happened?" Holly asked. "Why wasn't anyone aware of this electrical problem sooner?"

He was surprised her tone wasn't incriminating, especially since he'd been so abrupt with her. His gaze lingered on her lovely features. Her complexion was slightly golden, her high cheekbones flushed. Her lips were full, a deep vivid pink.

Slight and slim, she couldn't weigh more than a hundred pounds soaking wet.

And as he continued staring, he was utterly, inexplicably drawn to her.

In the silence, she waited for an explanation.

His hands dropped to his sides. "The electricity isn't up to code," he replied.

She nodded. "Go on."

His phone pinged, indicating an incoming text. He withdrew it from his pocket, assuming it was Felicia, his on-again, off-again girlfriend. He glanced at the screen. Sure enough, she was asking why he hadn't picked her up for dinner yet.

*Soon. Tied up at work*, he rapidly texted, then jammed the phone back in his pocket.

"Sorry," he said to Holly. "You were asking?"

"About the electricity for the building."

"The shelter lost power twice this week, and the ancient wiring presents a safety hazard."

She peered around. "Then all the more reason for me to find the family."

Lou stomped over. "You still here, Mr. Hot Shot Movie Star Inspector?"

"I was just leaving," Tim replied.

"Movie star?" Holly looked up at him. "I thought I recognized you."

"It was many years ago, and it was actually a television series." Tim dismissed her question by gesturing to Lou. "As I said, here's the guy to talk to if he can spare a minute."

Holly turned to Lou. "I'm Holly Kim. I'm aware this is a bad time, but I'm looking for—"

"Miss Kim, I'm so sorry I haven't been to my piano lessons." A girl about eleven years old raced to Holly and threw her skinny arms around Holly's waist. Her huge green eyes reminded Tim of a street urchin. "My mother lost your phone number."

"Jasmine, I'm so relieved you are here." Holly crouched down and cupped the little girl's face in her hands. "I was beyond worried. I called the number your mother had given me, then went to your address and—"

A woman with pinched cheeks and sunken gray eyes, her mousey-brown hair scraped back by a tortoise-colored plastic clasp, hurried down the hall. She gripped a self-improvement book close to her chest. She looked anxious, as if she never was able to catch up with life and couldn't quite handle it.

Tim recognized the look, for he'd seen it often enough on his mother's face. This woman had an addiction, most likely alcohol.

"Miss Kim, I apologize." The woman advanced toward Holly. "My truck wouldn't start tonight."

"I'm just glad you're okay, Emily," Miss Kim replied.

"Mommy." Jasmine tugged at her mother's sleeve. "We don't have a truck anymore. Remember at Sunday morning service the pastor told us not to lie?"

"Yes, yes." Emily's voice was quick and impatient. "I'm not perfect, you know."

Tim dawdled by the doorway, pretending to check his phone as he readied to leave. Yes, he was eavesdropping, but he couldn't help himself.

Thus, Miss Holly Kim was a piano teacher, and she obviously had an indisputable attachment to the young girl. And she didn't live in Snowflake.

He was familiar with Pine Cone Valley, recalling that the town boasted an excellent coffee shop rivaling the Cozy Coffee Shop in Snowflake. Maybe he could invite her for coffee and a sandwich sometime.

And why would he do that? Inwardly, he reined in his thoughts.

Complications, complications.

"Tim," Lou called. "Is there any other way?"

"I wish there were, Lou." He blew out a frustrated breath.

"To sum everything up, I'll be back first thing Monday to close the place."

He glanced toward the entrance. At least the good-natured giggling between two teenage residents, both wearing similar flannel shirts and torn jeans, took his mind off the problem for a moment.

"Thanks for nothing," Lou muttered, stamping away again.

*So now what?*

Tim lingered by the doorway. Should he say good-bye to Holly, mumble a "nice to have met you," or just leave the building?

He'd been curt with her but he'd apologized, hadn't he?

Umm, no, in fact, he hadn't. And the tension he'd felt all evening had spun an attraction to her he couldn't explain.

Really, tension could do that?

In his case, yes. Or rather, the real reason. He simply wanted to see her again.

He hung back, but merely for a second before he strode to her. She was conversing with Jasmine's mother, while Jasmine munched on a handful of chips the woman in the wheelchair shared with her.

"Holly?" He tapped her on the shoulder.

She excused herself from the conversation and curved to him. "Yes?"

"Can I call you?"

She blinked. "What?"

"Call you. You know, so that we can go out on a date."

"A date? Why?"

"I thought maybe we could go for coffee or something." He was talking like an idiot. Again, he reminded himself he'd had a very long day.

"Why?" she repeated.

"You do drink coffee, don't you?"

"Every morning. But only in the mornings."

"Are you dating anyone?"

"No. Not that it's any of your business." She combed a hand through her hair. "Are you?"

"Am I what?"

"Dating anyone?"

His conscience chattered for no reason, because he and Felicia had an understanding. No long-term commitments.

"I'm not the Grinch who stole Christmas," he said, "if that's what's holding you back."

"You're not grouchy?"

"Hardly ever."

She seemed to be holding in a smile. "So you don't live in a cave?"

"I've never stolen a Christmas, or any other item in my life."

Even at their lowest point, when he and his mother were desperate for a hot meal, at least they hadn't lifted any items out of the convenience stores they'd slipped in to escape a freezing winter's night.

"Thanks, but I'm not interested." Holly's reply was quick, dousing his enthusiasm.

"Why not?"

"I don't date."

A gorgeous woman like her?

Despite the facts that their paths might not cross again and her life was in the next town over, he was interested in getting to know her better. Nonetheless, after the crushing reality of being raised by a neglectful mother, he only dated women who didn't demand more than he could give.

Then again, Holly didn't seem like that kind of woman.

"I can call you," he heard himself saying. "Or text, if you give me your number."

"No call, no coffee, no texts. Understand?"

*All right then. This was a set-down he couldn't refute.*

He hid his disappointment behind a brief grin. "I understand, loud and clear." He should say more, something sharp and witty, something flippant, but words eluded him. Because in truth, he felt hurt and disheartened.

"Well, good night." He acknowledged the girl's mother and then noticed how Jasmine eyed the vending machine longingly.

He made his way to her. "Hold out your hand," he instructed.

She lifted her freckled face and chortled as he placed a fistful of loose change in her hand.

"Enjoy." He tousled her blond bangs that hung over her eyes. "Buy whatever you want."

She cast a furtive peep at her mother. "Can I get candy?"

"Yes," Emily replied, "since we've eaten supper already. Though don't eat it all at once."

"Yay! I love caramels!" As the change clinked into the machine, Jasmine whirled to give Tim a high-five. "Thanks, Mr. …"

"Stewart. Tim Stewart."

The woman in the wheelchair backed up, and he automatically gave her a hand, straightening her toward the hallway that led to the residents' rooms. Behind him, he overheard his name whispered, and not in a flattering way. Puzzled, worried glances were cast at him. Apparently word traveled fast, because he was already slated as the guy who was shutting down the place right before Christmas.

With an offhand nod, he turned toward the door and almost collided with a resident shuffling across the lobby.

He spun to find Holly watching him. He bid her and her friends a cordial good night and added a brief smile.

She smiled back, but the smile didn't reach her eyes.

She didn't want him to call her, since she didn't want to

date him, or anyone by the sounds of it. She didn't like coffee in the afternoon, or phone calls, or texts.

So that was settled.

He'd never had to pursue a woman before and he wouldn't start now, especially with one who wasn't interested.

He tugged on his wool tweed cap and wound a cranberry-colored scarf around his neck. Many had called him a fool when he'd headed for California as soon as he'd graduated from high school.

Sure, it was a year later than everyone else, but that he blamed on his constant moves. The main thing was, despite the years in between, he'd persevered.

And then, the poor kid from nowhere had landed an acting role.

Therefore, when had adversity ever stopped him?

"I hope to see you again, Holly," he called out.

She opened her mouth to reply, but he strode out the entrance, past the women smoking, the young twenty-some-things making their way inside, the piles of plastic bags jammed with folks' lives. He nodded at the police officer patrolling the area and kept walking.

Again, his cell phone pinged with an incoming text.

This time he ignored it.

# CHAPTER 4

*A*fter she returned to her apartment later that evening, Holly set Charity's letter on the garden stool in the living room.

With a mug of steaming chamomile tea and a slice of toast slathered with butter, she settled on her tufted couch with Butterscotch curled at her side.

When her landlord had granted permission, she'd wallpapered the room in faux, natural-looking grass cloth that sported a knotted, woven design. On the fireplace mantel, she'd tilted an antique beveled mirror picked up at the This and That Shop, a variety store in town. Beside the fireplace, she'd tucked a sizable, lush fern into a wicker basket, and a fabric-covered box near the piano hid an overflow of music.

Someday, she'd purchase her own place and decorate it exactly the way she preferred. But for now, since it was December, she'd draped a green garland along the mantel and added a splash of red spray paint to pinecones arranged in a clear glass bowl on her kitchen counter. On Christmas Eve, she'd set up a spindly artificial tree, then attend the six o'clock church service in Snowflake.

She made a note to herself to purchase a new tree topper. The year before, the previous one had shattered.

And then would come Christmas Day.

Since her divorce she'd spent it alone, a prospect she never looked forward to.

To chat about her eventful evening at the shelter, she phoned Aunt Clementine, who answered on the second ring.

"Hello, Holly," her aunt said. "Is anything the matter?"

"No, why?" Holly bit into her toast and chewed.

"You don't usually call me twice in one day."

"Are you busy?"

"A little."

Holly went along with her aunt, assuming she was joking. Typically at this hour she was snuggled on her flowered recliner watching her favorite game show, a rescue dog or two nestled at her feet.

"I called to tell you that this was easier than I imagined," Holly said.

"What was easier?"

Holly smiled. "How best to use the fifteen hundred dollars Charity gave me. I found a special charitable cause."

"That's the way the Lord works. Don't wear yourself out looking for something that God will place right in front of you."

A muted male voice resounded through the phone.

"Is anyone with you?" Holly asked.

Silence for a beat.

"Aunt Clementine?"

"Justin Kildred is here." Her aunt cleared her throat. "We're watching a game show together."

"The man who volunteered in the reception area the day you were admitted?" A vision of the portly elderly man with wiry white hair and a friendly, hearty chuckle, prompted Holly to smirk.

"The very same. While I was in the hospital, he came to my room and visited me, and before I was discharged, he asked for my number. He told me it took him a few days to gather up his courage to ask me out."

"And she was worth the wait," Justin called out in the background.

Holly gaped into the phone. "When did this all happen?"

"We went on our first date soon after you left, a celebration because of the good report I received from the doctor. And Justin brought me a bouquet of white roses. You know how much I love flowers. And white roses signify new beginnings."

"How romantic." Holly chuckled. "And more important, I'm thrilled about how quickly you convalesced."

"My faith is my greatest report, for God always puts us in the best place for our needs."

"Which includes placing you in the hospital so you could meet Justin?" Holly envisioned her aunt blushing like a sixteen-year-old girl. "You never spoke about him once during all our recent phone conversations."

"I figured you were heartbroken over losing your friend and needed the chance to talk about your friendship."

"Charity wouldn't want us to grieve, although I can't help myself." With a choked laugh, Holly curved her hand across Butterscotch's back and was rewarded with a low purr. "She wished everyone a long and happy life."

"Maybe God was bringing forth new life in her wishes," Aunt Clementine quietly said. "His timing is always perfect."

*New life. New beginnings.*

Her aunt was finally finding love, and Christmastime made it even more special. She'd lived her entire life alone, and she certainly hadn't been looking for love. But so what? Love at any age was praiseworthy.

Holly picked up Charity's letter and clutched it close to

her chest. It was tear-stained and raveled at the corners. Through Charity, God had given Holly and her friends an assignment. Surely God would see them through and provide assistance.

"Tell me about your special cause," her aunt prompted.

"It all happened so quickly." Holly set down the letter, wrapped her fingers snugly around her mug, and took a sip of the earthy chamomile tea. Then she explained what had happened at the shelter and her conversation with Tim. "Perhaps I'll use the fifteen hundred dollars to find a place for Jasmine and her mother, Emily, to stay."

"How long will that amount last to cover their rent?"

"Only a few months."

"So what about the other people at the shelter?" her aunt asked quietly.

"You're right." With a sigh, Holly set down her mug. "Of course that isn't the best use for the money. I considered donating it to the shelter for the rewiring, but I'm certain that money wouldn't even come close to the required amount."

"Then start a fund-raiser to make up the difference."

"Like what, for instance? A bake sale?"

"You're a musician, aren't you?" Holly visualized her aunt —the lines in her face, the caring heart that held infinite wisdom. "Ask your students to perform a holiday piano recital and solicit donations at the door."

"And where would I hold this recital?" Holly reached for a blank piece of notepaper and a pen she always kept close by. "The wintry weather is unpredictable for an outside performance."

"Why don't you talk to that building inspector and throw around your ideas? What's his name?"

"Tim Stewart." The memory of his tousled brown hair and deep, velvety voice when he apologized for being forced to close the shelter, had a curious effect on Holly's heartbeat.

"Surely he can refer you to an electrician," her aunt said. "Or that other man ... Lou. Can he help?"

"I tried to talk with Lou after I spoke with Jasmine and Emily, but he brushed me off. A few minutes later, he announced he was coming down with the flu and left. He suggested speaking with his assistant, which I did."

"And?"

"He was chatty but useless." Holly scribbled on the notepad, then fixated on her pen. "Basically, he encouraged me to do whatever I want, declaring all the while that nothing will save the shelter."

"Sounds like he was hardly helpful." Her aunt pushed out a heavy sigh. "So, find out where Tim's office is located. He's your guy."

*Her guy? Hah! Not if Holly wanted a man who truly cared about helping people instead of displacing them.*

"Tim didn't seem inclined to offer a solution," she said.

"What about dating him?" A whisper of mirth from her aunt kept pace with Justin's low belly laugh.

"Date him?" Holly sat up straighter. "Why? I've created a happy life here in Pine Cone Valley. I love my students and music and—"

Even as she refuted her aunt, the word swirled in her brain. *Dating.*

She put the phone on speaker, padded to the piano and braced her hands on the fall board. Dating was for others, not for her.

But how many years had she dreamed about having someone love her, an amazing guy she could love in return? A man to share her life with.

No, no, no. Tim was the bad guy, and she'd married one bad guy.

*"I'm not the Grinch who stole Christmas, if that's what's holding you back,"* he'd said.

Holly went to the couch and plucked up her list, blank save for the scribbles.

Picking up the pen, she wrote while saying aloud, "I'm waiting until God makes it clear I've made the right choice in finding someone extraordinary."

"You should start going out and experiencing life again. You haven't dated since your divorce."

"I'm far from a hermit, Aunt Clementine." Holly drew in a quiet breath. "I'm just not interested, that's all."

"Two years is a long time."

"I'm not desperate, and I won't date a guy who throws homeless women and children onto the street."

"He's hardly done that, dear. And may I remind you that you said he apologized. Tomorrow is Friday. Go see him. From what you've described, he's eager to help."

"He's the opposite of eager."

"Interested then. Let's just say he's interested."

Her aunt didn't elaborate, and Holly didn't press her. A half dozen times, her mind quarreled that she should tell Aunt Clementine about Tim Stewart being an actor—and that he was ruggedly appealing and charismatic. But her aunt hadn't remarked on his name being recognizable, although, in all fairness, she was probably preoccupied with Justin.

The prospect of their romance made Holly smile.

Justin and Aunt Clementine were proving that it was never too late to find love.

# CHAPTER 5

The following morning, Holly dressed in a turtleneck sweater and formfitting jeans, then tugged on her coat and snagged her leather bucket handbag over her shoulder. Instead of a wool beanie, she fitted a pair of leopard earmuffs over her ears and freshly washed hair.

Brisk air embraced her as she exited her apartment. A radiant sun cast sparkles on the icicles, a shiny twinkle on the picturesque landscape of mountains and valleys.

After setting her GPS for the building inspectors' offices in Snowflake, she started her Jeep on the snow-rutted side street, then veered onto the main highway. The road had been plowed, and she drove quickly to Snowflake.

The day's piano lessons didn't begin until early evening, which allowed time to brainstorm solutions with Tim. Or so she hoped.

When she reached his office, she parked at the curb. A plain boxwood wreath was fixed to the entry door, and Holly envisioned attaching pinecones, red berries, and moss, so that the holiday colors would be highlighted. She'd always had a flair for decorating.

In the office foyer, she inhaled a mixture of old cigarette smoke, a flowery fragrance, and stale coffee.

A receptionist sat behind an oversized mahogany desk and greeted her. The woman looked like she'd done everything she could to fight the aging process—tightening her face with plastic surgery, dying her hair a garish red, and applying a pair of spiky black false eyelashes. The result made her appear older, not younger.

"Timothy Stewart, please," Holly said.

"He's out on a call." The woman squinted up at Holly over pink reading glasses. "Do you have an appointment?"

"No. I met him last evening at the homeless shelter and wished to talk to him about my—"

"Henry, Tim's assistant is here," the receptionist interrupted. "Do you want to see him instead?"

"Certainly." At least, Holly thought, there was someone in the office.

The receptionist ushered Holly down the hall and pointed to a tiny cubicle.

Henry, with thinning hair dyed an iridescent purple, offered Holly a seat across from the messiest desk she'd ever seen.

"I heard about the homeless shelter, but I'll try to reach Tim for you as he's more familiar with the problem." Henry punched a number into his cellphone and kept up a stream of one-sided conversation. "I grew up in New York City, but wanted the tranquility of a small town so I relocated here. Did you know that New York has a population of over eight million?"

"That's a hefty percentage in comparison to—"

"Then I went through a complicated divorce and—" He set down the phone. "Tim isn't picking up."

"Well, thanks, anyway." Holly stood before he could begin his nonstop chatter again. "At least you tried. I'll come back after lunch." She slung her handbag over her shoulder and headed into the hallway, spotting a memorable broad-shouldered man with dark wavy hair. Tim's cheeks were reddened from the outside air, which only enhanced his chiseled good looks.

"Miss Kim. What a delightful surprise." An enigmatic smile swept across his face as he surveyed her, from the top of her earmuffs to the toes of her brown leather boots. He carried a cup of steaming coffee in one hand and his gloves in the other. "The receptionist said you were here to discuss the homeless shelter." He checked his watch. "But you should have made an appointment."

"This was spur of the moment and ..." Holly trailed off. He was obviously preoccupied. "Can you spare a few minutes?"

"For you? Certainly. Come into my office." He grinned and gestured to a door down the hall. "I assume you don't want coffee, since it's almost noon. You only drink coffee in the morning, right?"

"Your memory is outstanding."

"I've been told that before, but I'll let you in on a secret. I remember only certain things ... or certain people." He lifted his cup. "Can I get you anything?"

"I'm fine, thanks."

He flashed another grin and she was surprised by its warmth. She recalled that same devastating grin when it had spun across countless television screens, bringing up the heat level of every woman who'd watched him. But after a couple seasons, he'd abruptly left the business and disappeared.

So, he'd decided to settle in Snowflake to become a ... building inspector?

Rather than guessing his reasons for leaving a lucrative acting profession, she inched into his outdated paneled office and met his steady gaze.

He nudged the door closed behind them, set his coffee and gloves on a narrow dilapidated desk that had seen better days, then pulled out a chair for her. Papers were piled high, and half-empty coffee cups furthered the clutter.

He removed his parka, scarf and wool cap. His wrinkled, white button-down shirt strained across his muscled chest.

"Well, Miss Kim?" He slid into a chair behind his desk.

She wiped her sweaty palms on her coat, because for some reason she was nervous about being alone with him. He was, after all, an attractive man with impressively innate appeal. Nevertheless, her expectations had been high when she'd set out for Snowflake this morning.

Now she wasn't so sure. Now she was considering that their discussion might be unsuccessful at best and exasperating at worst.

She took a quick glimpse out the window. Tailor-suited men and women emerged from the entrances of multistory buildings, fastening their down coats and shoving fleece-gloved hands deep into their pockets. Even in this commercial part of town, dense pine wreaths trimmed with red bows decorated the businesses' steel doors. In Snowflake, the spirit of Christmas reached everywhere.

She glanced back at Tim. He stared at her intently, as if waiting for something.

"Well?" he repeated, folding his hands together.

Today he was all business. She sensed his standoffishness and couldn't understand why. Surely she'd done nothing to offend him since she'd entered his office.

She presented a level look. "Well what?"

"Miss Kim—"

"Holly."

"Holly, you're here at *my* workplace, so what can I do for you?" That velvety voice resembling a silky caress had changed to abrupt and businesslike.

In order for their meeting to go forward, she needed to speak, she told herself.

She swallowed. "The shelter needs our help."

"Ah, I see. The shelter needs *our* help." He glanced at his watch again. "Go on."

"There are countless ways to assist." She ignored his impatience with a good-natured smile. "I've brainstormed ideas with my aunt."

"And your aunt is—"

"My aunt Clementine," she flipped back. "She lives in North Carolina and we chat often. I try to visit her whenever I can."

"So your aunt is some sort of homeless shelter expert?"

"She's just my sweet, elderly aunt."

In the ensuing silence, his gaze slid to her mouth. Then he pushed out a deep sigh. "Therefore, you're not here to accept my offer for a date?"

*Absolutely not* was on the tip of her tongue, warring with an a*bsolutely yes.*

As her throat went dry, she reined in the enticing thought of actually going out with him.

A date ... with Timothy Stewart. At the same moment that the thought went through her mind, her heart thumped an erratic beat. She was in close quarters with him in his ten by twelve foot office, and the air was scented with leather and the outdoors—purely masculine scents.

She sensed there was an inordinate amount of life that he'd experienced beneath that handsome exterior, and for some reason, he'd sealed all of it behind a barrier of polite courteousness.

Besides, he was far beyond her reach. And she suspected he believed he was beyond God's reach as well.

She wanted to reassure him that God wasn't looking for perfection, and that Tim had made mistakes along with everyone else. God looked for people who were unsure of the next turn, not those who thought they knew it all and were full of their own knowledge.

Her fingers tightened.

So when it came to dating him?

Bad idea. The absolute worst idea.

Besides, she had a history of making poor choices with men, seeing the virtuous and never the unscrupulous. This had led her to marry a narcissistic man who cared only about what she could, or rather, *should,* do for him.

"I told you, Tim, I don't date." She managed a wavering smile. "As I mentioned, I'm here because of the shelter."

For a split second, disappointment flew across his rugged face.

He shrugged indifferently as his blasé mask slid back into place. "Did your visit with Jasmine and her mother go satisfactorily after I left the shelter?"

"As well as it could, considering the circumstances."

Along with a long-suffering look, he sighed. "Not my fault."

"I didn't say it was."

"Good, and Jasmine is an adorable child, by the way."

"She's quite out of the ordinary compared to other students," Holly replied. "For instance, she's mastered two-octave scales, both hands together. Her musicality is incredible for a child who practices only three times a week on an ancient upright piano in Snowflake's only music store."

"Encourage her to stick with it," Tim said. "Music can enhance verbal memory."

"How do you know that?"

"I've read articles, but my knowledge is all second-hand experience."

"Also important to remember is that when you play an instrument, you use both sides of your brain." Holly tried to sound human and not like a page out of a textbook. "I gather you don't play, Tim?

"I play the radio." He grinned and stretched out his long legs beneath the desk. "Other than that, I truly have no musical proficiency."

"You never had the opportunity?"

"That's one way to sum up my childhood. One sugary, polite way." The jaded drawl in his voice, his response immediate and conclusive, told her there was more, but she didn't pressure him.

Their brief cordiality floundered as Holly returned to the subject of the shelter and how to help the residents who were about to be turned out into the cold.

"They won't be 'turned out into the cold,'" Tim said curtly. "To begin with, the various lodgings in the area are willing to assist temporarily." He lifted the coffee to his lips and grimaced, muttering, "I forgot my three sugars." He set the cup to the side.

"Temporarily isn't the right answer," Holly said.

"*Temporarily* will have to do."

"It's a Band-Aid." Holly blew out a breath. She wasn't here to argue with him. "I'm assuming you can direct me to an electrician, the first rung in solving the problem. Do you have anyone in mind? I'm willing to help financially."

Understanding seemed to dawn, and Tim quirked a dark eyebrow. "Really? How?"

"A dear friend recently passed. Her name was Charity. She left money to me and several of our high school friends and tagged it for a good cause. This is certainly the case with the shelter needing all new electrical wiring." Holly struggled to stave off unanticipated hot tears. Wasn't grief supposed to subside with time? Would it never go away?

Tim's expression changed, the strain in his face replaced by compassion. He got to his feet and reached across the desk, touching her shoulders with both hands. "I'm sorry. Charity must have been young. My condolences for your loss."

"I take comfort from a sermon from Pastor Tom I heard a while back."

"Do you?"

"We must endure today's sadness. Remember, a blessed tomorrow is just around the bend." Holly wiped her eyes and repaid Tim's cool tone with a proud reply. "Charity wanted to strengthen her friends during her weakest hours by the gift of generosity."

Belatedly, Holly registered his unreadable expression. "What?"

He dropped his hands. "You won't appreciate my answer."

"Try me."

"I've attended church, and it didn't work for me. I found the people there were judgmental and insincere."

"Then try again."

"No."

His flat reply reminded her of the teenage rebellions she'd dealt with when her adolescent students refused to take piano lessons, but were being forced to by their parents. "Why not?"

"Because I have an aversion to artificiality," he replied. "Which is one of the reasons I'm not in Hollywood anymore."

If Charity were alive, she would encourage Tim to embrace the season of Christ's birth with joy and church attendance. But Charity wasn't here anymore.

Holly drew a fortifying breath in a futile attempt to stave off more tears. She missed her friend considerably.

Tim came around his desk. "Holly—"

There was no distance between them now.

"You must think I'm a woman who cries all the time. I

don't usually break down like this. I guess I'm not as strong as I should be."

"I sense you're very strong." He cupped his hands on her shoulders. "Whatever your ideas, I'll make them work." The tender sincerity in his tone, coupled with the touch of his fingers, comforted her.

She gulped, and her blurry eyes searched his face. Tim had made an assurance without asking for repayment. She tied this with the realization that she simply believed him. His voice had been sincere, his response heartfelt.

"Thank you."

He gave a last encouraging squeeze, then swung back and settled in his seat.

She groped for a handkerchief in her handbag. This weeping must stop, she scolded herself. Charity would want her friends and family to move on with their lives.

"So you're not some rich model with millions of dollars to spare?" he asked teasingly. "Because you're extraordinarily beautiful."

"I'm certainly well past the age to start modeling." She focused on his coffee cup, the coffee he'd hardly touched. "Is that a compliment, by the way?"

He didn't miss a beat. "Actually, it was. Genuine and sincere."

Her cheeks grew hot. Had he also been genuinely sincere when he'd asked her out?

Frustrated by the direction of her musings, she chastised herself. How could she contemplate dating him when she was in the middle of mourning her friend's death, worrying about Jasmine and her mother's calamitous circumstances?

Tim observed her closely. "Holly?"

"To be clear, I assume fifteen hundred dollars isn't adequate for the shelter's rewiring." She tucked her lace handkerchief back into her handbag and placed the bag beneath her chair. "However, my aunt and I discussed a fund-raiser."

"Your lovable aunt Clementine." He smiled. "Let me guess, you're planning a bake sale?"

"No." Holly stifled a discomfited laugh. "Instead, my piano students and I will present a holiday recital and accept donations at the door."

"Are they any good?"

"Who?" she asked innocently. "My students?"

"Yes." He reached for his coffee.

"Well, they're not professionals, although they're extremely diligent."

He took a swallow of coffee, grimaced again, and slid the cup to the farthest spot of his desk. "Are you a hard taskmaster, Holly?" He kept his features straight for a moment before he chuckled.

"I'm not here to describe my teaching methods." She met his chuckle with one of her own. "What's more important is that my students' parents and friends will support the performance, and I expect the community will rally as well."

"And you'll also perform?"

"I usually don't, but I could."

"I'd pay to see you. You could end the program with a Christmas song."

"How about a sing-along?" she asked.

"Even better. I bet you're excellent."

Her pulse jumped at his enthusiasm. Nonetheless, she reminded herself that he'd acted for a living. "I'm okay. I studied music at a distinguished university in New York."

"I presume you have a shiny black grand piano in your home."

"On the contrary, I have a spinet piano in my apartment

that works just fine. Someday, I'd like to learn how to play the accordion. The instruments are similar."

"Miss Holly Kim, you grow more interesting by the second." He rolled up his shirt sleeves and fixed her with a direct look. "Where will you hold this recital?"

"How about Golden Birch Manor on Cedar Lane?"

"The senior residents will love it." He rummaged through the top drawer of his desk. Extracting a stack of business cards, he handed her one. "Here's Ralph's information. He's the electrician I recommend, so let's start with getting a cost estimate for the rewiring. By the way, Ralph recently erected a neon sign for the new ice skating rink in town."

"And that's why you recommend him?"

"He's fully qualified and the best in the area. We've been friends a long time."

"If he can erect a neon sign, then clearly he can rewire a homeless shelter," she said humorously.

*A neon sign.* That was exactly the sign she needed from God, pointing to the right guy before she fell in love again. Inwardly, she shook her head. As if that would ever happen.

What? The neon sign or the guy?

Both, she decided.

"Are you familiar with the rink?" Tim asked. The aloofness was gone, any former brusqueness in his tone subdued.

"I've driven past on many occasions, but I've never iceskated before."

"You should try sometime. It's fun."

"Fun if you can stand upright on skates," she hedged. "I probably wouldn't even make it to the rink without falling."

He raised his eyebrows in a dare. "I'll hold you up."

She flushed, speechless. A vision of him and her iceskating together, laughing, the sounds of smooth blades gliding across the ice, the enticing scents of nachos and popcorn from the concession stand, ignited an expectant warmth in her chest.

She gave herself a resolved mental shake. Talk about a fantasy. Most likely, her ankles would wobble, while he would make skating appear fluid and effortless.

"If you ever want to learn, let me know." It seemed like he wanted to prolong their conversation, and she sat back in her chair while he continued. "I played hockey on two high school teams."

"You attended more than one high school?"

"I attended five."

"Why so many?"

"My mother and I constantly moved around." His eyes darkened, and he looked away.

"I assume this was all before you became an actor?"

He raked a hand through his hair. "I've been on my own for most of my life, and spent several years in a variety of professions, yet that's the one everyone brings up. Thankfully, that stint is long past."

Abruptly, he stood, a firm conclusion. Their meeting was apparently over.

Holly scooped up her handbag. "Shall I call the electrician?"

"I'll text Ralph to arrange a discussion." Tim tugged his phone from his pocket. After quick back-and-forth texts, he read, "He can meet at the town center on Saturday, December seventh, the night of the tree-lighting ceremony. He's slated to be there in case anything goes wrong."

"Like if the tree doesn't light up?"

"Something like that."

"I haven't been to a tree lighting in ages, but I remember it was always held the first Saturday in December." She hadn't been since she'd gone with Charity and their friends when they were in high school.

"Neither have I." Tim studied her and smiled, and she had the most surprising thought. He seemed to definitely be admiring her. "So, we can all plan to meet there."

"*All?*"

"I'll come too," he said. "What's your phone number?"

Did she have a choice? It seemed as if he'd asked numerous times already. She offered her number, he put it into his phone, and then her phone pinged with a text. It was from Tim.

*Five o' clock on December 7th?* he'd texted. *I'll meet you in front of The Little Corner Bistro in Snowflake on Main Street. Ralph will be with me.*

*I'll be there,* she texted back.

This was absurd. He was standing right across from her and they were texting each other. She looked up at him, and their gazes locked.

And then, the strangest thing happened. They both laughed at the same time.

# CHAPTER 6

*A* few days after meeting with Tim, Holly's thoughts continuously veered back to him—the strength of his fingers on her shoulders, his rich chuckle, his admiring smile. Everything about him melted her into an illogically thinking female. How could a man like him possibly be interested in a woman like her? She'd been told she was pretty, but she certainly didn't parallel a curvaceous starlet.

Surely she was the least stunning woman he'd ever bothered to flirt with. Did he assume he could lure her into a meaningless date with trite, empty flattery?

And then what, after he'd tired of her?

Why, he'd do what her ex had done.

She refused to dwell on the scenario, but had learned from experience.

Tim would abandon her.

At four o'clock on the day of Snowflake's tree-lighting ceremony, Holly gave herself a final once-over in the foyer mirror and smiled. She'd spent an hour getting ready, something she usually never did—opting for black mascara and a touch of blue eyeshadow to complement her dark eyes. Sparingly, she brushed on a light rose blush to her cheekbones, then applied lipstick in a sun-kissed mauve tone. Her reflection smiled back, and she attributed her shining eyes not to her makeup, but because she was seeing Tim.

She tucked her hair beneath a wool cap, and knotted a sumptuous blue cashmere scarf over her coat.

Snow had begun to fall when Holly stopped at the motel that was temporarily putting up Jasmine and Emily.

She insisted on bringing them to the tree-lighting.

At first Emily declined, her thin lips flattening, before finally complying for her daughter's sake.

They piled into Holly's car and arrived at the resplendently decorated town center where the unlit tree towered, and Holly snagged a parking space in a lot off Main Street. The town resembled an oil painting of a chocolate-box Christmas scene, enhanced by mouth-watering cocoa beans flavoring the air from Sheila's Gourmet Chocolates.

The dark green of the pines contrasted with their coating of pristine frosty snowflakes. Jasmine's breath left white puffs as she incessantly chattered, and the muted crunch of their boots on the hardened snow assured that the winter season had a firm hold on Snowflake.

As they approached the town center, they marveled at the winking silver lights in the shops' windows, and Holly ducked into the This and That Shop to probe their inventory of antiques before they closed. The observance of Christmas in a modest, Americana Colorado town was a sparkling and detailed affair. At one corner, a flashing red arrow pointed to Candy Cane Avenue, a side alley lined with candy canes.

"It even smells like peppermint!" Jasmine exclaimed, and the women smilingly echoed her enthusiasm.

At the end of the avenue the humane society had organized an 'adopt a dog' event. Multiple dogs wearing white-and-red velvet Santa hats chased an inflatable ball in a fenced-in area, while miniature piles of puppies, resting on each other, barked playfully and looked on.

Jasmine's cherubic face beamed, and she tugged at Emily's coat sleeve. "Can we adopt a puppy, Mommy? I always wanted a shih tzu."

"Maybe someday. And older dogs need companions too." Emily replied with cautious deliberation, which Holly attributed to an abundance of broken dreams. "Once we get back on our feet and have our own place, we'll see."

"That will happen," Holly encouraged.

"Will it?" Emily invariably had such a faraway stare. "It's difficult being a single parent, and I'm all alone."

"Not anymore. I'm here to help you." Holly offered an upbeat nod of confirmation. "In fact, the entire community is. Look at how the town rallied and found space for everyone."

As they proceeded, Emily declined Holly's offer of money so Jasmine could buy some hot chocolate or little trinkets. Respecting the woman's wishes, Holly placed her wallet back inside her handbag.

What made people too proud to accept a kindness, despite desperate circumstances? Didn't they realize it was a joy to give? Charity had often quoted a favorite Bible verse, 2 Corinthians 8:12: "For if the willingness is there, the gift is acceptable according to what one has, not according to what one does not have."

"Okay," Holly said. "But if you change your mind ..."

Emily twisted the cheap wristwatch around her skinny wrist and didn't answer. Holly had the urge to place her hand over the woman's, calming the anxious gesture.

Farther down the street, they ducked in and out of local shops and grinned at holiday shoppers sipping mulled wassail. Jasmine inhabited her own little space, taking it all in

—the fruity scents of apples, lemons, and oranges mingling with cinnamon.

Seasonal markets clustered together selling residents' handicrafts. Spotting a unique stand, Jasmine tugged them over to a craft booth where an older woman was making handmade dolls. Traditional and beguiling, each doll was designed with a whimsical smile.

The woman used coffee-brown colored yarn to knot two eyes, then cut out a heart-shaped piece of red felt for the mouth.

"I loved dolls when I was young, but now I'm too old for them." Jasmine sighed and cupped a tiny doll lovingly. She handled the thick braids of yarn and dashed her fingers along the doll's gingham dress, circling the wide white buttons.

"You're never too old if it's something you love," Holly said. "The fact that you appreciate a beautifully handcrafted doll means you're imaginative and artistic. Which we already recognize, of course." Holly and Emily exchanged a smile. "Because you're a quick learner."

Beaming, Jasmine drummed her fingers on the counter as she leaned in to inspect the other dolls.

"Please let me buy this doll for you." Holly immediately noted Emily's frown and chided herself for not asking her permission first.

Jasmine jumped up and down. "Please, Mommy?"

Emily's face filled with regret. She surveyed the doll, then her daughter. Finally, her silver-gray eyes met Holly's. "Are you sure, Miss Kim?"

"It's my pleasure and we'll call it an early holiday gift," Holly said. "Agreed?"

"Yay, yay yay!" Jasmine snuggled the doll close to her chest. "Thank you, Miss Kim." The elation in the child's eyes was a reflection of the true spirit of Christmas.

"This gift gives *me* more happiness than you can ever imagine," Holly said.

A chill was in the air, and the scent of fire-roasted chestnuts permeated every inch of space. Food trucks sold homemade candy, and Holly was drawn to Nancy's Caramel Station, selling delectable, buttery caramels. She bought a half pound and shared the candies with her companions. The caramels were dense and chewy, a gooey delight.

The magical holiday atmosphere was furthered by evergreen wreaths twined with eucalyptus leaves and emerald satin ribbons placed uniformly on each shop door. The distinctive woodsy scent unmistakably proclaimed Christmas.

"I don't recall the tree lighting being anywhere near as wonderful when I was younger," Holly murmured.

"Life's defining stages." Emily's hands flew through her thin hair, and her severe features relaxed. "I read about it in my self-improvement book. Each stage you're in gives you a different perspective of the world."

"See, Mommy. I told you tonight would be fun." Jasmine supplied a tooth-filled grin and wiped a glob of caramel stuck to the edge of her mouth. "Let's go visit the dogs!"

"You two run along," Holly attempted to keep the jump of excitement from her tone. "It's almost time for me to meet the building inspector."

Emily removed her square-framed glasses and polished the lenses with the sleeve of her drawstring jacket. "You're meeting the bad guy here tonight, Miss Kim?"

Holly bristled, immediately coming to Tim's defense. "The shelter's defective wiring isn't his fault, and he's working with me and a host of others to get it fixed. I'll catch up with you two afterwards."

"Sounds good. C'mon, Mommy!" Jasmine quickly ended the women's verbal duel. "See you later, Miss Kim."

A chorus of brass instruments—several of Snowflake High School's band students playing the tuba, trombone, and trumpet—rang a medley of well-loved carols with "It Came Upon a Midnight Clear," succeeded by a jubilant "God Rest Ye, Merry Gentlemen."

Meanwhile, other members of the band played under the gazebo, and the melodies brought a grin to Jasmine's pale face as she raced off with her mother in tow.

Armed with an animated smile, Holly reached The Little Corner Bistro a few minutes later. She lingered, mesmerized by the tiny candles illuminating each window. Assorted restaurants were open, and patrons wearing sleek parkas with fur-trimmed hoods perused the outdoor menus. Scents of flame-grilled meats melded with basil and garlic, beckoning them inside.

Women idled as they passed the bistro, feasting their eyes on Tim.

Which was how Holly spotted him, as he reigned tall and straight and unbearably handsome outside the bistro. Because of the admiring women.

That, and because his athletic physique filled out his familiar quilted parka flawlessly. His attractive face showed the beginnings of a dark beard.

He was conversing with an older, gruff-looking man wearing round eyeglasses and a plaid wool coat. Tim tilted his head toward the man, suggesting that he was attending to the conversation, although he examined the crowd as if he was searching for someone.

He was searching for her, Holly thought with an inner tingle.

Seeming to detect her presence, he lifted his head abruptly, and their gazes locked.

Before she'd scanned the crowd a second time, he'd reached her.

"Holly?" He offered his usual charismatic smile, and her breath caught. "I haven't seen you in what ... five days?"

She couldn't stand still and tried to relax her breathing. The magical atmosphere had transformed the night into one of enchantment, especially with a handsome, enigmatic guy at her side.

She stole a peek at him, appreciating the strength carved into his chiseled cheekbones and tanned face. Timothy Stewart was exactly what fairy tale princes were created from—broad-shouldered, hard-working, and compelling.

She bit back a grin. "But you text me all the time."

Since their initial meeting in his office, he'd texted each evening at eight o'clock when she'd finished teaching.

*How was your day?* he'd always begin.

*Jasmine is the most precocious and talented student I've taught in several years,* she'd texted back. *I only wish she had a decent piano to practice on, and a parent who was more invested in her progress. I've arranged to give her lessons at a music store in Snowflake.*

Slightly self-conscious by her chatty zeal for Jasmine, Holly described her other piano students and schedule.

Once, when silence lapsed, she'd informed him about how she'd subbed for the pianist at Snowflake Chapel. She'd been tempted to invite him to Sunday service, but didn't. He always brushed off every reference to church, changing the subject to inquire about her aunt or students or her cat.

*What is Butterscotch doing?* he'd ask, and she'd reply, *Nothing. Lazy, as usual. And your stray kitten?*

He'd confided that he'd revisited the shelter and adopted one of the kittens.

*She is company for me, because my place is lonely.*

Holly had studied the phone screen. Lonely? Him? What was he trying to tell her?

Hurriedly, she combed her thoughts for another topic but

fell short when she failed to think of anything. Finally, she texted, *Have you thought of a good name for your kitten?*

*Taffy.*

*Sweet.* For a man who was just as sweet.

As the days progressed, Holly clicked on her cellphone each evening with anticipation and delight.

The previous evening, she'd finished with, *Well, I'm calling it a night. I'll see you tomorrow.*

*Can I tell you how much I'm looking forward to it?* he'd asked.

Her pulse had given a leap of excitement.

*Why?*

*Because I like talking with you, especially in person.*

*Calm down,* she'd told herself after he'd sent that text.

And she was telling herself the same thing now. They'd arranged this get-together to figure out a solution to the shelter's dilemma. This wasn't about seeing Tim again.

The older man, who must be Ralph, approached, grinning broadly. "So this is the gorgeous lady you've been yakking about." Conspiratorially, he winked at Tim.

"Thanks for keeping my secret," Tim murmured.

"I didn't know it was a secret. Besides, you can't keep a beautiful woman under wraps forever." Ralph kept his unrepentant grin on Holly. "You don't live in Snowflake or I would have recognized you."

"I live in Pine Cone Valley," she answered. "I'm a piano teacher."

"So I heard."

"I teach a girl who lived at the homeless shelter with her mother."

"Jasmine, right?" Ralph quizzed. "She and her mother are staying at the motel in town at a heavily discounted rate until this electrical situation at the shelter is resolved."

"Yes. How did you learn about her?"

"Well, now, I wonder." Ralph sent a teasing look toward

Tim, then extended a hand to Holly. "Tim and I go way back. He was such a solemn little boy."

He really had been talking about her to his friends, she thought.

"You're a fountain of information tonight, Ralph," Tim said with an offhand laugh.

She smiled and shook Ralph's hand. "I'm Holly."

"Tim and I have texted the last few days." Ralph reached into his pocket, extracted a folded sheet of paper, and passed it to her. "I stopped by the shelter and the problem isn't as severe as everyone anticipated. But don't forget, the building hasn't been updated in twenty years, and chances are it will require upgrading."

Holly unfolded the paper and scrutinized it. "Three thousand dollars is your repair estimate?"

"Be warned. Rewiring is chaotic, disruptive work. Lou has a copy of my estimate too. It should be accurate, give or take any surprises."

"In this business, there are always surprises," Tim inserted. "So round out that number to thirty-five hundred dollars."

"I'll donate fifteen hundred toward the project," Holly said. "Somehow, we'll make up the difference."

"*We?*" Ralph's smile faded. "I'm working at a reduced rate already."

"I meant me and the business community, and anyone else who wants to contribute," Holly said. "I have various fund-raisers in mind."

"Like what?" Ralph countered. "A bake sale?"

Tim and Holly both laughed.

"Private joke," Tim explained.

Mayor Hardy, who prevailed at a podium by the tree, spotted Ralph and waved him over.

From where they stood, Ralph surveyed the tall, unlit

pine. "I'll catch up with you two in an hour," he called over his shoulder as he shuffled away.

"I brought Jasmine and Emily with me tonight," Holly said to Tim. "They're over on Candy Cane Avenue with the dogs. I'll meet them after the ceremony."

She regarded the steady stream of shoppers, the beginning of the retail rush. Why was the Christmas season so commercialized? Wasn't the holiday supposed to be a Christian holy day to mark the birth of the Son of God?

"How are they faring?" Tim's quiet tone jerked her from her reflections.

"Moderately well, considering the upheaval of moving into a motel." Holly placed Ralph's estimate into her handbag. "In addition, Emily is applying for a number of jobs this week."

"That's encouraging. I'm optimistic that she'll find a decent position soon." His hand on her elbow, Tim gently drew Holly away from the jam-packed sidewalk.

She glanced up at him. "Where are we going?"

He gestured to an outside seating area serving hot chocolate and tiny, fried cinnamon-glazed doughnuts. Portable heaters and a canvas canopy outfitted with Edison light bulbs created a snug, welcoming atmosphere.

"Do you want to grab something to eat?" he asked. "My treat."

This might be a date. She didn't want to date him. Or did she?

She hesitated.

"Do you prefer somewhere else?" He surveyed the various kiosks, looking like he could easily be hurt by her reply if she refused.

"No, this spot is ideal."

"Good." He guided her to a turquoise-colored bistro table and pulled out a chair for her. She liked that about him—

standing until she was seated, always courteous, calm, and considerate.

"It's not exactly quiet, and the menu is limited to beverages and doughnuts," he said. "It's more of a—"

"Everything is lovely. The vintage lights on the awning and the little place selling homespun sweets"—she gestured to the shop across the way—"smells wonderful."

He settled across from her. "So you're not teaching again for a couple days?"

His inquiry won him her astonished gape. "You remembered my text?"

He was so fine looking, and she loved the way he listened to her, honestly listened, as if every word she spoke—or texted—was important.

"I've learned a lot about you because I've been reading your texts over and over."

She tipped her head. "Why would you do something like that?"

His heated scrutiny of her sent her pulse into a double rhythm. "You really have to ask?"

On the tip of her tongue were the words, *Yes, I really do.*

But she really didn't, because that irresistible attraction tugged her ever closer to him.

In an attempt to avoid his searching gaze, she studied the menu as a freckle-faced teenage waitress started toward them.

"Hot chocolate and doughnuts?" Holly asked him.

"Sure."

After the waitress took their orders, Holly leaned back in her chair. "Hot chocolate reminds me of sledding, or simply sitting by a window and watching the snow fall." She smiled. "What about you?"

"Nope." He did the opposite of echoing her enthusiasm by

pressing his lips together and grimacing. "Hot chocolate isn't part of my childhood memories."

"Oh, I see."

Although she didn't see anything of the sort.

After they were served the piping hot cocoa laced with whipped cream and yeasty deep-fried doughnuts, Holly bent her head to say grace. Tim supported her lead. Granted, he didn't pray, but he bowed his head.

"Do you always say a blessing before every meal?" he asked when she whispered "amen."

"Absolutely. It's a way to show respect to God, and gratitude for our blessings."

Thoughtfully, he took a sip of hot chocolate. "So, tell me more about your fund-raiser."

"My students are all on board to play piano for the benefit recital." Holly savored a mouthwatering taste of whipped cream, finishing with a bite of her warm doughnut. "Jasmine and I are working on a difficult duet arrangement of 'Silent Night.'"

Tim averted his head. "Duly noted."

"You don't like Silent Night'?"

"Everyone likes 'Silent Night.'"

"Is it because you don't like church?"

He shrugged. "Like I said, it's not for me."

"Did you ever attend church?"

"What do I look like, Holly? The Grinch again?"

"Sorry."

"We went, but certainly not often." He picked up a spoon and stirred the hot chocolate in his mug. "While we lived near Denver, we visited my grandparents. When we did, my mother often argued with my grandmother."

"What did you do? I mean, while they argued. You were a little kid."

"My grandfather was a contractor, and he'd bring me

along on his jobs. He taught me all about the building trade." Tim raised both his hands and grinned. "And thus, here I am. All that on the job training paid off, plus four years of taking college courses at night, multiple certifications, and passing licensing exams."

"You're a great guy."

"Me?"

She threw him a comic sigh. "You're not as cynical and hardhearted as I first suspected."

"Hmm. Gee, thanks."

"But we were talking about your grandfather."

"He was the best," Tim said quietly. "Unfortunately, there were days when he didn't take me with him and I'd be subjected to a firsthand blow-out between my grandmother and mother. My grandmother would go on and on about church, insisting religion was precisely what my mother needed—a clergyman to set her on a respectable path and enable her to overcome her many addictions."

"Which were?"

"Alcohol, pills, whatever she could get." He hesitated. He couldn't seem to find his words. "As usual, my mother expelled the idea as quickly as my grandmother fired it at her."

"She wasn't in favor of getting help?"

"She wasn't in favor of anything my grandmother suggested. They had a prickly relationship, which is stating it mildly. Grandmother disapproved of my mother's lifestyle, and looking back, I can understand why. My mother only visited when she was out of money."

A silence lapsed as Holly collected her thoughts. Nearby, the brass band launched into a jazzy rendition of "A Holly Jolly Christmas."

"Were you out of money often?" Holly asked.

"What do you think? Let's just say she would have fit in

seamlessly during the flower child era. She drove around in a Volkswagen bus with her friends like life was a never-ending party, while I hung out in the back seat."

"How old were you?"

"Eleven, twelve." He reinforced his recollection with an indifferent head shake. "My mother even changed her name from Sally to Astra. As you can imagine, my grandmother wasn't thrilled about that, either."

"Pretty name."

"Astra means star—derived from the star. My mother said it reminded her of Christmas. Ironic, in view of the fact that we didn't celebrate."

"Where is she now?" Holly surveyed his mug and half-eaten doughnut. He'd pushed both to the side.

"She passed away from pneumonia and a hard life." Tim's voice trailed off into silence. "Years ago."

"I'm sorry."

"Thanks." He swallowed hard. "The next day I headed west. I was nineteen when I arrived in Hollywood."

*Hollywood at nineteen.* A lively discussion about his adventures in that shiny town should have ensued. Instead, Holly felt an unexpected sadness for him.

"Forgive me, Tim." She concentrated on the festivities—youngsters carrying bags of buttery popcorn and skipping backward, their watchful parents close behind. "My questions were too intrusive."

# CHAPTER 7

S he was right, Tim thought. Her questions, their confidences, brought up painful memories. They'd only known each other a few days, and he'd always kept his personal life off limits. Yet, as she watched him expectantly, he wanted to talk with her in spite of his inner hesitancy, in spite of his vow to never dwell on his childhood.

He inhaled, his memories peeling back fifteen years. "I remember sitting in the passenger seat of a rig after I'd hitch-hiked," he said softly.

*"Where are you going?" the truck driver had asked.*

*"Wherever you are," Tim had replied.*

"The trucker was driving to Hollywood to drop off some costumes for a movie set. He introduced me around, so I was able to get some work the next few years, doing various odd jobs at the studios and construction. I started auditioning for acting roles too, and even hired an acting coach." Tim shrugged. "Eventually I got a minor role on a TV show. That led to another, and finally I landed a spot on a popular television series."

"Congratulations," Holly said.

He smiled. Nodded.

Way before that, there were the do-gooders, the authorities who threatened to separate Tim from his mother. Sure, as an adult he understood that children should be safeguarded, but as a child, he only wanted to stay with his mother. And because of the fear that he might be taken from her, she often switched into protective mode and avoided appealing to the powers that be for help.

But this was Holly.

Sitting across from her, sharing the celebratory nature of the evening, compelled him to tell her more about himself.

And that was a first for him.

Besides, he wryly reflected, he didn't want to dampen her enthusiasm for their upcoming fund-raising conversation by answering her questions with curtness.

He steepled his hands and leaned forward. "I don't mind. Honestly. Next, I suppose you'll ask me about my father."

"If you'd like to talk, I'm here to listen."

Clad in a crimson-red coat with a thick blue scarf wrapped around her, she was breathtaking—all fresh-faced complexion and enormous eyes framed by thick lashes and gracefully arched eyebrows. Her black hair was tucked beneath a wool cap and a stray wisp fell across her cheek. The glow of the vintage light bulbs highlighted her soft skin and softer, enticing lips.

"Tim?" Holly propped her small chin on her palms, suspending his delightful observation. "Your father?"

"I didn't know him well." His account was lacking, and Tim allowed a pause before continuing. "All my mother used to say is that he ruined her life."

*Because she'd had a baby. And she'd named the baby Tim.*

Holly slid her hand across the table. "Did your father desert you and your mother?"

"On the contrary, my mother left him." Tim closed his

hand over hers. Holly offered reassurance and comfort, and he decided to accept it. Another first. "My mother was a free spirit. Everything was done her way."

"Where is he now?"

"My father?" Tim tried to smile. "For many years he was absent from my life, and then he reappeared when I was cast in that television series. I suppose he was after money, assuming I was a rich and famous actor." He stared off, noting Ralph chatting with the mayor, the families gathering near the enormous tree.

Holly nodded toward his mug. "Your hot chocolate is getting cold."

He detected sympathy welling in her eyes, although she strove for a heartening smile. She'd clearly caught his distasteful tone at the mention of his father.

He picked up his mug. "I'm sure it's fine."

The last time he drank hot chocolate he'd been in grade school. These days, his likings ran toward a refreshing beer after work. Fearing she would disapprove because she was obviously a churchgoer and his mother had repeatedly lectured that God had strict rules you were supposed to follow, he amplified his sip with a smile. "This is excellent, especially during the Christmas season."

A season he hadn't celebrated in years.

Wait. There was that one Christmas when they'd arrived at his grandparents' house. Or rather, he'd arrived. He'd never been certain where his mother had disappeared to. He only knew that he'd bought her a gift with the money he'd earned working with his grandfather.

He shook his head. Those memories, that gift, were too difficult to deal with, and he shoved them aside, preferring happier reminiscences. His mother had loved him, but if she was pushed, she loved the drink more. Surely by now, he'd accepted that.

And then there were the pleasant emotions, the giddiness of waking up Christmas morning in his grandparents' secure home, despite he and his mother always being despairingly broke.

That remembrance of a happy Christmas gave birth to a heartening possibility; and a chunk of his resistance, the barricade he'd firmly erected from one end of his broken dreams to another, began to split.

Was a real Christmas in the future for him—that elusive spirit of goodwill? Was Christmas about receiving, like the child he'd been as he'd contentedly unwrapped his grandparents' gifts? Or was Christmas truly the season of giving, per Holly's intent?

And was it about God's love and forgiveness, as Christians proclaimed?

He kept his hand around Holly's, studying her lips, rosy from the invigorating air.

"What people don't understand," he said, "is that just because an actor gains a modicum of success doesn't mean he's amassed a fortune. Especially if you give most of it away."

"You gave the money you earned away?"

"Just about." He gentled his reply with a smile. "I didn't make millions, as most assumed. I wasn't the lead in the series. Actually, I got the role of a secondary character when the actor who originally had the part opted to work on a different show."

"So who did you give your money to?"

She didn't seem interested in the amount of money, which surprised him. That was initially the first thing everyone wanted to know.

He focused on the brass band performing a rousing rendition of "The Twelve Days of Christmas" while the crowd chimed in with, "'And a partridge in a pear tree'" at the end of each verse.

Holly toyed with her doughnut, apparently waiting for his reply.

"Who do you guess I gave the money to?" he asked.

"Your father?

"He claimed he was in a jam." Tim gave a derisive snort. "But my grandmother had stated countless times that he was constantly in a jam, which she blamed on compulsive gambling." Tim scrubbed a hand over his face, as if he could rub away the memories of his father's betrayal. "He was supposed to use the money to check into a treatment program. By the time I reached out to see how he was doing, he'd disappeared. I haven't heard from him since."

Tim caught Holly's expression of understanding, the slight slump of her posture, and tugged his hand from hers. He didn't need her sympathy, he cautioned himself. He didn't need anything from anybody. He'd made his own way and had done just fine.

She blinked.

"Holly?"

"Hmm?" Her eyes welled with tears.

"You're crying?" he asked skeptically.

She flapped a dismissive hand. "Don't mind me. I cry when the commercials appear on television about sponsoring an abandoned puppy in a shelter."

"Please don't feel sorry for me." He tipped up her chin. "My mother cared about me and my grandparents were wonderful. I don't have any emotional wounds. I promise."

"You must. Your parents were neglectful, and—"

"No more talk about me or my past." With an indifference he didn't feel, he blew out a breath.

"You're important too Tim."

He dropped his hand. "Let's discuss your fund-raiser, all right?"

"All right." She faltered, then plucked a sheet of notepaper from her handbag. "I consulted the internet and discovered that it's best to start with a name."

"And what name did you come up with?"

"I hadn't decided on any until now, but what about Astra?" She perked up. "Because we're reaching for the stars to create a better and safer shelter."

"No, no." He crossed his arms. "You initially blamed me for the electrical problem, and now you're thinking about naming your fund-raiser after my mother?"

"It's a lovely name and ideal for the season. The star of Bethlehem guided the three wise men, and a star is the glowing symbol of hope."

"Astra. My mother. A star of hope." Tim sucked in a quick breath. "And then what?"

"Then we formulate a plan. But wait. Are you okay with the name?"

He saluted.

"Good."

Her infectious smile, her eagerness, made it challenging to concentrate on their conversation, or take a nibble of his doughnut or a gulp of tepid chocolate. Holly was unabashedly enthusiastic, and her energetic voice captivated him.

He uncrossed his arms, taken aback at how his heart spun in his chest, precisely the same as when he'd first laid eyes on her at the shelter.

"There are state regulations and building permits," he murmured, half to himself. "I'll look into them."

"And I'll solicit the parishioners in my church for donations. They're always generous. Plus, I'm going with the idea of a Christmas sing-a-long at the conclusion."

"Okay." He raised his mug for a toast, feeling slightly foolish for his youthful excitement. "What about a tree decorating? Ask the attendees to contribute money, plus bring an ornament to hang on a Christmas tree."

"I like that." Deliberately, she nodded. "But where is this tree? There was a pine at the shelter, and Jasmine and the other children trimmed it before they left."

A Christmas tree. He'd never hung ornaments on a tree before, not even at his grandparents' house.

"We'll set up a tree at the nursing home. I'll donate it." He took her hand, drawing the shape of a pine tree on her palm with his thumb.

He feasted his gaze on her glistening eyes, her ready smile. Could she truly be genuine and so different from the do-gooders he'd dealt with when he and his mother were homeless? Individuals who claimed they would help, but did so only for publicity?

"I phoned the Golden Birch Manor, and the director said she is thrilled to support us." Holly lifted her face, shimmering with delight. "The residents will enjoy hearing the students play holiday carols, and the facility will place the donation box at the entrance."

He squeezed her hand in encouragement. "Thank you for sharing your vision with me. You're an inspiration."

"Because this is my vision and my mission," she declared, with a satisfied wag of her head. "I've scheduled the recital date for December twenty-third at three o'clock, which gives me a little over two weeks to raise the funds. Will Ralph allow the shelter any leeway if he doesn't receive the full payment when the work is completed?"

"He's a hard man to get to know, but once you do, you'll discover he's good-hearted," Tim replied. "Though I can't predict what he'll say because he must pay his employees too."

"I'll donate my fifteen hundred dollars immediately, and that should move things quicker." He was aware she looked to him for a smile to soothe her unspoken concerns. He obliged, then stated he was ready to render assistance to Ralph and the shelter, and that he was well-connected to the community because of his job. Moreover, her fund-raiser seemed feasible.

"I'd like all the residents to move back by New Year's Eve," she said.

"That will make for a happy New Year?"

"A very happy New Year."

"Attention." The mayor's microphoned voice boomed, accompanied by a drum roll from the band's percussionist. "Our very own Snowflake High School chorus is singing Christmas carols by candlelight, and the tree-lighting ceremony begins in fifteen minutes."

"Ready?" Tim checked the time on the town clock. At Holly's affirmation, he signaled for the check and paid the bill. As they rose, he took her hand as if it was the most natural thing in the world.

She stalled when they passed a candy stand. "I'd like to buy Jasmine a bagful of caramels. She loves them."

"Whenever you mention her, your face lights up," Tim said. "And being well-acquainted with Mayor Hardy's fondness for speech-making, I guarantee there's plenty of time."

"I feel a love for Jasmine that's difficult to explain."

He chuckled at her sincere smile, then gestured toward the candy stand. "Will you buy candy for me too?"

"I suppose I can spare you some." She purchased two separate pounds and provided him with his own bag.

"You're a generous woman, Holly." He popped a caramel into his mouth, offered her one, then shepherded her to a quiet area behind the crowd. "This spot is just right."

"We can't see the tree lighting from back here."

"We will once the tree is lit."

"Shouldn't we move closer?"

"I can't imagine why, when here is perfectly fine." He leaned against a tree trunk and nestled her in his arms.

"Jasmine and her mother are here." Holly squirmed and went up on her tiptoes. "I told them I would meet them afterwards to bring them back to their motel. I pray that her mother—"

"If she's struggling with an addiction, she'll need support. The shelter offers excellent resources, and seeking a job is admirable."

She prompted him to look toward a booth selling beverages—bottled water and warm cider and soft drinks.

"They don't serve alcohol at these events, Holly."

"It's just that … I would do anything for that little girl."

"So you mentioned." Tim scanned the crowd. "I don't see them and the ceremony hasn't started yet, so they're probably playing with the dogs on Candy Cane Avenue and it's all good."

"Maybe we should—"

"Holly." He inclined his head and brushed a kiss on her temple, his lips gliding down her cheek and settling on her mouth for a kiss. "Thank you."

She drew back. "Why?"

"Because you are kind and determined and thoroughly gorgeous." He smoothed his hands across her cheeks to lighten the moment before he recognized that the look in her glistening gaze wasn't confusion. She felt the same tug of emotion that he did.

"I should get another bagful of candy for Jasmine before the stand closes, and—"

He grinned, not intending to change his plans in the least.

"Tim? Did you hear what—"

"Holly." Again, he touched her lips with his, exquisitely gentle. "Let's stop talking."

# CHAPTER 8

*S*he must have dined at the Cozy Coffee Shop a dozen times, Holly thought as she snagged one of the few empty tables, tucked by the entrance. Invariably, she appreciated the comfortable interior—sunny and lively with light-colored walls and a splash of brilliant-red poinsettias decorating each table—and detected the aroma of freshly ground coffee beans and the daily baked baguettes. A rolling jazzy arrangement of Christmas music played softly in the background.

Tim strode to the table and set down their tray. "Eggnog latte and a peppermint brownie for lunch?" He raised his eyebrows.

"Technically, eleven thirty is still morning." She smoothed down her red V-neck velour sweater that matched her red slacks as she defended her choices, which were startlingly lacking in nutrition. Unapologetically, she inspected his plate. "Should I have ordered your selections? Double smoked-bacon on a croissant and a cup of black coffee?"

"What's wrong with it?"

"Black coffee cancels out the calories of a buttery croissant and bacon?"

Amusement flicked over his features. "If you recall, I take my coffee with three sugars, so there goes your calorie-counting theory."

She took a swallow of latte—steamed eggnog, dark-brewed espresso, and a dash of cinnamon. "You should try to look a little embarrassed by your choice of food groups."

"I will if you will," he teased in response. When he smiled, his eyes crinkled up at the corners, flashing with wit and keen intellect.

The same overheating of her senses she'd experienced the night of the tree-lighting ceremony flooded through her. She avoided his gaze and focused on his navy-blue parka as he hung it on a rack beside her coat.

"I'm paying for lunch," she reminded him, "because you treated last time."

"That's why I ordered the early luncheon special, to save you money," he teased. "In fact, I might order the daily dessert too. Muffins are half price on Saturdays."

"Be my guest," she said graciously. "But first, let's say grace." She bent her head. Tim didn't participate, but he kept his head bowed until she completed the prayer.

The shop's glass door swung open heralding a burst of wind, casually teasing his coarse, dark hair. Thick and rich and the color of root beer, she decided. His hair was styled to lay flat on the sides, fairly long at the nape, the waves sweeping against his shirt collar. Over his shirt, he wore a fisherman knit sweater.

She sampled her brownie and briefly closed her eyes to savor the sweetness of mint chocolate laced with peppermint buttercream icing. "It's delightful. Do you want a bite?"

"Only if you let me pay for lunch." He slid onto the seat across from her so that their knees touched.

"I told you—"

"It's the least I can do to thank you for your commitment to the homeless shelter."

"You mean the Astra project," she corrected.

"My mother wasn't exactly the poster child for Christmas." Wryly, he smiled. "And may I point out that we were talking about lunch and concluded with my refusal to allow you to pay?"

"Tim, you agreed to let me treat today."

"I don't recall ever actually agreeing." His dark eyes glinted with mischief. "In any case, I changed my mind."

"Are you the persistent type who won't quit badgering me until I agree?"

"I'm known for being extremely tenacious, especially if I want something." The serious tone of his voice robbed her of any retort, and she avoided his roguish expression by staring at the poinsettia.

She'd been thrilled when he'd suggested meeting at the coffee shop, hoping all week that he'd ask her out. And with that hope, she'd questioned herself.

What was she doing? These feelings, these rose-colored glasses, were completely out of character. She'd sworn off men after her unpleasant experience with her ex.

"A bite of your brownie?" he repeated. "Or do you intend to eat it all by yourself?"

Obligingly, she offered him a nibble.

"Just like I imagined." He laced his fingers through hers. "Delicious."

A hazardous warmth invaded Holly's bloodstream. Warily, she lifted her hand from his.

In the days since the tree lighting, she'd taught a full schedule of daily piano lessons, and Tim had put in a seventy-hour workweek. Still, he'd texted or called nightly, and they'd compared notes on the progress of the fund-raiser, whom they'd spoken to that could help raise funds, and the arrangements with the nursing home that was hosting the performance.

And in those texts and calls, an easygoing companionship had developed between them which was established by spur-of-the-moment remarks and mutual laughter, peppered by recurring, relaxed silences.

She arranged a napkin on her lap. "So what was your urgent need to see me on this sunshiny morning?"

"Well, the first urgent need was that I was hungry. Starved, actually, but not only for food."

Pointedly, she ignored his innuendo, as well as the flush of heat creeping up her cheeks. Self-consciously, she tucked a strand of hair behind her ear.

Earlier that morning, she'd taken particular care with her appearance, applying rosy lip gloss. Then she'd brushed her black hair until it gleamed and refrained from wearing her usual woolen beanie.

"Well, I'm starved for conversation," she joked.

"I told you about myself." He dove into his croissant. "Now I'd like to learn more about you."

"We've corresponded nearly every day since we met."

"And from the little I gathered from your brief responses, you were adopted from South Korea when you were six months old." He reached for his coffee cup. "Is Holly the name you were born with?"

"I didn't have a name. I was dropped off on a church's stairs."

He stopped in the middle of drinking his coffee. "Truthfully?"

"Many children in Korea are abandoned. Many more are abandoned all over the world."

His stunned expression prompted Holly to explain, "Nonetheless, I believe I was loved by my birth mother. She chose to give me the advantages of adoption—a healthy home and solid education—opportunities she couldn't have provided as a single parent. Most likely she had limited choices, and she 'abandoned' me in a way that permitted me to be found."

He sent her a blank look. "So, who named you? Your adoptive parents?"

"Yes. I was born four weeks premature and required hospitalization in South Korea, which was why I wasn't adopted immediately. Because my birthday is January first and near Christmas, my parents called me Holly. They were Asian as well."

He put his cup down. "They must have been thrilled with an adorable baby girl to cherish."

"Perhaps in the beginning." She nibbled at her brownie. "But as I grew older, I acted out. I assumed I was the only Asian adoptee in town and felt out of place."

He set down his croissant and regarded her. "Were you?"

"No. There is an extensive Asian community in this area. Still, as a child I was bullied for being homely and awkward."

"Surely not?" He leaned forward and gently cupped her chin. "Looking at you, that's hard to believe."

Airily, she waved him off. "The teenage years are difficult for a girl who hasn't figured out where she belongs. Maybe my insecurity showed."

"You were special. You were chosen by your adoptive parents." His brown eyes reminded her of the finest chocolate, and involuntarily, she memorized them. Oftentimes, the scorching heat of his gaze melted her. Now that gaze was slightly hard, as if he was ready to protect her from the insensitive actualities of the real world.

She repaid his protectiveness with a sincere smile.

"You must have fought off the boys in droves once you hit

high school." He threw a quick, grim laugh, and the thought crossed her mind that he might be jealous.

"I was short and skinny, and no guy even looked cross-eyed at me." She reflected on those distressing, uncomfortable years, knowing she'd been thankful for Charity's friendship. Later on, when they'd reached adulthood, Charity often reminded Holly that God was in everyone's heart, even the classmates who had cruelly tormented her. Often, she spoke about sadness and happiness growing together.

*"Praise God when things go perfectly,"* she'd advised. *"And praise God when they don't."*

"Fast forward, and you could be a model on a runway," Tim was saying.

Though she glowed at the flattery, Holly reverted to their earlier conversation. "Certainly, Snowflake and the surrounding areas are welcoming and diverse. The residents are down-to-earth and genuine."

Tim responded by folding his arms and leaning back. "Tell me about your parents. I spoke honestly about mine over hot chocolate and doughnuts."

She caught the aloofness that threaded his tone whenever he mentioned his mother or father, and perceived the hidden frustration and sadness and, yes, bitterness.

"They were loving and bighearted. Both were missionaries and adopted me later in life." Holly fiddled with the charm bracelet on her wrist, hearkening back to her father's chuckle, her mother's arms enfolding her. The delicate scent of violets and shared giggles and bedtime stories enveloped her.

"You mentioned in one of our phone conversations that they passed away?" he asked.

She took a deep breath. It was a question that was challenging to answer, despite the five years that had gone by.

She'd learned a hard lesson the day they died—that the people she loved could be taken away from her in an instant.

Precariously close to tears, she fingered the silver charms. "Their small plane went down on a missions trip in Asia. I was supposed to go, but my work schedule interfered at the last minute."

Soon afterward, she'd met Jim and plunged headfirst into a hasty marriage. With hindsight, she'd figured out that she'd coped with the void in her life, seeking to fill it with love and companionship, and had married a man incapable of either.

Tim's steady fingers covered hers. "I expressed my sympathy the other day, but I'm truly sorry for your loss."

"Thank you. This bracelet was a gift from my mother. She bought all the charms too."

He lifted her wrist and inspected each charm individually as she described the momentous occasions in her life.

"By the way, did I mention that you look as beautiful as your charm bracelet?" His intimate grin, the way he adeptly piloted the conversation in a different direction, prompted her heart to do a little flip in her chest. He lifted her hand and kissed it.

"I remind you of a charm bracelet?" she challenged with a jaunty smile.

"A beautiful one."

She busied herself with stirring her latte and beamed. "Thank you. Again."

Many folks had complimented her beauty once she reached college, a respective number of men poetically expressive. She'd extended a gracious acknowledgement while harboring the belief that they weren't speaking the truth. With clear precision she would flashback to the tongue-tied girl she'd been, the girl who'd worn glasses and been nicknamed a studious geek. And sometimes, even if she didn't entirely admit it to herself, the baby who had been abandoned in South Korea.

While she'd attempted to tuck away those long-ago memories of youth, as an adult she placed little significance on something as fickle as external prettiness.

"I've learned from God that I'm sufficient just the way I am. I'm sufficiently attractive and sufficiently tall."

Tim grinned. "You're five feet."

"That's tall." She recited a favorite pastor's message that had been her mantra through those difficult adolescent years. "God made me, and He is perfect."

"I'm not following."

"I'm enough because God is in me. My talent and intelligence are sufficient."

Without taking his gaze from her face, Tim replied, "I agree."

"It took me a long time to come to peace with that. And Tim, you're enough too."

"With all my baggage?" Despite his outward unconcern, his voice caught ever so slightly.

She clutched her hands together. "I'm subbing at Snowflake Chapel for Sunday's service. I'll be playing Christmas carols, and you're welcome to attend. You mentioned you like 'Silent Night.'" She kept her tone neutral, but inwardly entertained the wish that he would accept her offer.

"Nope. Not my thing, Holly." Idly, he traced his forefinger along the table's wooden surface. His fingers were rough and callused. He was a man who worked with his hands. This charismatic man sitting across from her wasn't a television star anymore. "Thanks for accepting my invitation to see me today," he added.

Accepting? No decision there.

*Anytime,* she wanted to blurt. Instead, she viewed his

239

guarded expression, his unswerving approach to navigating their discussion away from church.

They ate in quiet camaraderie, interspersed with Tim's queries regarding Jasmine and her mother.

When they finished, a college-aged woman with spiked blond hair wended past the other tables to them, ready to whisk off their plates. "Dessert?" she suggested, and Holly debated. The excellent service in the shop made her wish they had dined somewhere else. Her time with Tim had gone by much too fast. They'd been in the coffee shop less than an hour.

"No dessert for me," Tim told the waitress, grinning at Holly's quirked eyebrow.

"I thought you said—"

"Seeing you is a heap full of sweetness for a Saturday morning, and enough for any man."

Holly rolled her eyes. "Uh-huh. Me and your three packets of sugar."

With a smirk, the waitress placed the check between them.

Neatly, Tim covered the bill with his hand before Holly tugged it toward her.

"My treat, remember?" He reached into his pocket and laid several bills on the table. "No change," he instructed the waitress.

"Thanks, Tim. Annie is cooking in the kitchen but saw you come in. She said hello." Friendly and breezy, the waitress swept up the bills and carried their plates away.

"Who is Annie?" Holly asked. Through the large glass window, she watched pedestrians with ruddy cheeks hurrying along the sidewalk.

"The owner of the place."

"And the waitress knows your first name?"

"I've lived in Colorado ever since I was born, except for

my stint in California." He gave an unabashed smile. "When I was a child, I came here with my grandfather."

"Where was your mother? Was she with your grandmother?"

"Sometimes. Other times, she'd take off for a spell and leave me with my grandparents. We never quite knew when she'd come back."

*Or if.*

She expected him to say more.

How long did his mother leave him? Days? Weeks? Months? Unnerved, Holly waited while a hush took up the space between them.

"Tim?" she eventually said.

"Did you want to ask anything else?" He looked at her as if he'd practically forgotten she sat across from him.

"Not unless you want to tell me more about yourself and—"

"Let's move on to your fund-raising business, all right?" It wasn't a question. The discussion concerning his mother was clearly over.

Holly didn't think she could ever learn enough about him to be satisfied, but she understood that his feelings about his past needed to be respected.

"Yes, of course." She picked up her latte and gazed at him over the cup, attempting to banish the downhearted mood that had settled. "Is Ralph making progress on the shelter?"

"He began the initial-stage fix, which is installing cables and wiring." Tim slid his coffee cup to the side of the table. "His crew removed furniture and carpeting and are running wires under the floorboards, through the walls and in the ceiling. New back boxes have been fitted, and sockets and switches are being rewired."

"The shelter needs all that?"

"Present-day demands are different from the past. High-tech is a part of everyday life, so might as well do it now when they're rewiring."

"So that's just the first stage?" She shook her head. "There's a considerable amount of work involved."

"Ralph and Lou are using a graph, so they're literally on the same page."

"What's the second stage?"

"The floor, ceiling, and walls are replastered, modern light fittings, switch plates, you name it."

"How is the timeline?"

"So far, Ralph and his crew are on track." When she reached for her cup, Tim lightly touched her arm. "Holly, your contribution is an immense help. You came at exactly the right time."

"God's timing is perfect, and every moment matters." She quoted another beloved saying from her pastor.

"Every moment matters," Tim repeated with a wide smile. "I like that. So let's make the most of it by spending the afternoon together."

"Don't you have to work?"

"Not on Saturday." Boyishly, he grinned. "And you aren't teaching any lessons, so you're free."

She swallowed a last gulp of latte. "Are you certain you know my schedule?"

"I memorized your texts, remember?"

She couldn't help her smile. He seemed to regard their texts as a higher form of communication, to be studied, analyzed, and gauged. "Tim, I may not be teaching, but I arranged to stop by the nursing home to prepare the final recital arrangements. Consequently, I'm not free."

"You're an educator, correct?"

"Yes."

"Educators are fond of learning new skills, right?"

She eyed him warily. "What did you have in mind?"

"The nursing home is right down the street from the ice-skating rink."

"So?"

"So, Miss Kim, we can visit the nursing home first and spend time with the residents." He grinned, extending his hand and bringing her to her feet. "Afterward, I'll teach you how to ice skate. And I'm looking forward to your reaction when you see the neon sign that Ralph installed."

# CHAPTER 9

*F*our days later, Tim was still grinning when he parked his truck near town and walked the short distance to Musical Notes, the local music store.

Flurries were blanketing Snowflake in a fresh covering as evening neared. It was as if he'd phased into a scene from Norman Rockwell's colorful oil painting, *Main Street At Christmas*, complete with the faded brick town hall and country store. All Snowflake lacked were the vintage automobiles.

Sprigs of mistletoe and holly intermingled with whiffs of pine, and candlelight spilled across the pathways.

Taking Holly ice-skating had been a splendid idea, he decided as he neared the store. The rink had been a cacophony of giggling children and adults, and the bustle of hockey and figure skaters competing for ice time reminded him of his limited seasons as a high school hockey player.

Despite having never ice-skated before, she'd been a good sport.

She was infinitely appealing—her dark almond-shaped eyes and black hair flying with abandon over her shoulders—

and she possessed an elegant poise when she'd eventually skated around the rink twice without falling.

Her movements had been graceful, the gentle sway of her hips alluring.

"I did it!" she exclaimed as she skated back to him, her pert nose held high, her fine, sculpted cheekbones flushed with excitement.

Wholeheartedly, he'd applauded.

Because, why not? She was stunning.

He'd been attracted to her since the first night they'd met at the shelter. He recalled her stunned stare when he'd asked if she was homeless and needed a room.

In the ensuing days, she'd occupied all his attention. Brilliant and gifted, righteous and honorable, all wrapped up into one mesmerizing package.

He'd missed seeing her, understanding that she was entrenched in organizing the final fund-raising details and juggling a demanding full-time teaching schedule. Still, he had texted her numerous times each day and phoned her in the evening.

And now he wanted to buy her a gift. Nothing elaborate, just a thank you for all she'd accomplished, and the happiness she'd given him.

In jovial spirits, he brushed a fluffy snowflake off his face and couldn't contain the expanded emotions in his chest. He was behaving like an infatuated adolescent boy.

His mind went back to their day together. After they'd ice-skated, Holly had requested that he build a snowman with her. With her hair tucked beneath a forest-green beanie and her clear complexion devoid of makeup, she was magnificent, and thoughts about anything other than her vanished.

"Sure," he replied, although he never remembered ever actually building a snowman before.

Because again, why not?

And then she did the most childish thing as they strolled toward Cedar Lane Park. She stuck out her foot and tripped him, and he fell into a pile of snow like a piece of sawed timber.

As he lay sprawled on the ground, he'd gaped up at her cherubic grin. "What was that for?"

"Let's call it payback for teaching me how to ice-skate while the entire town of Snowflake watched me fall a half-dozen times."

"But what about when you got up? Do those times count?" He brushed snow from his jacket and advanced on her as if he were a silent leopard ready to pounce.

"Don't you dare, Tim." Stifling a giggle, she backed away.

He made a grab for her, she twisted, and he tumbled forward into another high snowdrift.

Hands primly on her hips, she hovered over him. As ever, her eyes held him spellbound, an intense dark brown, fringed by long lashes. Eyes that were pure and tender.

However, as he was quickly understanding, the true glimpse of the woman was her determined chin and alert gaze.

"Are you lounging there all afternoon?" She rocked on her heels and tossed her hair back, and all he craved was to gather her in his arms and kiss her full lips.

Instead, he fixated on the trees standing starkly above him and the dove-gray sky covered in clouds. "It depends on whether you'll try to push me down again."

"I didn't push you. I tripped you, and it was bad of me." Her gaze sparkled with mischief. "Are you hurt?"

"Only my pride." He gave a guileless smile and held out his hand. "Will you help me up?"

Exactly as he figured she would, she extended her hand, and he pulled her down beside him. With a shriek of merriment, she paused to catch her breath as he curved her onto her back.

"That's the thanks I get for teaching you how to ice-skate?" he challenged.

She giggled and squirmed. "Yes."

"Say thank you."

His answer was a face full of snow while she giggled louder.

"Now I deserve a thank you *and* an apology." He mopped the snow from his face, but when she started to scramble to her feet, he linked his arms around her waist.

"I didn't hear you," he whispered in her ear.

"I'm sorry." Out of breath with laughter, she gasped, "And thank you."

"A vast improvement." He nuzzled her nape. "Kiss me and we'll make up." His lips slanted over hers, and he tightened his hold. With a quiet sigh, she molded herself to him. "Holly, you are so beautiful," he murmured.

And the thought came. If only they could stay like this.

She was with him, he could see her, feel her enticing lips on his.

But then snowflakes began to fall, swirling in all directions, and he feared he would lose her in the thickening flurries. Just as he'd feared losing everyone he loved—his mother, his father, his grandparents. And he had, for they were gone.

He cautioned himself that this was present day and here was Holly. She was honest and vital and kissing him back in delightful surrender. Their future was unexplored, their pasts filled with obstacles, but with her he felt entirely at peace and in agreement with a world that hadn't lived up to his expectations.

That is, not until now.

A few minutes later, the snow stopped, and the clouds

cleared. He helped her to her feet and reached for her hand—two people falling in love, strolling outdoors beneath the dazzling vastness of a winter sky, holding hands. They were surrounded by a Jack Frost wonderland.

He squeezed her gloved fingers. Her hand fit into his as if she were made for him.

And there was no mistaking his feelings, because he was in love with her.

She was free of the pretensions he'd witnessed in Hollywood. She was funny and enthralling and generous. And she was bursting with affection for her students, most notably Jasmine.

Her love for God was forever present, and she clearly accepted God's gift of salvation. "Faith and love begins on the inside," she'd declared, and he was humbled by her attributes, particularly kindness.

Once they arrived at the park, they located a flat, shady area near the gazebo. Nearby on Snow Hill, a popular hilltop ideal for sledding and inner tubing, children zipped down and landed at the bottom. Their parents watched, cheered and hastened down the hill.

"Tim?" Holly said as she shaped and flattened the top of a medium sized snowball.

Whenever she spoke his name, the melodic sound of her voice had a hypnotizing effect on him.

"Hmm?" He evened out the edges of a gigantic snowball and fixed it on the ground. To his astonished pleasure, she made a great show of liking his creation, though he'd only just started. But then, as he'd discovered, she had an ability for making even the ordinary seem extraordinary.

"We've been acquainted only a short while, yet it seems like we've been friends forever," she said. "We shared a great deal about ourselves."

"I've revealed more to you than anyone. We're certainly

never at a loss for words." He paused, observing her. "I like to think we're more than friends."

She polished the angles of the snowball she'd placed on top of his, then gazed up at him. "I would too," she said quietly.

He heard the uncertainty in her voice and his breath halted. Unreservedly and effectively, she was beginning to thaw his heart.

Briefly, he closed his eyes, pondering why she had this magical effect on him. A few seconds later, he managed to speak. "How does the phrase, *a couple,* sound?"

He was surprised at how effortlessly the words came. He'd avoided serious relationships with women and any endearments he'd used were surface only.

"I like it," Holly was saying. "We're a couple, then."

"Let's shake on it." He extended his hand. "Deal?"

She laughed and shook. "Deal."

He lifted her into his arms, twirled her around, and thoroughly kissed her.

As he held her, he reflected on her biggest surprise, which had occurred when they'd parked in front of the ice-skating rink.

Tim had hurried around his truck to open the door for her, looking forward to her reaction when she saw the neon sign Ralph had fixed to the entrance of the rink.

Lips parted, she stared, while he suppressed a chuckle.

"Every moment matters." She enunciated the words she read in a shaky tone, then veered to him. "The owners of this rink must attend my church. They obviously chose this phrase after they heard the pastor's sermon."

"Could be," he said with mild cynicism. "I'd wondered where they got that slogan, and then when you said the same thing in the coffee shop ..."

"*Every moment matters* is more than a slogan, Tim." Their

gazes held. "It's a way of life whether you attend church or not."

Their silence was charged with a growing, mounting awareness for each other. He felt it, because there was no denying its existence; and by the softening of her expression, Holly felt it too.

Now, Tim rehearsed exactly what he'd say to her when next he saw her. He wanted them to spend Christmas together. He didn't usually celebrate the holiday, save for serving meals in a Denver soup kitchen in the morning. He didn't cook, so he'd usually bring leftovers back to his apartment, or order a takeout pizza and spend Christmas afternoon reading by himself.

Of course Felicia, his ex-girlfriend, would observe the holiday in high style. Fortunately, that high style didn't include him, and there was no wandering through that mine field anymore of struggling to satisfy her with lavish dinners at overpriced restaurants.

He'd broken things off with her shortly after he'd met Holly. It had been insanity to get involved with Felicia in the first place, but he knew she cared for him.

The breakup had been quick and honest. He saw her in person and tried to do everything right.

She'd been angry. She'd screamed at him. And then it was over.

At the intersection of Main Street, Tim crossed at the stoplight. Outside the entrance to Musical Notes, he paused and rubbed the back of his neck. He hadn't purchased a gift in years, and then only once, when he was twelve and waiting for his mother's recent disappearance to end. Had she been in a treatment program, or run off hot-rodding with her latest boyfriend? He couldn't remember.

It had been mid-December, and the weatherman forecasted a massive storm producing significant snowfall. He'd tried not to upset his grandparents by asking where his mother had gone and spent the empty hours staring out their front bay window at the whirling snowstorm.

He'd watched. He'd waited.

"She'll come back," he'd determinedly told his grandmother. Why wouldn't she? He was an exemplary son, a son to be proud of, so of course his mother wouldn't leave him.

Two days later, Ralph, who worked with his grandfather on construction jobs, had taken Tim shopping. He'd earned a few dollars by running errands for his grandfather at the construction sites.

That day, he'd bought his mother a Christmas gift.

Tim shook his head, chiding himself for overthinking.

This wasn't the same. He wasn't buying a Christmas gift for Holly. He was buying a thank-you gift because of her generous contribution to the community.

And because they were ... a couple.

Besides, his mother and Holly were entirely different people.

He pushed the door to the shop wide open and banished the old memories.

The timbered space was crammed with musically themed gifts, from pencil pouches to statues of composers, to frames embellished with string instruments and posters of Beethoven and Bach.

"Do you sell charms for a bracelet?" he asked the middle-aged salesclerk behind the counter, rushing his words. Thoroughly engrossed in scrolling through her cell phone, she gave a start and swiveled around.

"Yes." She beamed. "And anything musical you can imagine."

Tim took a step forward. "I'd like to purchase a charm."

"Brilliant." She ushered him to a display stand. "Any particular instrument?"

"She plays piano, but she already has a piano charm." He picked through the charms, examining each one.

"Gold or silver?"

"Silver. But she wants to learn how to play the accordion." He perused the display and selected a sterling silver accordion charm polished to a shiny finish.

"This charm is accordion accurate," the sales clerk said.

"Music isn't my forte." He chuckled a little too loudly at his pun. His insecurity about purchasing a gift for someone was showing.

*Suppose Holly didn't like it? Or worse, suppose she discarded his gift in search of something more appealing, as his mother had done?*

"See?" The clerk rode her thumb across the accordion's tiny keyboard. "Complete with white and black keys similar to a piano."

He nodded. "I'll take it."

"Our store offers gift wrapping at no extra charge."

"Sure." He'd only wrapped one gift in his life, a young boy's clumsy attempts using the Sunday newspaper comics and string.

"Hello, Mr. Inspector! I mean, Mr. Stewart."

A chirpy young voice prompted Tim to spin around. "Jasmine, what are you doing here? And please, call me Mr. Tim."

Jasmine, carrying an armful of music, sprinted to him. "Okay."

"What are you doing here?" he repeated.

"I just finished practicing in the back room. Miss Kim and I are playing 'Silent Night.' It's a duet arrangement."

He grinned. "So I heard."

"And I counted the beats out loud for each measure so I don't go faster than Miss Kim." Perky-pink flags of color enhanced Jasmine's pale cheeks. "I'm preparing a solo too. 'We Three Kings of Orient Are.' Have you ever heard it?"

"Yes. Many times." He paid for the package, carefully wrapped in ivory paper embellished with lime-green musical notes, and he placed it in a purple bag embossed with the store's logo.

His gaze strayed. "Where's your mother?"

"Working." Jasmine scooped up a heavy quilted coat from a peg rack and traded her shoes for a pair of glittery shearling boots. "Mr. Tim, guess what else?"

"What else?"

The slight girl fairly beamed with excitement. "I won't need to practice at the music store anymore because I'm going to live with Miss Kim. She's been alone since her divorce, so I'll keep her company."

He froze, nearly gasping while his brain recorded disbelief. *Holly had been married? Never once had she mentioned it.*

*And what was this about Jasmine living with her?*

"Is that what she said?" he casually asked.

"Yep. It's all arranged."

"How?" He struggled to assimilate everything. "Miss Kim lives in Pine Cone Valley."

"I know. I went to her house every week for piano lessons."

"When?" He heard his voice. He'd raised it. "When are you moving in with her?"

"This afternoon."

"With your ... mother?"

"No." Jasmine filed her music into a canvas bag and hoisted it over her shoulder. The strap slipped off, and she slid it back up her arm. "My mother isn't coming."

*Then how ...*

Unable to extend any more than a head bob, he kept his features bland.

Once he exited the store, the questions exploded in his mind.

Had Jasmine's mother relapsed? Was that why Jasmine was staying with Holly? Or was Holly planning to take over the little girl's life?

His muscles quivered and his body tensed.

Memories of the incidents when the "men in suits," as his mother had called them, threatened to remove Tim from her home, or rather, lack of home, whenever she lost the battle to her addictions, climbed to the surface.

No. It couldn't be. That wasn't Holly. She'd never take Jasmine away from her mother. She loved the girl and wanted what was best for her. And a child belonged with a loving, caring parent. Holly knew that. Everyone knew that.

His heart hollered the denial. But his mind mulled over Holly's words, the smidgens of conversations regarding Jasmine, and his pulse raced.

*"I would do anything for that little girl."*

# CHAPTER 10

*S*eated on the tufted couch in her living room, a pen in hand and a mountain of paper beside her, Holly studied her list of things left to do. The baby grand piano in the nursing home had been tuned, a donation box set up, and her students were prepared. The media had publicized the fund-raiser on television, radio and newspaper at no charge, and colorful brochures noting the date and time were posted in shop windows everywhere.

Plus, an extensive three-part email marketing event had begun, with an announcement sent to area businesses. The first was a Save the Date; the second, an Event Reminder; and the third, a Last Chance email.

*The Astra Project Fund-raiser to benefit the Snowflake Homeless Shelter*

*Holiday Piano Recital at Golden Birch Manor*

*5 Cedar Lane, Snowflake, Colorado*

*December 23rd at three o'clock*

*Bring an ornament for the residents' tree!*

*Donations accepted at the door*

Tim had mentioned that he'd provide the tree, and Holly counted on him staying true to his word.

Luckily, she'd started her annual winter recess, which meant lessons were scheduled only for students who opted to participate in the fund-raiser.

But she hadn't finished decorating her apartment, nor hoisted her "Charlie Brown" tree from the attic.

And she hadn't heard from Tim.

Her hands fluttered, and she set the pen aside. She sagged against the couch, trying to ignore the prick of anguish that came with a stark realization. Tim was avoiding her. He hadn't reached out in days, and her texts had been greeted with replies so short and clipped that she'd actually flinched.

Why had he suddenly lost interest in her?

All the jubilant expectation of spending the holidays with him had drained out of her. And that awareness left her shocked and rejected.

Unfocused, she stared vacantly at the paper.

She'd done it again. She'd placed her trust in a man. A man who obviously considered her nothing more than a diversion that had run its course.

Her chin quivered as she succumbed to a rush of tears. These days, she did that a lot. When at last her tears subsided, she dried her eyes and went in search of a soft cloth to press over them.

That morning, her views had swung the opposite way, and her battered pride had prompted her to push her shoulders back and silently banish him.

Of all the nerve. Of all the insensitive nerve.

She'd thwarted her heartache by telling herself that there was no reason for her sadness. He'd go on to solid-gold charm another woman and … And so what?

So what if that thought caused her to feel hollow inside?

She rubbed her temples and swung her legs to the side of

the couch, weary of the mental conflict harboring her disbelief and bewilderment.

Finally, she'd decided not to contact him anymore. No
longer did she leave him cheery voice mails, or any voice
mails at all.

*"How does the phrase* a couple *sound?"* he'd asked.

She'd detected the revealing huskiness in his voice and
believed his admission sincere. Apparently the actor could
carry off a deliberate deception without a second thought.

Determined that the recital would be a success, she'd
resolved that nothing, not even a shattered heart, would
preclude her from achieving her goal. Her aunt had pegged
Holly's quest as a personal penchant, a private pursuit to
raise all the money the shelter needed. And that was exactly
what she intended to do.

Nevertheless, she also had an eleven-year-old girl living
in her apartment. A girl who left scuff marks on the tiled
floor in the foyer and often seemed despondent. A precocious child who chatted only when she was in the mood,
Jasmine spent hours after school practicing the piano in
Holly's living room, or straggling her legs out in front of her
as she flopped on the couch. Hands jammed into jean pockets, she resembled a tiny pixie with round, impish eyes as she
declared how bored she was.

Holly suggested she read a book or play with the cat. That
occupied the girl for about ten minutes.

The previous afternoon, the principal of the elementary
school had phoned because of a discipline issue. Jasmine, it
seemed, had a tendency to associate with the wrong crowd,
claiming that she should stick with "kids who understood
her best."

Considering her age and how she'd been displaced and
lived in multiple homes, the principal assured Holly that
Jasmine's behavior was normal, and her scores on intelli-

gence tests rated higher than average. Still, Holly spent numerous hours on the phone with Jasmine's mother discussing the situation.

The last morning before winter break, Holly phoned her aunt while Jasmine was in school.

"Try to relate to the depth of Jasmine's plight," Aunt Clementine advised. "Understandably, she misses her mother. Focus on the good news. She secured an excellent job with a generous salary and benefits, and they'll be reunited soon. But I'll continue to pray for them, of course."

Silence surged for a beat.

Holly tapped her foot on the floor. To split the stillness, she inquired, "Are you still seeing Justin, Aunt Clementine?"

"His arm is looped around my shoulders as we speak."

"You both fit in the recliner?" Holly teased with a delicate chuckle.

"We're a perfect match."

Holly smiled at the mental image of two seniors ultimately finding love. "Are you housing any new rescue dogs?" she asked.

As if on cue, a dog bayed.

"One adorable long-eared beagle, and a Yorkshire terrier who insists on yapping at everything."

Holly giggled and then immediately sobered when her aunt inquired, "What's new with Tim?"

She tightened her grip on the cell phone. "I … I wouldn't know."

"I understood that you texted or saw each other every day." Holly heard a smooch and assumed Justin had kissed her aunt.

"Tim isn't talking to me," Holly replied.

"Why not? What's the problem?"

It was useless to hide the facts. Her aunt was extremely discerning.

"The problem is he's avoided me ever since ..." Frowning, Holly sat up straight as a notion struck her. "Ever since Jasmine moved in. I assumed he liked children. Apparently not."

"So he's aware of the situation with Jasmine?"

"Yes. She met him in the music store in Snowflake and told him before I had the chance." Holly gulped to steady her emotions. "It all happened so quickly when her mother was hired for her dream job in Denver."

"And now along with caring for a youngster, your fundraiser is in a couple days," Aunt Clementine said.

"Tim is supposed to donate the tree. I hope he will."

"If he said he will, then I have no doubt he will. He seems a man of his word, so I wouldn't worry. Have faith."

"I do."

"Then the odds are in your favor. Tim will come through."

Holly collapsed against the back of the couch. "Will he?"

"Your expectations flow from God. In the end, it is God who provides."

Holly gained strength from her aunt's belief, as well as her conviction regarding Tim's solid character.

"I invited him to the recital so often that I lost count, but his replies were always noncommittal."

"What did he say exactly?" her aunt asked.

"Just something about working that day." Holly bit her lower lip. "But the town offices are closed for the holiday break, so he wouldn't work unless he was on call."

"From the sounds of your romance, I presumed you were falling in love."

"You were wrong." Unconsciously, Holly pressed a hand to her heart. "We only met a short while ago."

"But still, it sounded wonderful."

*But still, it WAS wonderful.*

So wonderful, in fact, that when Holly clicked off, she curled her arms across her chest and wept.

FORTY-EIGHT HOURS LATER, Holly entered the lobby of the Golden Birch nursing home, carefully balancing a pile of music with a container of Chinese Christmas cookies stacked on top. Garland outlined the door, spelling out the words *Noel* and *Joy*.

She'd chosen to wear cashmere slacks in a rosebud-pink, and a notch-collared faux wrap blouse in a vibrant silk print. She'd arranged her hair into an elegant chignon at her nape, secured with a faux diamond clip, and a pair of tiny diamond earrings. Her gingerbread-colored tote bag doubled as a handbag.

Jasmine, endearing in a red ruffled lace dress and black patent leather shoes, her blond hair styled in ringlets, skipped beside Holly. Clutching her music to her thin chest, she glowed with optimism when her mother hugged her.

As arranged, Emily had met them at the recital and would take Jasmine home with her to Denver when it was over.

"Thank you, Holly, for allowing Jasmine to finish the semester in Snowflake while I started my new job," Emily said. "It was helpful that you drove her to and from school every day."

"No worries," Holly said. "Jasmine even helped me set the table for dinner two nights in a row. That is, when she didn't practice or play with my cat."

Holly realized that Jasmine's mother deserved whole-hearted accolades. She was a single parent who'd resolved to make a better life for her and her daughter and raising a child certainly wasn't easy. "I'm happy this is all working out for you."

The previous afternoon after church service at Snowflake

Chapel, Holly and Jasmine had baked Christmas cookies. They'd snacked on leftover butterscotch chips and velvety chocolate that melted on their tongues, and Holly had explained that the Chinese Christmas cookie recipe was from Tina, her college friend.

And they'd discussed Pastor Tom's sermon based on John 3:16, concerning God's unconditional love. "The outlook in your heart replicates the judgments in your mind," he'd preached. "God sees how your narrative begins and ends. He loves us, even though we oftentimes feel inadequate and make mistakes."

Holly had taken the message to heart and prayed for forgiveness. She'd recognized that she'd lost patience with Jasmine on occasion.

She was brought back to the present when she shifted to allow a professional caregiver to pass. He wheeled a white-haired fellow in a wheelchair and both extended a smile. Inspired, she smiled back. The home was evidently devoted to its seniors.

To celebrate the holiday, multicolored lights in the shape of an angel were affixed with tape to a blank wall, and individual stockings were tacked on each resident's door. Down the hall, an engaging game of bingo sounded over a loudspeaker, and an outdoor area beyond the dining room enabled residents to enjoy the gardens when the weather was warm.

While parents made space for the residents, Holly's students guided the elderly men and women, some with canes, others with walkers, to the enormous parlor where the recital would take place. The glossy ebony-black piano commanded center stage.

In the meantime, Holly conferred with the director about organizing the refreshments and donation box, and reminded the attendees to hang their ornament on the eight-foot-tall tree.

"The crowd is larger than we expected and donations started pouring in yesterday," the director informed Holly. Her ash-blond hair was coiled in an upsweep, a bouffant hairstyle that Holly hadn't seen in years. She headed toward the hallway and began setting up extra chairs.

"Yes, I'm thrilled." Holly tailed her. "Thank you for allowing us to perform."

"Our pleasure. And the tree." The director regarded the tall pine. "The tree was donated by Mr. Timothy Stewart. A local Christmas tree farm delivered it this morning."

"Is he here?" Holly couldn't help herself, her anxious gaze pinned to the front door. Then she foolishly regarded the tree, as if Tim might materialize from behind it. "The man who arranged the delivery?"

"He was here earlier, but disappeared shortly before you arrived."

Holly stopped herself from asking any more questions about him. "Right. Thanks." She reverted to her professional teacher tone and stepped into the parlor.

A half hour before the recital, Holly knelt by each of her thirty students, who ranged in age from six to eighteen years old. She offered encouragement and reminded them to sing along with the Christmas hymns for the finale. However, she was no match for their eagerness, their love of music, which, she ascertained with a tinge of pride, she'd helped to instill in them.

At five minutes before the hour, Holly's heart rate doubled in nervous anticipation. She seated herself in the front row and creased the page turn of the first piece, "Silent Night." She'd decided to commence with a strong opening, foreseeing a seamless performance because she and Jasmine had practiced the duet for hours.

*"You don't like Silent Night?"* she'd asked Tim.

*"Everyone likes Silent Night,"* he'd replied.

Her eyes burned with tears. A lump settled in her throat, and she swallowed determinedly. She certainly couldn't break down here. She was a woman with mettle and resolve.

Something caused her to swivel, and her stomach fluttered. Privately, she wished that a broad-shouldered handsome man had shown up at the last minute to support her and her cause. Instead, she locked gazes with a recognizable fellow sporting a plaid coat and wearing round eyeglasses. He'd planted himself at the far end of the parlor and passed her a sociable nod.

"Ralph?" She chewed on her trembling lip and prayed her disappointment didn't show. She came to her feet and hastened to him. "What are you doing here?"

"I finished work early, and I'm always up for supporting a good cause." He gave a half-laugh. "After the recital, let's meet in town at The Little Corner Bistro. Say, seven o'clock? They close at eight."

It was a subtle order, not a request.

"All right."

"Will you be bringing Jasmine?" he asked.

Startled, she shuffled back. "No. She'll be with her mother."

"Excellent. That's where a child belongs." He stepped away. "Be prompt. I have some news you'll want to hear."

# CHAPTER 11

They'd done it. The recital was over. By the ringing applause from the residents, friends, and family, the students' performances and sing-along were an emphatic success. Even better, they'd raised an additional five hundred dollars, and the director assured Holly that donations would continue throughout the holiday season.

Holly kissed Jasmine and her mother good-bye, and congratulated the girl on a flawless recital. She promised to send recommendations for piano teachers in the Denver area. On their way out, Holly overheard Emily reveal to Jasmine that they were heading to the humane society. A seven-year-old shih tzu named Leo had been given up for adoption because the owner's landlord didn't allow pets.

"But our new landlord does?" Jasmine asked tentatively.

"Yes. He gave the okay. Merry Christmas, Jasmine!"

The girl flung her arms around her mother's neck. "Merry Christmas, Mommy!"

After lemonade was served and the remaining students and parents departed, Holly lingered to converse with the residents and joined in a high-spirited game of bingo.

At six o'clock, she yanked on her coat and headed for the exit. An hour was enough time to drive the short distance to The Little Corner Bistro in town.

"Holly?"

She swiveled at the recognizable male voice, deep and achingly familiar.

Tim perched on the edge of a folding chair, arms crossed, the color rising in his handsome, tanned face. She struggled to still the traitorous responses unfurling within her, struggled to keep her expression blank in the same way he had mastered.

"Excellent recital." He stood and came forward. "You were magnificent."

Guardedly, Holly contemplated him. "How would you know?"

He brushed his hand along her cheek. "I was here."

"I didn't see you." She'd scanned the parlor countless times.

"Do you think I'm lying?"

"I'm not certain what to think anymore when it comes to you."

He reached out to take her hands.

She jerked aside and spun for the door. The director at the front desk peeked up, and Holly ignored her soft bark of laughter.

"She's watching us," Tim murmured. He'd beaten Holly to the door. He propped his hand on the frame, successfully delaying her departure.

Holly sent a commendable imitation of a smile toward the director, committing to revisit on Christmas Eve at three o'clock, which would allow ample time to attend the church service at six. She'd made arrangements to play carols for the residents.

She placed her fingers on the door's brass handle. "Even

more of a reason to let me pass, then," she sputtered.

His jaw hardened. "Where's Jasmine?"

"She left already."

"I'll walk you to your car." His tone was as unmoving as his stance. "I ... I bought you a gift."

Her breath caught as she stared up at his earnest, attractive face, and once again she cautioned herself that he'd been a successful actor. "I'm not interested in your gifts. Please excuse me." She wrenched the door open and held a stiff posture as she marched past him.

The nursing home's parking lot was silent and nearly empty. A nipping, icy sleet had begun to fall, fierce and relentless.

Across the street, the neon sign of the ice-skating rink flashed *Every Moment Matters.*

She thrust her freezing hands into her coat pockets and observed the nursing home. Frost clung to the windows and night had fallen. In December, the days grew short so rapidly.

She hurried to her Jeep.

Tim quickened to keep up with her. "Why are you ignoring me?"

Holly grabbed her beanie from her tote bag and drew it over her raw ears. "Now there's a million-dollar question."

"What's that supposed to mean?"

"You're the person who disappeared."

His forehead creased into a scowl. "I've been around the nursing home all day."

"Where? Invisibly?"

"I stayed in the hallway for the entire recital, and rushed out the minute it was finished because I was called to a job in town. I assumed you'd chat a while with your students. I intended to return within a couple hours, and I did." He grasped her forearms. "So, can we talk?"

Meticulously, she wrenched free from his grasp, first one arm, then the other. "No. Not anymore."

"Can I give you ... this?" Undeterred, he smiled, but the smile wavered. "I thought you might like a little something."

She drew a trembling inhale at the sight of the miniature box wrapped in ivory paper, embellished with lime-green musical notes. "Why?" Rubbing a hand over her heart, she readied to end the conversation. Being near him hurt too much.

His smile faded, his eyes bottomless pools of anguish. "Don't you like gifts?" His voice sounded very odd, very unsure.

"Not your gifts, Tim. Please keep it."

With a proud tilt of her head, she whirled, striding away on legs that felt too weak to support her body.

# CHAPTER 12

*A* hollow numbness settled over Holly as she drove the few blocks to The Little Corner Bistro. Instead of being emboldened by refusing Tim, she was despondent, and heavy with remorse for her inexcusably bad behavior.

Negotiating the busy traffic into the center of town took longer than she anticipated, compounded by waiting at an intersection until there was a break. Nonetheless, she reached the bistro before seven o'clock and parked at the curb. The street was dark save for the bistro's muted pendant lighting stretching from the rustic interior.

As she got out of the car, she hardly noticed the sting of icy pellets on her heated cheeks. Unblinking, she shivered and clutched her coat closer, half hoping that Tim had pursued her. He hadn't, and she shook her head in mock derision, feeling foolish for thinking otherwise.

She shuffled to the front entrance. An illuminated reindeer in the lobby greeted her, along with background instrumental music, a classical rendition of "Silver Bells." White pine roping adorned the mantel of a crackling fireplace, and each tabletop sported a mason jar chock-full of red and green ornaments.

Ralph sat at a table near the back. He sprang to his feet, took her coat and hung it on a coat rack.

"Where's Tim?" He asked so casually that Holly was immediately put on her guard.

"I have no idea." She tugged off her wool beanie and flattened back the wet hair plastered to her cheeks. They both slid into chairs across from each other at the table. "Why?"

"I expected he was coming with you." Ralph's gray eyebrows rose at what he evidently assumed was an oversight. "Didn't you see him after the recital?"

"Only for a short while." Somehow, she kept her tone nonchalant.

A waitress scurried over, gripping a pad to take their orders.

"Peppermint tea for me," Holly said.

Ralph nodded agreement. "The same."

After tea was served, Ralph silently observed Holly while he stirred in cream and sugar.

"Do you want to discuss what happened at the nursing home and why he's not with you?" he asked.

"And spoil a perfect chat? Let's just say we had a disagreement." Ruefully, she shook her head and fixated on the mason jar between them. "Truthfully, I've thought about him so much, I've run out of words."

Ralph's forehead furrowed. "In my opinion, you two care a great deal about each other. However, I'm not certain who is more stubborn, you or Tim."

His reproof made Holly straighten. "It's Tim. He's impossible. I assumed I understood him, but he's an enigma."

Ralph hunched forward. "He was angry when he found out you had taken Jasmine in."

"First, that was none of his business," Holly said. "Second,

Jasmine's mother secured a job in Denver and asked me to keep Jasmine at my apartment so that Jasmine could finish out the school semester. Of course I was happy to help."

A gleam sparked in Ralph's eyes, partially hidden behind his round glasses. "Ah, so that explains it."

"I don't understand."

"Tim's mother wasn't the best, but she was fiercely protective." Ralph bent his head and surveyed Holly. "She instilled in him a deep fear of being taken by the authorities, an 'us versus them' philosophy. Because of Tim's previous experience, he probably assumed you intended to pull Jasmine away from her mother for good. He's got deep feelings about subjects of that nature."

"So in his mind he charged me with a crime, and the verdict was guilty?" Holly drew in a small breath. "All without actually speaking to me?"

"And yet he still came around today and forgave you."

She studied her hands. "For a crime I didn't commit."

"Why didn't you explain Jasmine's situation to him?"

"Well, to begin with, he's completely ignored me these past few days. He didn't respond to my texts or phone calls." Holly broke off, unable to put her heartache into a coherent sentence.

"And that hurt you, because you're in love with him," Ralph replied.

"Yes." Her face heated. She'd blurted her admittance too quickly.

She couldn't bear to face Ralph's perceptive smile and averted her gaze, peering out the double-hung windows facing the street. Sleet had frosted the overhang, and the hand-painted stone fountains flanking the entrance were glazed with ice.

"Good news." Ralph didn't hide the delight in his gravelly voice. "He's in love with you too."

Suppressing the flare of optimism in her chest, Holly kept her gaze on the outside fountains. There was nothing else to say, but in all honesty, there was everything.

"Does Tim ignore every woman he loves?" she finally asked.

"To my knowledge, he's never loved another woman. Sure, he dates women and treats them with respect, but he never reveals anything about himself. But you—you touched a nerve. You brought out a part of his past he's tried to suppress." Ralph shook his head. "Instead of confronting you, he closed up. That's what he does."

"Why?" Holly's mouth went dry. "We've spent hours talking about our lives."

"But not talking about everything." Ralph fairly swooped down on her reply. "Tim is a complex man, Holly. I first met him when he was a little boy. He was lovable, appealing, and into mischief at every opportunity despite his attempts to appear angelic."

Holly smiled and leaned forward. "Please tell me more."

"He was smart, sharp as a razor." Ralph grinned. "And solid and sunny. Any mother would be bursting with pride to have him as her son."

"Any mother except ... his?"

"Oh, she was proud, all right. Sometimes. Sometimes not. It all depended on if her addictions got the better of her. Tim never knew where he was going to wake up from one week to the next—under a bridge or at his grandparent's house. His mother was an original and even called herself Astra for a spell. When I saw the name on your advertisements, I knew Tim had told you about her."

"A star of hope," Holly said. "I must have explained the significance of that name a hundred times this week."

"Or a falling star."

"I refuse to believe that." She frowned. "Where did you and Tim meet?"

"His grandfather and I were friends since we were both in the building trade." Ralph lifted his cup to his lips, and Holly noticed a subtle tremor in his hand. "We all called him Timmy back then, that is until he forbade it."

"How old was he at the time?"

"Probably nine."

"And his mother?" This close, Holly counted the numerous lines on Ralph's wide forehead, the gray whisker stubbles on his chin. "From what I gather, she was everything to him, although he shuts down whenever it comes to actually discussing her."

"Despite her lifestyle, she was the center of his life." Ralph folded his hands. "Can I tell you a story?"

"Of course." There was the tiniest catch in her voice. She wondered if Ralph noticed.

"His mother was drop-dead gorgeous until her addictions wore her looks away. One Christmas soon after I met them, she left him with his grandparents, and, after a few days, he begged me to take him shopping. He'd saved some money by working for his grandfather, doing odd jobs at the construction site, and he wanted to buy her some jewelry. He found an adorable charm on clearance that was engraved with the words *Mama Bear*."

"Precious."

"To you. To me." Ralph fell silent for a heartbeat. Firelight cast dim shadows on his creased cheeks. "Tim didn't have the money for the store gift-wrapping, so he wrapped it himself with old newspaper and string."

"His mother must have been thrilled when he gave her the gift."

"I was at his grandparents' when she finally showed up on Christmas Eve. Tim was so excited he could hardly keep still.

He grabbed the gift from beneath the tree and pressed it into her hands. 'Mommy, I got you a gift,' he said. He looked so small standing there." Ralph's tone rang with sadness. "I assumed she would welcome him into her arms and apologize for being gone so long. And that she'd make a big show of opening it."

"Didn't she?"

"No. A car horn, her latest boyfriend, and off she went out the door."

Holly's entire body tensed. She was unable to hide her sadness and righteous anger for the little boy Tim had once been, for the man she loved.

For she had, indeed, fallen in love with him.

"What happened next?" She dabbed tears from the corner of her eyes.

"He called out to her, he still held the gift. She dismissed it. Dismissed him." Ralph's eyes were damp. "Sure, he probably spent exorbitant amounts of money on women when he was in Hollywood, but he never actually bought them a present. He's been blessed in his professional life because of his exceptional looks and hard work ethic. In his personal life, not so blessed."

A painful silence emerged, despite the bustle as the bistro began shutting down for the night. Holly was perilously close to weeping, recalling her heated discussion with Tim only an hour before, and the contemptuous way she'd informed him to keep his gift.

She covered her face with her hands. "Did he ever forgive his mother for her callousness?"

"In one sense, yes, but forgiveness is difficult. Tim's heart is kind, but he's careful. Understandably so. It takes a big person to forgive."

"'As far as the east is from the west, so far has he removed our transgressions from us.'"

"Psalm 103:12," Ralph responded. "I'm a church-going man, and listened closely to Pastor Tom's recent sermon. Does that surprise you?"

Holly smiled at the reference to church. "Not at all. You strike me as a compassionate man, who has obviously formed deep friendships."

"I never married. I wanted to."

Holly chuckled. "Until a few weeks ago, I might have matched you up with my aunt. But now, in her sixties, she is dating a wonderful man."

"I never found the right woman." Ralph held up his left hand, devoid of a wedding band. "Fortunately for Tim, he has."

"I appreciate what you're trying to do, Ralph." With a ragged laugh, Holly reached for her tea. It was cold. "However, your efforts are wasted."

"I read a study once. Within three days, you'll be able to identify whether or not you're attracted to another person."

"Hardly a lifetime. I didn't go to the homeless shelter looking for love."

"Let's call it a fortunate accident then."

"A fortunate accident." She sought to match his upbeat tone. "What's the good news, by the way?"

The waitress pointedly placed a check on the table and peered at her watch, then posted the closed sign on the entrance door.

Ralph paid the bill and got to his feet. "An anonymous businessman in the community has offered to pay the entire rewiring project, and the work should be completed by the end of December. Lou will deposit the money you've given toward services, food, and clothes for the residents."

"Ralph, that's wonderful." He helped Holly on with her coat, and she swung her arms in excitement as they exited. "Who's the businessman?"

He winked. "Anonymous, remember?"

"Is it Tim?"

"I'm not at liberty to tell. But since you mentioned Tim again ... I watched the way he looked at you the night of the tree lighting, and in truth, I was surprised. When he acted in that popular television series, women swarmed all over him. They still do. He's always been immune, which hardly shocks me, given his history. Still, despite the fleeting fame, he's a street kid at heart. Nonetheless, that man is deeply in love with you."

And Holly, in turn, was in love with him.

But would he ever forgive her for being so insensitive—rejecting not only his gift but the man himself?

# CHAPTER 13

*E*arly on Christmas Eve day, Holly hoisted her spindly tree from her apartment building's attic and arranged it by the living room window. Outside, luminous rays of sun highlighted wintry trees, and a light snowfall resembled crystal lace.

She hadn't heard from Tim, and although the possibility existed, she certainly didn't expect to.

Consequently, she pondered how best to approach him.

Phone? Maybe. Maybe not. Suppose he ignored her calls?

Text? Probably the same.

There was so much she wished to say, so much to explain. But where to begin?

Completely immersed in her musings, she balanced on the garden stool to hang tinsel on the higher branches. From the corner of her eye, she glimpsed the box of ornaments on the floor—the glittering baby-blue icicles, the winter angel, and the lighted manger.

*"How does the phrase a* couple *sound?"*

Tim's rugged face seared in her mind, and she recalled each detail of their afternoon building a snowman. The scene jerked her from her task, and the restraint she'd relied upon crumpled.

She sank onto her tufted sofa. The tears she'd vowed not to shed streamed down her cheeks.

"I'm sorry, Tim." She wept hot, broken sobs. "How do I ask for your forgiveness? How do I know you won't reject me?"

With a semblance of control, she grabbed her cell phone. Butterscotch skirted across her ankles, purring and flicking his cream-colored tail. She reached down to scratch his head. "I'll stop at the This and That Shop before the nursing home, then I'll return here after the church service," she informed him.

Already wearing a red crushed-velvet dress that skimmed her curves, Holly styled her hair long and loose. Her silver bracelet decorated her wrist, the charms gaily jingling.

The only thing left was to contact him. Easy. She'd invite him over for Christmas Day. She paused, swallowed and cradled the phone to her chest.

And how would she begin that invitation, exactly? Her courage dissolved as she anticipated his curt reply. Or worse, if he didn't reply at all.

SEATED IN HER FOUR-WHEEL-DRIVE JEEP, Holly focused on the road to the nursing home and arrived at three o'clock. Streetlamps misted beneath a fine snowfall, and the sun struggled to appear through gray clouds.

Earlier, she'd ducked into the This and That Shop to purchase a tree topper. On the spur of the moment, she'd requested the topper be gift wrapped because she planned to give it to a special someone.

Voices were muted as she entered the nursing home. When she walked into the parlor, she noticed quite a few of the residents visited with family members. Holly sat at the piano and introduced herself before launching into the first Christmas carol.

After the sing-along ended, she reminded each man and woman individually how remarkable they were and wished them all a joyous holiday.

After embracing the last resident, she stepped out of the home. Pausing, she hesitated in the parking lot and stared at the unpretentious yet expressive words flashing from the ice-skating rink's neon sign.

*Every moment matters.*

But it was the person standing beneath the sign who captivated her.

There it was. And there he was.

From his dark furrowed eyebrows to the sturdy jut of his jaw, he was her beloved. The mark of his strong physique, the same potent appeal that had chased her nightly dreams, caused tears to slide down her cheeks.

His hands were at his sides, the familiar cranberry-colored scarf around the neckline of his navy-blue parka.

Silently, he acknowledged her.

The director stepped out from the home, calling to Holly that she had forgotten her music, flapping it in the air. Holly hardly heard her. She rushed through the snow, the parking lot, quicker now, then raced across the street into Tim's outstretched arms.

"What are you doing here?" Her shoulders quaked. Her face nestled against his chest as he embraced her.

"I came for you. I waited." His deep, gripping voice. She'd ached to hear it again. "I wanted to wish you a Merry Christmas. And to tell you I'm sorry. I'm so very sorry."

"I planned to call you, to text." She swallowed the lump of remorse in her throat and curved her arms around him. "I was afraid you'd reject me. There were things I wanted to say, beginning with my apology for the way I treated you yesterday."

"You're forgiven. Now please forgive me." His tone was a raw whisper, hoarse and sincere.

"I forgive you." Her eyes moistened as she gazed intently into his. "You're a good man. You inspire me to become a better person."

"You inspire *me*." He pressed his forefinger to her lips to prevent her from speaking. "To care. Really care, even if I get hurt."

"You won't. I promise." She placed a hand on his chest. Beneath his jacket, his heart beat vital and solid.

He brushed a strand of hair off her cheek. "If I could undo—"

"There's nothing to undo." Her heart constricted with a love so deep that she held him ever closer. "An hour earlier, I felt alone and sad. Now I feel like dancing."

"And singing?" he teased.

"Yes." She sniffed, and a tear trickled down her cheek.

"Then why the tears?"

"Because you're here," she whispered. "And I'm happy."

"Has anyone ever mentioned," he kissed her, leaving her breathless, "that your smile lights up the entire town?"

Her merriment muffled against his chest, before she glanced around at the empty sidewalk. "It's probably wise if we go to my car. I have something for you."

The director still stood on the nursing home's steps, apparently impervious to the cold.

"She isn't going to go inside until she sees us kiss again," Tim murmured.

"Again?" Holly offered a winsome grin. "All this kissing in front of the entire town?"

"Yep." He tightened his hold and lowered his head, and she encouraged his stirring kiss with one of her own.

He was here, Holly thought. On Christmas Eve, Tim was really here.

A HALF-HOUR LATER, evening had fully descended.

Tim and Holly were seated in her Jeep, in the parking lot of the nursing home. She sat in the driver's seat, he settled beside her in the passenger seat.

A dozen questions raced through his brain and he drew in a breath.

"I've missed you very, very much," he began.

"I've missed you too."

He responded with a kiss, trailing his fingers through her silky black hair and holding her near. She reacted with the same yearning that had awakened him from sleep and kept him up at night.

"Tim, we need to talk," she said.

"For a while," he granted. But not for long, he grinned.

"When I told you to keep your gift …" Her features swelled with anguish, her tone subdued. "I was hurt and baffled and lashed out at you."

His grin sobered. "I assumed you were seeking to take Jasmine away from her mother. My judgments were uncalled for."

"Don't ever shut me out like that again. You didn't even allow me a chance to explain."

"I'm sorry." He enfolded her in his arms and kissed the top of her head. "And you were married. You never told me."

She shuddered. "I assumed I would never get over it."

"Did you?"

"Thoroughly. Charity was correct. A joyous tomorrow is straight ahead."

He smiled at her infectious tone. "Because?"

"Because I found you."

"And I found you." He fished in his pocket for the small wrapped gift and presented it to her.

"For Christmas?" she inquired.

"Guess again."

"My birthday?"

"January first is a week away and I'm buying you something special." He would ask her to marry him, to embark on their future together as *a couple*. "This gift is for you for being ... you."

Silently, she unwrapped the package, broke into a wide grin, and leaned forward for a closer look.

"Do you like the charm?" he asked.

"I love it. But how did you remember I wanted to learn how to play the accordion?"

He fastened the charm onto her bracelet and kissed her wrist. "Because, if you recall, I memorized all your texts and our conversations."

"I have something for you too." She reached behind her, then handed him a bag imprinted with the words This and That Shop.

He gazed at the star he unwrapped, a simple five-point design with gold glitter, and smoothed his forefinger along the sleek edges. At one of the most touching moments of his life, he could only smile.

"Thank you." His voice was husky and he cleared his throat.

"It's a tree-topper. At first I bought it for myself—for my Christmas tree. But in my heart I knew it was for you."

"Astra," he murmured.

"A shining beacon of hope."

This was Holly's gift. An act of generosity, the true spirit of the holiday, an acceptance of Christian grace and love.

"Will you spend Christmas with me?" she asked. "Will you help me decorate my tree? More often than not, I'm alone."

"So am I."

"I usually order a pizza."

"Me too. Takeout."

Her beautiful face brightened with color, her almond-shaped eyes glistened with love. Tenderly, she touched the tiny accordion charm.

"And I accept," he added. "In fact, I thought you'd never ask." He smiled and peered through the foggy windshield. Arms crossed and a cardigan sweater thrown over her shoulders, the director remained on the nursing home's steps and glared at them. Or was she grinning? He couldn't tell.

"I'm guessing she aims to throw us out of the parking lot," he said.

"Should I tell her I'll pick up my music some other time?"

"You can text her. Tomorrow."

The peal of Snowflake Chapel's church bells made him pause. The first star appeared in the sky, radiant and twinkling.

"Church service begins at six o'clock," Holly said softly.

"I'd like to attend."

He couldn't judge her reaction at first. That is, until she gazed up at him with a radiant smile. "Really?"

"Really."

"God is calling. He must've found you."

"I'm easy to find because I'm with you. If He will take me with all my shortcomings—" Tim wavered. "He's bound to be disappointed."

"You can't disappoint God." She started the car, letting it idle as she hummed "Silent Night." He chuckled. She glanced at him. "You don't like 'Silent Night'?"

"Everyone likes 'Silent Night.'" Laughing quietly, he nuzzled her neck. "And Holly Kim, I love you."

She skimmed her hand against his cheek.

In the midst of a wondrous Christmas Eve, he reflected

on the unexpected circumstances that had brought this exquisite woman into his world.

At the age of thirty-four, when he was toughened by what he'd seen as a child, by what he'd done in Hollywood, he bowed to a consideration he'd never allowed himself.

He was good enough for God. And he was good enough for the woman he cherished.

**THE END**

# A NOTE FROM JOSIE

Dear Friend,

Thank you for reading *Holly's Gift*, set in the charming fictional town of Snowflake, Colorado.

If you loved this sweet inspirational holiday romance as much as I loved writing it, please help other people find *Holly's Gift* by posting your review.

I've always looked forward to the holiday season, and wanted to give the title, *Holly's Gift*, personal meaning when Holly offers the hero, Tim, her most precious gift.

A gift of faith.

Like Holly, I am also a pianist, and I happily brought music into the season. Holly's students, notably Jasmine, were an inspiration.

Many of my readers will chuckle about the shih tzu who is adopted in the story, as my shih tzu, Henry, occupies a special corner beside me while I write. He is a sweet dog!

Josie Riviera

My Spotify Play List for Holly's Gift is here.

# RECIPE FOR TINA'S CHINESE CHRISTMAS COOKIES

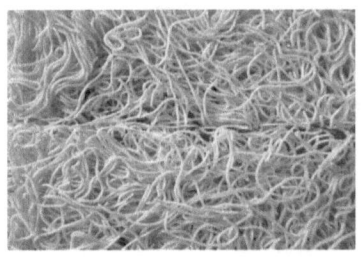

Ingredients
- 1 cup semisweet chocolate chips
- 1 cup Butterscotch chips
- 1 cup chow mein noodles
- 1 cup dry-roasted peanuts

Preparation Steps
1. Melt chocolate and butterscotch chips until smooth.
2. Put chow mein noodles and peanuts in a large bowl.
3. Pour chocolate mixture over the noodles and peanuts and stir until well coated.

4. Drop rounded tablespoonfuls of mixture onto wax paper. Refrigerate until set.

Enjoy!

# RECIPE FOR NANCY'S CARAMELS

6 cups sugar
  3 cups light corn syrup
  6 cups cream
  1 cup butter
  1 ½ Tsp. Salt
  1 Tbsp vanilla

Combine sugar, syrup and 3 cups cream in a large heavy saucepan. Cook over medium heat: boil about 10 minutes. Add remaining cream slowly, keeping at a boil, stirring constantly. Boil 5 minutes longer.

Add butter, 1 teaspoon at a time; stir in.

Lower heat so mixture remains at a slow boil and cook to a firm ball stage (248 degrees) (45 minutes to an hour).

Remove from heat; add salt and vanilla. Let stand 10 minutes, then pour into greased (about 12" x 17" pan). Let sit for several hours to cool before cutting and wrapping in waxed paper.

You can make 1/3 of this recipe and pour into 2 greased bread pans.
Enjoy!

# ACKNOWLEDGMENTS

An appreciative thank you to my patient husband, Dave, and our three wonderful children.

# ABOUT THE AUTHOR

Josie Riviera is a USA TODAY bestselling author of contemporary, inspirational, and historical sweet romances that read like Hallmark movies. She lives in the Charlotte, NC, area with her wonderfully supportive husband. They share their home with an adorable shih tzu, who constantly needs grooming, and live in an old house forever needing renovations.

Become a member of my Read and Review VIP Facebook group for exclusive giveaways and free ARCs.

To connect with Josie, visit her webpage and subscribe to her newsletter. As a thank-you, she'll send you a free romance novella directly to your inbox.

josieriviera.com/

josieriviera@aol.com

# ALSO BY JOSIE RIVIERA

Seeking Patience

Seeking Catherine (always Free!)

Seeking Fortune

Seeking Charity

Seeking Rachel

The Seeking Series

Oh Danny Boy

I Love You More

A Snowy White Christmas

A Portuguese Christmas

Holiday Hearts Book Bundle Volume One

Holiday Hearts Book Bundle Volume Two

Holiday Hearts Book Bundle Volume Three

Holiday Hearts Book Bundle Volume Four

Candleglow and Mistletoe

Maeve (Perfect Match)

A Love Song To Cherish

A Christmas To Cherish

A Valentine To Cherish

A Christmas Puppy To Cherish

A Homecoming To Cherish

A Summer To Cherish

Romance Stories To Cherish

Romance Stories To Cherish Volume Two

Cherished Hearts Six Book Volume

Aloha To Love

Sweet Peppermint Kisses

Valentine Hearts Boxed Set

1-800-CUPID

1-800-CHRISTMAS

1-800-IRELAND

1-800-SUMMER

1-800-NEW YEAR

The 1-800-Series Sweet Contemporary Romance Bundle

Irish Hearts Sweet Romance Bundle

Holly's Gift

A Chocolate-Box Christmas

A Chocolate-Box New Years

A Chocolate-Box Valentine

A Chocolate-Box Summer Breeze

A Chocolate-Box Christmas Wish

A Chocolate-Box Irish Wedding

Chocolate-Box Hearts

Chocolate-Box Hearts Volume Two

Chocolate-Box Double Hearts

Recipes From The Heart

Leading Hearts

New Year Hearts

SENIOR HEARTS

Summer Hearts

Christmas in the Air (1-800-Book)

A Very Christian Christmas

Most books are available in ebook, audiobook, paperback, Large Print paperback and Hardcover.

Many are FREE on Kindle Unlimited!